# SPLATTERFEST

ROBBIE DORMAN

Splatterfest by Robbie Dorman



www.robbiedorman.com

ISBN-13: 978-1-7336388-5-2

Cover design by Bukovero

For EZG.

# 1

"No, Marty, of course I don't want to do *Splatterfest*," said Dave Barclay, sitting on his couch, phone to his ear. "I want to work. I want to sink my teeth into a *performance*."

"Well, I'm sorry to say, old pal, but those offers aren't coming in," said Marty. It sounded to Dave like he was in traffic, but he could be anywhere. Marty hated to sit still, even if it meant stewing in LA gridlock.

"I know, I know," said Dave. He looked around his living room, surrounded by memories of his glory days. Movie posters with his face, front and center. Busts and statues of him in costume adorning every shelf. Even the full suit from Painmaker 3: Hell on Earth. The critics had ripped it apart, but he had loved it the most of all. It had given him character. It had made Nailface more than just a monster.

But the critics didn't care about that.

It still did well at the box office. No one mentioned that all of his movies earned back their money.

"I could always try and find some auditions," said Marty. "If you want to work that badly. At least Splatterfest is a festival."

"It's a convention, Marty. There are signings and photo ops. Sure, they show new films there, but it's all promotional. It's not Cannes."

"No, but it's guaranteed cash. Your appearance fee, plus a cut of all the signings and photos, plus any merch they buy from you—it adds up."

"I know," said Dave. "And Diane isn't going to suddenly stop asking for her alimony. Tell them I'll do it. Where is it, again?"

"This is the weird part," said Marty.

"What do you mean, weird?" asked Dave. "I'm not doing any fan films, Marty, I don't care how much they pay—"

"It's not that," said Marty. "They're showing Joe Banshee's next film at the festival. About the Midnight Star cult."

"That's his new project? Seems kind of tasteless," said Dave.

"Yeah, because the rest of Joe's output is the epitome of class," said Marty. Joe mostly released low-budget torture porn, endless rip-offs of Saw, and occasional reboots of old horror properties that never recaptured the magic of the original.

"I know, but still," said Dave. "Midnight Star wasn't Heaven's Gate. They killed people. I don't think I trust Joe to tell it correctly."

"Well, it's already made," said Marty. "And it's debuting at the festival. More than debuting. It's sponsoring the thing. It'll be plastered all over the place, so if you're going you'll have to make peace with it."

"Fine," said Dave. He had eaten worse frogs in his life.

"That's not everything," said Marty.

"What else could there be?" asked Dave.

"The location," said Marty. "It's Texas."

"Okay," said Dave. "So it'll be hot. I'll pack shorts."

"It's more than *that*," said Marty. "It's taking place at the Kalman compound. The former Midnight Star HQ."

"Christ," said Dave. "Where they all killed themselves?"

"Yes," said Marty. "And you'll be staying in the compound itself. All part of the deal."

"I have to sleep where hundreds of people died?"

"Only if you want the paycheck."

"Who else is going?"

"Frank Buchanon, Steven Hellman, Nancy Slaughter. Levi Stark."

"The usual suspects," said Dave. He knew them all, to varying degrees. They were guests on the convention circuit as often as they could, even if they hated it. Steven had become intolerable to be around lately, he detested it so much, but Dave understood his frustration.

"Mary Jo Carter," said Marty.

"Wow, really?" asked Dave. He thought Mary Jo was above it all. Maybe she just wanted the thrill. "I assume Joe will be there. With Abel by his side?"

"Yes," said Marty. "There might be others, but that's what I remember off the top of my head."

"I'll do it," said Dave. "Bills won't pay themselves."

"I'll call them tomorrow," said Marty. "And send over

your plane tickets. Let me know if you have any problems."

"Thanks, Marty. Bye." Dave ended the call, and his house was silent again.

He sighed and got up, leaving his cell phone on the couch. He paced through his living room.

What kind of publicity stunt is this? Having a horror convention in a cult compound? No wonder why they couldn't get any respect.

*Don't worry about it, you idiot. Take your paycheck. Be happy to be remembered at all.*

Dave wanted more than a paycheck. He wanted respect. He had been classically trained. He stood in front of the costume, the reflection off the glass display case creating an optical illusion, making it appear like he was wearing it again. He *had* been more than a monster. He had given the character a calmness, a tension that wasn't there in other horror movies. Nailface had been different.

"You look ridiculous, old man," he said aloud to the reflection. And he did. He wouldn't fit in that damn black leather any more, anyway. He weighed fifty pounds more than he did then and was thirty years older. He was almost seventy.

He *should* be glad they remembered him. That they still wanted his autograph and their picture taken with him. Hell, they dressed up like him and the other demons, and did a spectacular job of it. Better costumes than those awful sequels.

To be fair, he starred in a few of them. He turned away from the costume and went to his kitchen to get a drink of water. What did he have to complain about? He had his dream house. He had made his name. He lived comfortably.

So what if he wasn't Robert Deniro or Ian McKellen? Very few were. He took a sip.

*Clank.*

He paused, waiting. Did he hear that noise, or did he imagine it? He waited, cup in his hand.

*Clank.*

It happened again, and he knew that it was real this time. The sound of metal scraping against metal, or concrete.

"Damn raccoons," he muttered to himself.

He looked out the kitchen, toward the noise. It was night, and he had a few lights outside the home. He saw nothing, but he hustled to his bedroom, slipped on some sandals, and went out his back door, hurrying toward his trash cans. There were two of them, metal, specifically metal because he thought the lids would be too heavy for raccoons to disturb. Fat little bastards, they were, and they had been knocking over the trash for months. Smart too. They always scampered away before he could stop them.

He hurried around the side of the house, grabbing a broom on the way, hoping to catch them in the act so he could give them a thrashing. He reached the cans, and they were undisturbed. The Los Angeles air was humid and damp, and he wiped the already beading sweat from his brow.

"Damn it," he whispered to himself. He went over and touched the trash cans, and they were as he left them. Maybe the metal *had* been too heavy for them. Dave walked back to the house, through the sliding glass door that opened into his backyard.

*Clank.*

He heard the noise again. And then a series of them.

*Clankclankclankclank*

He recognized it, now. He had heard it many times in his life. The sound of chains. They rattled against each other, dangling in the air. It's what Nailface had used to kill his prey, for so many years, in so many films. Chains, with hooks at the end. Dave had controlled them, summoning them from the ether and shooting them toward his victims, until they were ripped apart.

The noise was at the edge of his hearing, but he knew it now, and goosebumps raised on his arms. He felt the terror his character had spread for the first time.

What was happening? Was he imagining this?

He turned on all the lights in his living room and kitchen, and grabbed a knife before exploring the rest of the house. He couldn't tell where the sounds were coming from. They sounded like they were outside before, but now they came from everywhere, from all around him.

He sneaked through his home, the blade outstretched in front of him. Was it some fan? Some obsessed nut who wanted to meet Nailface in person? Dave would turn down a hallway in his house and come face to face with some guy in cosplay, holding chains in his hands.

His heart beat harder and harder as he cleared more and more of his house. He moved down the central hallway, peeking his head carefully into the guest bedroom, and then the guest bathroom. Nothing in either.

Dave came to the T-junction of the hallway, with shorter hallways leading into the final two bedrooms, another bathroom ahead of him. He turned right and flipped on the light. He held his breath.

Nothing. The room only held a bed. He left the light on,

the door open. He turned around, and quickly opened the bathroom door, flipping the light on. Nothing again. The last guest bedroom was in front of him. He pushed the door open and turned on the light. Nothing *again*.

He was imagining things. There was no one in his house.

*Clankclankclankclank*

He wheeled around toward his master bedroom. The last room. They were waiting for him, and there was all the sexual stuff in the movies. *Christ*. He hated to imagine what they wanted to do with him.

His brain was telling him to call the police and get out of the house, but his guts told him to deal with the problem now. They were intruding on his home. He wouldn't let it happen.

Maybe they were deluded, and he could get them out without violence. He *hoped* he could get them out without violence.

He moved. The noise of the chains filled his ears.

*Clankclankclankclank*

*Clankclankclankclank*

*Clankclankclankclank*

It was getting worse. He felt them all around him, just as Nailface's victims once had. The horror of his films had never affected him, not like it did most people. Maybe it was because he was in them, but he only had eyes for the symbolism, the metaphor, the themes. He barely saw the violence anymore. It suddenly seemed much more real.

*Calm yourself, David. It's just some obsessed fan.*

He moved toward his bedroom, his knife at the ready, if anyone tried to attack. Step by step, he approached the door, open, the lights off within. He peeked his head into the shadowy room, trying to keep his breath silent even as his heart thudded in his chest. A dark shadow loomed in the corner. His breath caught inside him.

"Whoever you are, I want you out of my house this instant!" he said, with as firm a tone as he could muster.

The shape stayed still.

"I'm serious. I'm armed, and I will defend myself!" he said again, raising his voice.

The shape did not move.

His other hand went to the light switch and flipped it on, Dave still holding his breath. He turned on the lights.

A sweatshirt hung in the corner. His breath came out in a big sigh when he saw the dark shape. He had thrown it there after a jog the other day and forgotten about it.

*Goddamnit, Dave. You're losing it.*

He had been putting too much pressure on himself. There was no noise of chains.

Maybe he should go get a checkup. It had been over a year since he had seen a doctor, and at his age, he should really go more often. He inhaled and exhaled slowly, trying to calm his thumping heart.

He walked back into the living room and then a sharp thud to the back of his head sent him spiraling into darkness.

Pain brought him back.

He tried to move, tried to ease the sharp pain in the back of his head, but that only brought more agony, but in his hands. As he gained more coherence, the misery coalesced, harder and harder. He opened his eyes, and struggled to get a hold of what was happening.

He was in his living room, on the floor. All the furniture

had been pushed back, but his eyes went to his palms, trying to figure out the source of his torture. And then he saw it, and his stomach dropped out of him.

Hooks were pulled through his palms, attached to chains, which had been embedded in any firm surface. The walls, the floor. He tried to move his feet and they screamed with anguish. Dave craned his neck and saw the hooks through them. He could try to pull them, but the hooks were heavy, and they would rip his hands and feet apart if he moved.

Something moved in his peripheral vision, and he turned to look at it. A figure, dressed in black, their face obscured by a hood.

"Please, please, don't do this," said Dave.

The figure didn't respond. It only walked toward him. They stopped at the costume, and Dave heard a chuckle emerge from them.

"Please, I'll give you whatever you want," said Dave. "Please, just let me go."

The figure turned and removed their hood, revealing their face.

"You? Why are you doing this? Please, please," begged Dave. They dangled a chain from their hand, a heavy hook at the end of it. They finally spoke, crouching over Dave's restrained body.

"Your suffering will be legendary, even in Hell."

# 2

"You're out of your minds," said Gary Morton, his hands on the wheel of the van. "Both of you. Out of your minds. I can't believe I brought you along. I can't believe I hired you in the first place." Gary was in his late 50s, his gray head of hair trimmed short, with a giant bushy beard in front of him. He wore slate-colored corduroys and a green shirt, with suspenders. His brown eyes peered out through thick glasses.

"We are not crazy," said Stephanie Watts. She sat in the passenger seat, her dark brown skin contrasting with her flowery sun dress. Her hair was cut close, in short braids. "We just weren't born in the '60s, so we don't worship at the feet of Romero like you do."

"I respect him, I do," said Dan. "But—"

"No buts! How can you like the remake of Dawn of the Dead better than the Romero version? How? From that hack Snyder? He ruined Superman, and now the youth of America have been deluded to think his Dawn of the Dead is better than Romero's? Heresy!"

"I'm thirty-three, Gary," said Steph. "I don't think I qualify as a youth."

"Regardless, please explain to me how Snyder's version is superior."

"It's a better movie," said Dan. Dan sat in the back seat of the van, almost shouting up to them. White, tall, and lanky, Dan wore jeans and a t-shirt, his long legs stretched out in front of him.

"You're fired," said Gary.

"It's a better movie," said Steph. "It looks nicer. It has better actors. The writing is tighter. It's not full of sloppy scenes that serve no purpose."

"It's saccharine mush," said Gary.

"You mean it's pleasant to watch," said Dan. "And it's coherent."

"It's a product of a studio system," said Gary. "Romero was a maverick."

"And I respect what he did for film," said Steph. "But please explain to me, in what world does a biker in the middle of a zombie apocalypse smash a pie into a zombie's face? Or stop to get their blood pressure taken?"

"That—" said Gary, struggling with his words. "That was Romero showing the character of the times."

"It's goofy for no reason," said Dan.

"It's bad," said Steph. "And I won't apologize for it. And the makeup for the zombies is all over the place. I don't buy into the danger."

"Oh please, the zombies kill a lot of people," said Gary. "It feels plenty dangerous."

"Not anymore," said Steph. "It's outdated. And that's okay."

"Heresy," said Gary. "You're *both* fired."

"You aren't going to fire us," said Steph. "Who's going to work Splatterfest if you fire us?"

"Oh, please, you both would work it for free if I let you," said Gary.

"I don't know about that," said Steph.

"What were your exact words when I told you Frank Buchanan would be appearing?" asked Gary.

"I don't think I really said any words," said Steph. "It was more inarticulate joy."

"Exactly," said Gary. "And Dan, what did you say about Bill Chancellor?"

"I said he was the world's greatest living director and I worship at his feet," said Dan, in a monotone voice.

"Thank you," said Gary. "You're both rehired."

The van roared down the highway, Texas scrub and hills ripping past them.

"Why is Texas such a big state?" asked Steph.

"We're not that far away now," said Gary. "Only a few more hours."

"Is there really no closer airport?" asked Dan.

"Not one that would get us there today," said Gary. "Renting the van was cheaper and faster."

Steph looked down at her phone, her Instagram feed not loading. "My service is dying."

"I don't think we'll have service out there," said Gary. "I

think there's wi-fi, but I wouldn't count on actual cell service."

"So no phones?" asked Dan.

"There's a land line," said Gary.

"I still can't believe we're staying at the Kalman compound," said Dan, a tinge of excitement in his voice.

"It's creepy," said Steph.

"I know," said Dan. "It'll be awesome."

"Hundreds of people died there," said Steph. "It's awful."

"Yeah, I guess," said Dan. "But they were cultists."

"Most of them weren't evil. They were just normal people who got caught up in the middle of something bigger than them."

"They killed people, Steph," said Dan. "I can't feel too bad about using their place. Or about feeling sad, for that matter."

"It's not that I feel sad about it," said Steph. "It's just real horror, and I'm not too much into that. Not anymore."

"I'm not exactly excited about it either, Stephanie," said Gary, his eyes still looking at the road in the late-morning sun. "But Mr. McGrath was very specific about the details of our partnership. Midnight Star would be the featured film and get first placement on all materials. And finally, he was very explicit about us using the Kalman compound as the location."

"Is he going to be there?" asked Steph.

"Yes," said Gary. "And you are to treat him just like the stars. A Super VIP, so to speak. Without his money, this wouldn't be happening."

"But he's an asshole," said Steph.

"You talked to him one time—"

"Come on, Gary, you know he is. You don't have to talk like he's sitting in the van with us. He's not listening in."

"Okay," said Gary. "Maybe he's an asshole. But he's an asshole that is sponsoring this event and keeping both Splatterfest and the store alive with that money. It's going to keep us going for the next year, and without him, well… we would be in trouble. So grin and bear it, whatever his demands are. Treat him like you would Frank Buchanan. Or Bill Chancellor. Okay?"

"Okay," said Steph and Dan, almost simultaneously. Steph looked at Gary, his hands tight on the steering wheel. She could sense the stress in his voice. The Video Store had always been an iconic location in Austin, and Gary was a local legend, with the vast array of videos available in the store, and the variety of special events he would hold there.

No one saw the books but Gary, but it had been awful quiet lately. Event attendance was still great, but few people bought physical media at all. She knew the rent was rising around the city, and places like the store were closing left and right. If Gary thought it was necessary to bend to the whims of Mr. McGrath so they could keep their doors open, and keep Splatterfest going, then that's what they had to do.

Splatterfest was his baby. It had started out in the back room of the store, with Gary curating a list of little known horror movies to a small audience. Soon local filmmakers were coming to him wanting to show their films, and it grew and grew, until genuine actors and directors were premiering their movies and doing signings. It had grown and grown, but Gary was always worried it could collapse at any moment. And he never raised ticket prices, even if the audience could afford it. He wanted a kid off the street to see the movies as much as an urban yuppie.

"So are we just assisting them, or what?" asked Dan, from the back seat. Dan had started briefly after her. He was a little younger than her, but he loved film, and would argue about it with Gary for hours. It's honestly why she thought Gary hired him.

"You're doing literally anything the guests need," said Gary. "Helping them at screenings, signings, and panels. Getting them fresh towels. Showing them around, escorting them through the crowds. If they want iced tea, you go get it for them."

"Anything?" asked Steph.

"Within reason," said Gary. "Anything short of murder."

The road stretched out before them, and after a period of her cell service going in and out, it just went out, and never came back.

"I think that's the end of cell phone service," said Steph.

"You'll have wi-fi," said Gary. "Typical millennial."

"I'm sorry that this device that contains my entire life is important to me," said Steph. Gary had never bought a smart phone, or made a Facebook account. He was proud of both facts.

"We're getting closer," said Gary. He had repeated that every twenty minutes the whole way, almost to reassure himself as much as them.

"Why the hell did Kalman have his compound built so far out here anyway, in the middle of bumfuck, Texas?" asked Steph.

"I mean, he hated the government," said Dan.

"Because he was a con-artist scumbag who didn't want to pay taxes," said Gary. "Who made enemies wherever he went trying to coerce people into following his bat shit philosophies about magic and purpose. Who conveniently had all his women followers be his sex slaves."

"Jesus, I didn't know that," said Steph. "Gross."

"Like I said, I don't like that we're going there either," said Gary. "Or that Splatterfest is going to be connected to it because of some publicity stunt. But it's their way or the highway."

"But we are on the highway," said Dan.

"Oh shut up, smart-ass," said Gary.

"God, it's empty out here," said Steph. "I can't imagine living out here, with nothing but scrub grass, trees, and middling hills. Your closest neighbor being miles and miles away."

"Kalman wanted the cult to be isolated," said Dan. "He thought it would protect them."

"I'm pretty sure that after you kill some people, they're not going to just leave you be because you're out in the middle of nowhere," said Steph.

"It makes it a little more difficult," said Gary. "But it doesn't matter where you are, the old Jim Jones special can get you anywhere."

Steph shuddered to herself. She had heard about Jonestown, and the poisoned Kool-Aid, but the Kalman compound and Midnight Star cult was even worse. Being on American soil somehow made it creepier. That something like that could happen so close to home.

But traveling out here didn't feel like home, even if home was in the same state. It felt like no-man's-land.

Gary had to only say they were almost there a few more times, and then they *were* there, turning down a long and winding road made with crumbling pavement, probably paved thirty years ago when Kalman first built the place. The van bounced up and down as it winded far off the highway, multiple miles off into the arid grasslands.

"Will that thing support us?" asked Steph, looking at the road ahead.

"I hope so," said Gary. "It's a long way down. I would suggest not to look."

The van crossed onto a bridge that spanned a narrow canyon, only perhaps 50 yards across, but one that's bottom lay hundreds of feet below them, a spindly strand of water somewhere far below. Steph couldn't help but peer over the side, even though it hurt her stomach and made the back of her knees ache. Gary's hand gripped the steering wheel harder. Every bump made them gasp.

But the bridge stayed intact, and they crossed over. The compound was another mile farther out, big metal gates lying open, waiting to welcome them. Stephanie pictured the people crossing into the compound thirty years ago, not knowing it would be the last place they would ever live. An ache grew inside her stomach. She tried to ignore it, but it wouldn't go away.

"God, this place is creepy," said Steph, as they crossed the threshold.

"It's home for the next few days," said Gary. "You'll get used to it."

Steph said nothing, but she hoped she wouldn't get used to it. She didn't want to get used to the way it made her feel.

She didn't believe in ghosts, or the supernatural. It was the stuff of horror movies. But it wasn't right here. The land knew something bad had happened, and it warned them.

Steph felt the weight of the dead.

# 3

"Welcome to the Kalman compound, Mr. Morton. I'm William Joseph, the caretaker," said the stout man, wearing overalls over a flannel shirt with no sleeves. His eyes were closed against the sun, and he stooped as he moved, with short, slow steps. He reached out for a handshake with Gary, and Gary shook, and Steph could see the coils of muscle in William's forearm curl and flex.

"Nice to meet you. Not shying away from the history, Mr. Joseph?" asked Gary.

"What do you mean?" he asked, his eyes open only a millimeter. His accent had a faint Texan tinge, but Steph couldn't place it beyond that.

"You mention the name Kalman already," said Gary.

"No one coming here has forgotten what happened," said

William. "There's no point in trying to hide it."

"Makes sense," said Gary.

"Let me show you to your rooms, and then I'll give you the dime tour. Give you a lay of the land, so to speak."

They unloaded the van and followed William as he led them from the small parking area and onto a huge ATV.

"Too far to walk," said William, as they loaded up their luggage, jumped on, and sped through the massive open area that separated the multiple gigantic buildings throughout the compound. After a couple minutes of passing smaller structures, they arrived at a three story building which looked more ornate than anything they'd seen before. It was brick, with a huge wooden door.

"This is where y'all are staying," he said. "Where all the stars are staying too, I guess. It's where Kalman and his family stayed, back in the day."

"You mean his consorts?" asked Gary.

"Whatever you want to call 'em," said William. He keyed off the ATV, and they jumped off. He pulled a keyring loaded with keys off of his belt and unlocked the door. The deadbolt thunked heavily to one side.

"It's got everything you need," said William. "Each suite has a bathroom. A huge kitchen on the first floor. A big den too, with TVs."

"Is there wi-fi?" asked Steph.

"Yep," said William. "Whole place has satellite internet and wi-fi. It ain't great, but it's a fair hair better than a kick in the pants."

They walked inside, the massive door swinging open, and Steph was immediately struck by her surroundings.

*Holy shit, this is the mansion from Clue.*

The place was hardwood everywhere, with candelabras and chandeliers.

"Kalman had expensive tastes," said Gary. "Has it been renovated at all?"

"Not since I've been on staff," said William. "It's been kept clean, but that's about it. It's barely been lived in, to be honest. Kalman and his followers were only here a few months before it all fell apart."

Steph tried to envision life here, during that short time. Was it happy? Were Kalman and his followers enjoying every moment? Despite the infamy of the events, there were no survivors from the Midnight Star, and that only made the stories that came out about the place more exaggerated.

All her thoughts about the history only devolved back to the ending. Of everyone dying, rotting for days until the feds arrived, finding nothing but death and despair.

He walked them to the rear of the first floor, past carved wooden decorations and rooms filled with bookshelves.

"You are technically staying in the servant's quarters," said William, showing them to a group of bedrooms tucked away. "You can choose amongst yourselves."

"Where are we sleeping, Gary?" asked Dan. Gary looked at the three rooms.

"I'll take the small one," said Gary. "I won't be in it very often. You guys can fight it out for the other two."

"Which has the nicer shower?" asked Steph. She threw her stuff onto the bed after a brief inspection.

"I guess that's decided then," said Dan.

"You snooze, you lose," Steph said with a smile.

Dan went into the other room and tossed his worn duffel bag on the bed.

"You ready for the grand tour?" asked William.

"Let me change real quick," said Steph. She shut her door, quickly shed her dress, and changed into khakis, a polo shirt, and some tennis shoes. Something more suitable for work.

Soon they were back on the ATV, and William drove them out farther, talking as they passed anything.

"A lot of these homes were never occupied," said William.

"Built for a future that never came," said Gary.

"True enough," said William, "and I assume you won't have much use for them."

"No, probably not," said Gary. "Only a select few are staying overnight, aside from the actors and directors themselves."

"I'll show you the VIP quarters soon enough," said William. "We can see the back forty first."

They zoomed away to the largest building in the compound. Most of the buildings were limestone, with all the others looking rag-tag. Some were mobile homes, others normal wood construction with vinyl siding, some cabins, and others brick. The vehicle skidded to a halt in the dirt.

"This was the temple," said William. Steph looked up into the sky, seeing the peak of the building rising forty feet into the air. There was no cross, only a star adorning the tip of the building. She didn't know much about the Midnight Star beliefs. It was all urban legend when she was a kid. She was sure the info was out there, but a part of her didn't want to know.

William unlocked this door, just like the first, and they went inside, through a small antechamber into an enormous hall, with doors leading off of it in every direction.

"We'll have the new films screened here," said Gary, looking around. The space was vast, with room for hundreds of people. "The tech guy will be here early tomorrow. The chairs and tables should be here later today."

Steph looked around the giant space, her eyes drawn to the pulpit. A small set of wooden stairs led up to a platform. She could see row after row of pews in her mind, filled with followers, wearing simple clothes. John Kalman stood on the pulpit with his arms pointed to the sky, pointed to the star above him.

The star was the only thing that remained in the room, made of hardwood. It appeared as if it was growing from the wall. Its angles could cut, it looked so sharp, with five points, the top point the largest. Gary continued to talk, but she heard none of it. She only saw the Kalman phantom yelling at his followers, who he would kill en masse before the end of the year.

"You alright, Steph?" asked Dan, touching her shoulder, pulling her out of her reverie.

"Yeah," she mumbled. "I'm fine."

"This is so weird," said Dan. "Being here."

"What did the Midnight Star actually believe?"

"Typical doomsday cult stuff," said Dan. "Kalman kept the 'true' dogma secretive, available only to the most innermost members."

"Like Scientology?" asked Steph.

"Kind of," said Dan. "But it was mostly the world was ending, and a star god of some sort would come down and save the ones who believed."

"What is a star god?" asked Steph.

"Good question," said Dan. "I doubt Kalman himself knew. Some cosmic being greater than us. That's all that leaked out. But he preached a lot about humility, and the corruption of pride, money, and fame."

"He would love that his former compound is the grounds for a film festival."

Dan looked over to Gary, who was pointing around the room, asking William something.

"Honestly," said Dan. "Fuck Kalman, and fuck Midnight Star. I am sorry that all those people died, some of whom were probably innocent, but frankly, if having the festival here is a good excuse to rub it in the face of some dead cult leader, I'm fine with it."

Steph glanced over to Gary and William. Gary talked while William stared at Dan. Had William heard what Dan had said? Impossible. But still William glared at him with malice, before turning to look at Gary, his face blank. They walked back and joined Steph and Dan.

"Time for the next stop," said William, his voice a passive drawl again.

The next stop was a smaller building, also made of limestone. *Ka-thunk* went the lock as William unlocked it.

"This is Kalman's private ballroom," said William. The word ball came out of his mouth like bowel, and Steph's stomach suddenly turned. She took a deep breath and then it was gone.

Gary was looking around the space, imagining the setup. "We'll have the legacy screenings here," he said. It was a sparse, large room, with wooden floors.

"Legacy screening?" asked Dan.

"Did you not go over the notes I sent you?" asked Gary.

"I mean, I looked at them," said Dan. "Maybe I didn't *read* them, per se…"

Gary rolled his eyes. "It's watching classic movies with one of our guests, who either directed or starred in it. They talk over it, almost like a live commentary track."

"Oh, that's neat," said Dan, smiling. The strange nausea had disappeared, and Steph looked around the room. Private ballroom. Such a a bizarre notion.

They moved on, to a wooden building, relatively close by. The other buildings had some decorations, but this one was just wood, unfinished.

They went inside, and the size surprised Steph. It seemed much smaller from the outside.

"This will be for panels and signings," said Gary. He looked to William. "Do you know what they used this for?"

"For meditation," said William. "Focusing in on yourself. Sitting quietly."

"How do you know that?" asked Steph.

"I was here," said William. "Back when they took everyone away." His eyes glanced away at that, and Steph felt her face turn red. He had seen the bodies.

"Did you visit, you know, before?" asked Dan.

William's eyes only glanced at Dan and then returned to the floor. William didn't answer, only walking away.

Gary said nothing, ushering the two outside. They joined William on the ATV again.

"One more stop," said William, and drove off, this time a longer trip than any they had taken. They left most of the buildings behind them, passing a few small mobile homes and sheds before the landscape turned to rocky hills and sparse trees.

"Where are we heading?" asked Gary.

"The mine," said William.

*The mine?*

Steph hadn't heard of any mine on the property.

"Why?" asked Gary. They shouted over the drone of the engine.

"Because you should see it," said William. He left it at that, and no one asked him questions.

They arrived soon enough, the unkept trail leading to a chain-link fence surrounding an opening in the earth, a gaping maw that eternally hungered. William turned off the ATV once again, and the silence here felt darker. Their footfalls on the rocky ground echoed more. Stephanie could feel the emptiness here.

"I saw the mine on the plans," said Gary. "But I assumed it was a remnant from the nineteenth century. What did they mine? Silver? Gold?"

"Nope," said William. "This is newer than that. They dug for Kalman."

"Dug for what?" asked Dan.

"I don't know," said William. "They just dug. The more you dug, the better you were."

"Empty work," said Gary. "To keep them occupied. Dig more, and you get more favor. How far down does it go?"

"A mile or so," said William. "I went down there once, all the way. Do you want to go in?"

Steph walked up to the entrance, but kept herself in the sunlight. A mile of digging in just a few months. They would have had to work night and day. Hundreds of them, bleeding into the rock.

"I think we'll pass," said Gary.

"Did they find anything?" asked Dan.

"Not that I know of," said William. Steph looked down into the darkness, into the rough rock mouth. There was nothing. She turned from it quickly, moving back to the rest of them.

"Can we leave?" she asked.

"I want to go into it," said Dan.

"There's nothing down there," said Steph. "It's a mine of nothingness."

They returned to the main part of the compound where they were once again surrounded by buildings. Steph already felt better, just getting away from that mine, but her general unease wouldn't leave her. William showed them to a fleet of golf carts.

"To get around," he said, before handing them all keys.

"Awesome," said Dan.

"To drive the guests to their rooms," said Gary. "They should be here soon." He checked his phone. They had all switched over to a messaging app to circumvent the lack of cell service. "Shit. Henry and Linda are already here. Let's go meet them. They're handling all the celebrity guests."

They all drove over, three golf carts in a row. Dan weaved back and forth, glancing at Stephanie with a smirk, sticking his tongue out. She laughed despite herself. Dan could be an idiot, but he always knew how to cheer her up.

Soon, they were at the front of the compound, near the parking lot. Two people stood nearby, stretching their legs. A man and a woman. Henry and Linda, Stephanie presumed. They were dressed professionally, Henry in a full suit, with Linda in a blouse and a knee-length skirt. Henry was scrolling through his phone when he looked to see them approach.

"Henry?" asked Gary, leaving his golf cart behind.

"Hi," he said. Henry was tall, with broad shoulders and narrow hips. The suit fit him well. His haircut was sharp, and Steph could feel herself staring at him. He was stunning, and then he caught her eyes and she looked away quickly, embarrassed. "Glad to meet you and your team. This is Linda."

"This is Stephanie, and Dan," said Gary. "They'll be happy to help with whatever you need."

Henry smiled wide, his face genuine. "That's great to hear." He turned to them. "Nice to meet you," he said, shaking each of their hands. "Do either of you get star struck?"

"No," said Steph, speaking for both of them. "They're just people, right?"

"Good," said Henry. "Because they'll be arriving in about five minutes."

4

Steph told herself that she wouldn't geek out over Frank Buchanon. He had only starred in her favorite horror movie franchise, and she had cosplayed his character Axl at multiple cons over the years, and she was geeking out, *oh my god, that was Frank Buchanon, in the flesh, right there—*

*Calm your tits, Stephanie. He's just a person.*

Frank emerged from his ride, a luxury sedan, one of many that were chauffeuring the celebrities from the airport out to the isolated Kalman compound. He was dressed in a red velvet suit, despite the heat. His sunglasses blocked out the mid-afternoon sun. Stephanie hadn't known what to expect from the celebs, but Frank didn't seem to turn off his personality. His sideburns were perfectly trimmed, and his black hair, white at the temples, looked just like it did in her mind. His famous dimpled chin stood out, just like it appeared on screen. She couldn't believe he was here.

And she was the one helping him get settled.

She couldn't find her tongue, mumbling through an introduction, and then he kissed her hand, and she was going to faint. She could feel her face redden, and she was sure she said something, but nothing came out. Soon they were on her golf cart together, his luggage and clothes draped in the back. It seemed like a lot for three days. Frank didn't pack light.

"God, this really is out in the middle of bumfuck, nowhere," he said, as she sped away from the entrance. "All of this for that damn movie, huh?"

*Make small talk, idiot.*

"That's what I heard," said Steph, forcing her mouth to form words.

"I bet it was Geno's idea," said Frank. "It feels like one of his ideas."

Steph remembered Gary's comment about Geno in the car.

"Gary told me he's behind it all," said Steph. She didn't know if she should have said that.

"Oh, really?" asked Frank. "Doesn't surprise me. What a bastard. Pardon my French."

"Do you not get along?" asked Steph.

"Ha. No one *gets along* with Geno," said Frank. "Either you do what he wants and he does you favors, or you don't. I don't do what Geno says. Probably explains why Joe didn't put me in the movie."

"Joe?" asked Steph.

"Joe Banshee. Directed the Midnight Star flick. They told

me he'd be here," said Frank.

"Oh! Yeah, Joe. Yeah, he's arrives today," said Steph. "Were you supposed to be in it?"

"You know how it is," said Frank. "Everyone tells you you've got a job, and then suddenly, poof, you don't got a job anymore. Joe loves casting older horror actors, except not Frank, ole Frank isn't good enough for Midnight Star. Can't even get a cameo."

"I thought you were great in Hell or High Water," said Steph. Frank had played a supporting role, but it was the last new movie he had been in, a couple years ago.

"Thanks, kid," said Frank. "It was a fun picture. But they come few and far between these days. That's why I do these things." He motioned around him. "Not that I don't like the fans, but you know, I'm an actor. I want to act."

"I keep seeing talk about another Vile Buried movie," said Steph.

"Yeah, so do I," said Frank. "And yet I haven't been contacted once about it. I love Sam, I do, but I don't think I'm in his future anymore."

"What? They can't re-cast Axl!" said Steph, catching herself almost shouting.

"You're telling me," said Frank. "He's *me*. What are they gonna do? Get some simmering young stud, like that boy back at the car? They don't get it anymore."

The golf cart cut through the dirt, getting close to the lodge where they all were staying.

"I think you're still great," said Steph, trying to muster come compliment. "I watch everything you're in."

"Thanks, kid," said Frank. "How much farther do we have to go?"

"We're close," said Steph. "It's the nicest place in the compound. The guy who ran the cult used to live there."

"That just gives me the warm and fuzzies," he said.

The cart skidded to a halt, and Steph went to grab Frank's luggage.

"I'll get it, kid," he said. "You can get the door, if you want to help." Steph opened it for him, and they walked inside.

"Not too shabby," he said. "Where am I staying?"

"On the third floor," she said, leading him up the stairs. "No elevator."

"No kidding," said Frank, his voice dripping with sarcasm. Steph pulled out the sheet that had all the room assignments on it. They walked upstairs, Frank starting to huff behind her. It was easy to forget that he was approaching 60 years old.

They got to the third floor, and Steph looked at the small map on the paper. "You're in the third room on the left," she said, walking to the door and opening it for him. "The keys should be inside."

He walked in, and Steph got a peek of his room. It was massive, with a window that looked out on the hilly terrain. The king-sized bed dominated the space. Frank dropped his stuff onto it and scoped out the place.

"Not bad," said Frank. "You know, considering where we are."

Steph handed him his keys.

"One should work for the front door, the other for your room," said Steph. "The wi-fi password is on the dresser. And they do have satellite television. Is there anything else you need? Would you like a tour of the rest of the grounds?"

"Would you recommend it?" he asked.

"Honestly, not really," she said. "It creeped me out."

"Then I'll pass," he said. "Can I ask about security? I know there will be VIPs sleeping onsite as well, right? They can't just wander in here, correct?"

"There'll be security on site during the day, and they'll be staying in the dormitories in the evening. The VIPs have a strict curfew. Plus they don't have golf carts to get around."

"So it's not impossible for them to get in, it's just really, really difficult," said Frank.

"Yeah," said Steph. "If you see anybody that doesn't belong, call any of us and we'll help."

"Fair enough," said Frank. "I'll be here until dinner."

"Then I'll get back to the entrance," said Steph, going to close the door. "It was nice to meet you, Mr. Buchanon."

"Wait, kid," he said. "You can call me Frank. Before you go…can I see that paper you got there?"

"This?" she asked. "The room assignments?"

"Yeah," said Frank. "I'd like to see who my neighbors are."

"Sure, I guess," said Steph, handing him the sheet.

"Oh, wow," he said. He sighed. "Mary and Nancy, on either side of me. Guess I wasn't lucky as I thought."

Mary Jo Carter and Nancy Slaughter, both former scream queens. Mary became a very successful actress in comedies and dramas. Nancy, not so much.

"What's wrong?" asked Steph. Frank handed the paper back.

"I don't kiss and tell, kid," said Frank. "But I don't have a great history with either of them. It'll be alright. It's only a few days, right?"

"Right," said Steph. "If you need anything, just call Henry."

"Will do," said Frank, turning his back to her. Steph closed the door and exhaled.

*You didn't do half bad.*

The rest of her charges were alright. Mostly because she had gotten the worse case of star struck out of the way, right off the bat.

She escorted Bill Chancellor next. He was the oldest of the guests, in his mid-seventies, wearing black jeans and a black shirt, with unkempt flowing white hair underneath a black hat. He wore black sunglasses, and stooped slightly, most likely because of his age. He only had a small carry-on. Steph assumed it was full of more black clothing. As they sat in the golf cart, Steph could faintly smell weed on him.

Sure enough, within a minute of the ride, Bill had taken out a joint and started smoking it, guarding his lighter against the breeze.

"Would you like some?" he asked, after taking a long hit.

"Uh, no thanks," she said. "I don't smoke."

"Fair enough," he said. "I won't get in trouble out here, will I?"

"I think you're okay," said Steph.

"Good," he said. "God, what a fucked up place."

"It's pretty creepy," said Steph.

"Christ, Geno is such an asshole," said Bill, taking another hit.

"It doesn't seem like anyone likes him," said Steph.

"Oh, no, everyone fucking hates him. And if they say they like him, they're lying. But he's one of those assholes who enjoyed being feared, instead of loved. Fucking sociopaths, if you ask me."

"Does anyone say they like him?" asked Steph.

"I'm sure Joe would, if you asked him while Geno was around," said Bill. "But Geno gives him work. And Joe can handle the ass-kissing."

"You can't?" asked Steph. Steph only knew some of Bill's movies. They were great, some of them classics, but he also hadn't directed anything in twenty years.

"Oh no," said Bill. "It gives me indigestion. Last time I was in a meeting with studio heads, I got a nosebleed. My body can't handle it. So I called it quits. My health is better." He took another long drag off the joint.

They arrived at the lodge and Steph got Bill settled. She passed Dan on the way in. He had dropped off Nancy Slaughter, and the look on his face told her he hadn't enjoyed it.

Steph couldn't believe the next person she was escorting, because she recognized him. More than that, she *knew* him. It was Ted. Ted Nowakowski.

"Ted?" asked Steph. Ted threw a massive duffel bag and a backpack into the back of the ATV.

"Hey, Steph," said Ted, displaying his awkward smile. Ted wore his normal uniform, which was skate shorts and an ironic t-shirt. Today it was a Britney Spears concert shirt. His long blond hair was tied in a ponytail. He jumped into the passenger seat of the golf cart.

"How's it going?" he asked.

"What are you doing here?" asked Steph.

"I'm a director," he said.

"Yeah, but—" said Steph, but she stopped herself, because the rest of her sentence was going to be "but you're not a *real* director." Ted made movies, but they were all terrible. He always showed them at Splatterfest, but she wasn't sure if he realized that most people laughed *at* them, not *with* them. He also unashamedly flirted with Steph long after she'd made it clear she wasn't interested.

"But what?" asked Ted.

"Nothing," said Steph. "I'm just surprised. Let's go." She sped off, heading for the mansion.

"You're staying with us at the lodge?" asked Steph.

"Yeah, why wouldn't I?" asked Ted.

"No offense, Ted, but you're not quite Bill Chancellor," said Steph.

"Bill's here?" asked Ted.

"Yeah, I just drove him out," said Steph.

"Holy hell," said Ted. "This is so awesome. Have you seen Joe yet?"

"Joe?"

"Joe Banshee," said Ted. "You know, the guy who made the movie that's sponsoring the festival? The whole reason we're out here at this creepy compound?"

"Right. No, I haven't seen him yet," said Steph. "Dan is handling some celebrities."

"I want to talk to him," said Ted. "This is my chance."

"Your chance for what?" asked Steph.

"My chance at a break," said Ted. "To finally pitch to someone with some power." Steph glanced at him, and Ted's eyes gleamed with excitement. He really thought it would make a difference.

"You're going to pitch a movie to Joe Banshee?" asked Steph.

"Yes," said Ted. "This is my chance. Gary got me in, and all I have to do is execute."

"Right," said Steph. They pulled up to the lodge.

"This is where we're staying? This place looks awesome!" said Ted.

"It's pretty neat," said Steph. She got out to help Ted with his bags. She lifted the duffel bag off the back of the cart.

"There's a party tonight, right?" asked Ted.

"Yeah," said Steph. "Everyone will be there."

"Do you have a date?" asked Ted.

Steph sighed and dropped the bag on the ground. "Still not interested, Ted." She threw him his key. "You're on the second floor. Room three."

Ted caught the key. "I—"

Steph pulled away. Ted was relentlessly optimistic. She wanted to like him, but he made it very difficult.

Steven Hellman was next. Frank and Bill had their complaints, but they were both pleasant.

Steven was not.

"I can't believe I'm doing this," he said as Steph loaded his luggage onto the back of the golf cart. "Can we hurry up? I'd like to be in my room as quickly as possible."

"Yes, Mr. Hellman," said Steph. His baggage was big and unwieldy, and didn't want to stay on the cart. She strapped it in, and they were on their way.

Steven wore designer jeans and a t-shirt. His hair was dyed jet black, and it didn't suit him. Steph was never the biggest fan of the Sleep Terror series, but she didn't hate them or anything. But it had been almost twenty years since Hellman had played the main villain, with multiple reboots attempted in the time. She doubted he'd ever play the character again.

"How far away is where I'm staying?"

"Only a few minutes drive on the cart," said Steph.

"Jesus," he said. "Geno said nothing about this."

"I don't—"

"First, we have to fly out to a little misbegotten airport in the middle of Texas, and then drive out even farther to this shithole, where a bunch of assholes killed themselves. Just to please a few fans."

"It'll only—"

"And the nerve of Geno to invite me, after centering this entire show around Joe and that damned movie of his. After what Joe did to *my* character and *my* franchise. Joe didn't even give me a damn call. He didn't even ask for my blessing!"

Steph didn't answer. She wanted to drop him off and get rid of him. They arrived soon enough, with Hellman ranting nearly the entire way.

"Here we are," said Steph, stopping the cart and unloading Hellman's stuff.

"Christ, we're far out," he said. "What if there's an emergency?"

"We have medical staff on the premises," said Steph, even though she didn't know if that was true.

"I'm going to fucking die out here," he said.

"Your room is upstairs," said Steph. She grabbed his luggage with two hands, leaning it against her hip just to get it up the stairs. Hellman stomped up ahead of her.

"Fourth room on the right," she said, trailing behind him as they reached the third floor.

He opened the door in front of her, disappearing inside. Bill, who leaned against the door frame of his room, the door open, still smoking. He watched as they passed.

"This is not acceptable," he said, as she entered.

"What's wrong?"

"I specifically asked for a mini-fridge," he said.

"There's a full kitchen downstairs, I'm sure—"

"I don't want to go downstairs," said Hellman. "I don't want to have to talk to anyone. I want a mini-fridge. And this painting."

"What about it?" asked Steph. Steven gestured toward a landscape that hung above his bed. It was a desert, from somewhere out west, with cacti and mountains in the background.

"The energy in it—it's all wrong," said Steven. "I can't sleep with that thing hanging above me."

"What do you want me to do?"

Steven sighed. He reached up and grabbed the painting, pulling it down, and shoving it toward Steph. She took it awkwardly.

"And a mini-fridge."

"I'll see what I can do," said Steph. She remembered Gary's words about doing whatever the celebs needed.

"Jesus, is everyone here inept?" he asked out loud. "Also, this mattress is not firm enough. I have severe back issues, and if I don't have a firm enough mattress, I can barely walk—"

"Give the girl a break, Steve," said Bill, now standing in the doorway. "You were the one who came."

"Bill," said Hellman. "I see you're still doing drugs."

"I see that you're still an asshole," said Bill, his face plain.

"My attendance was contingent on very particular conditions—"

"I don't think they keyed poor Stephanie in on any of those," said Bill. "Maybe just try asking nicely."

"Asking nicely hasn't ever worked for me," said Hellman. "If you'd be so kind, I'd like some privacy. And get that terrible smoke away from me. *Please*."

Bill shrugged and retreated, with Steph right behind him.

"I'd apologize for him," said Bill. "But I've given him the benefit of the doubt enough times."

"Thank you," said Steph.

"Oh, no worries," said Bill. "We're not all bad seeds."

Steph took the painting downstairs, and dropped it off in the lounge, having nowhere else to put it.

Steph returned to the front entrance, to find Dan, Gary, Henry and Linda all there, waiting.

"Who's left? Any more celebrity guests?" she asked.

"Nope, we got 'em all," said Gary.

"Technically," said Henry, with a slight grimace.

"Then what are we waiting for?" asked Steph.

"Geno," said Gary.

They waited, and soon enough Geno was there, not in a luxury sedan, but in his own stretch limo, looking ridiculous out on the Texas dirt.

The driver opened the door, and Geno got out. He wore a white suit, with snakeskin boots and a ten-gallon hat. He looked absurd. He stared at the five of them, waiting for him.

"What the fuck are you all looking at? Hurry up. We've got a show to run."

# 5

"Hello, Henry," said Geno. "Gary. Everything going well so far?"

"Yes, Mr. McGrath," said Henry. Steph and Dan both grabbed luggage from the trunk of the limousine and loaded it onto the golf carts. The baggage was heavy, and there were six of them, each weighing fifty pounds or more.

"All the stars here?" asked Geno.

"Dave Barclay hasn't shown up. I got word that he missed his flight," said Henry.

"Make sure he doesn't get paid," said Geno.

"Yes, sir," said Henry.

"Careful with those bags," said Geno. "They're crocodile. They're worth more than your life." Steph and Dan exchanged a glance between each other. Her one conversation with him hadn't been an outlier. She understood why every-one disliked him now.

"Have you gotten all the stars squared away?"

"Yes," said Gary. "All are in their rooms."

"Where all the banners?" asked Geno, looking up and around the entrance. "I wanted Midnight Star banners at the entrance."

"They'll be up early tomorrow morning, before most of the crowd arrives," said Gary. Geno sneered, a quick motion before his face returned to normal, but Steph saw it.

"Stephanie will drive you to your room," said Henry.

"Your chariot awaits," said Stephanie, mustering the best smile she could. She remembered Gary's words about Geno's movie. She thought about the video store.

"Golf carts, huh?" he asked.

"It's what they have," said Steph, the wheels spinning a second before grabbing hold of the dirt and propelling them forward.

"Christ, be careful," he said.

"Sorry, Mr. McGrath," she said. He shook his head, look-ing out over the various outbuildings.

"What a fucking place," he said. "This is brilliant. Bril-liant. I can smell the money already. Premiering the film at the actual compound."

"Gary told me you produced it?" asked Steph.

"Nothing would be done without me, sweetheart," he said. "I talked with Joe, got him his money. I got Joe the stars he wanted. I kept it on schedule. Wouldn't have happened without me. And now we're here. God, beautiful. I mean, not the land. It looks like spoiled shit. But I mean, hell, the publicity will be beautiful."

"But will it be good?"

"No such thing as bad publicity, girlie," he said.

"But all those people who died. Some of them were innocent," she said. The feeling that had washed over her earlier, the vision of hundreds dead, including children. It was there, just a fingertip away, at any moment. She only had to reach out, and she would find it.

"Boo-fucking-hoo. That was what, twenty-five years ago? Longer? Who gives a shit about some dead brainwashed morons? If they wanted to stop me, they shouldn't have died in the first place. I'm sure Kalman told them whatever they wanted to hear, and then they all committed seppeku to go their alien god."

"He drugged them," said Stephanie. "They didn't want to die."

"They were here willingly," said Geno. "They didn't think they were in any danger out here, getting corralled by that nut job? Gotta defend yourself, you know. Who do you work for?"

Steph's stomach soured. She shouldn't have said anything.

"Gary," said Steph.

"Ah, I see," said Geno. "I remember now. You're the one from the video store, who was uppity on the phone. Well, remember that your precious store is getting funded from this damn event. So keep your mouth shut and your opinions to yourself."

A pit of anger rose within her, but she pushed it down. She squeezed her lips together. Steph had never been the best at keeping her thoughts private, but she would have to suffer with Geno. They all would.

They arrived at the lodge, and Steph pulled the golf cart up to the front door, and began unloading Geno's many bags. He watched her as she did it. He could feel his eyes on her, lingering on her butt. She knew when a man was leering at her. She did her best to ignore him, and shouldered the luggage, pulling them inside one by one. She would have to carry them all upstairs.

She pulled them up, one at a time, feeling Geno's gaze on her the entire time. Her heart beat hard in her chest by the time they were all up on the second floor, where she could luckily use the wheels on them. Steph opened the door to his room, a massive suite.

"This is the biggest room, right?" he asked, as she pulled all his luggage inside.

"Yes," she said.

"Good," he said. He rubbed his hands together, taking a quick look around. "You know, we don't have to be antagonistic. We could be friends."

"I—"

He got closer to her, smiling, his teeth visible. She felt the anxiety raising in her gut. She balled her fist. *This motherfucker. If he touches me—*

"You know, I have a lot of power. I can make things much easier for the video store. For you."

"I need to get going," she said, forcing a smile. "The VIPs are about to arrive."

"I'm sure Henry has got it covered," said Geno. He still rubbed his hands together.

"Mr. McGrath—"

He got closer.

"You can call me Geno," he said. "All my friends do."

One more step, and she would hit him. She thought of Gary, of the video store, of this whole thing. Of all the money gone from it.

He took another step. Her fist silently shook.

"Please—" she mustered.

"Did you make that poor girl carry all that luggage upstairs by herself?" asked a voice from the doorway. Steph recognized it, turning to see Mary Jo Carter still cutting a trim figure in her 60s, her hair cut short and silver. She wore a simple white blouse with green capris. Of all the people here, she was the biggest name. She had been nominated for an Oscar. But her first big break had been in horror, in the granddaddy of all the slashers.

None of that really mattered to Steph. She was just happy to have someone else here.

"That's what she's being paid for," said Geno, who had reflexively taken a step back from her. Steph didn't stand on ceremony and quickly retreated out the door. She could feel the heat in her cheeks. "It's good to see you, Mary Jo."

"I bet it is," she said, and smiled, and hurried up behind Steph as she started down the stairs.

"Thank you," said Steph.

"Try and not be alone with him," said Mary, looking back up the stairs.

"I'll try, but—"

"It's hard when he has so much power," said Mary. "I know. Believe me. And he's not even the worst."

"I need to get back to work," said Steph. "It was nice meeting you."

Mary nodded at her and returned upstairs.

Steph took a deep breath and went back to the golf cart.

The VIPs would show up soon, and she needed to help them. She knew more volunteers and employees would arrive too, but they would need all the help they could get.

Steph parked the cart and walked back to the front entrance, where the shuttle buses would pull up soon enough. More workers had arrived on another shuttle. Linda and Gary were giving them a quick walkthrough of procedures for the rest of the day.

"Any problems?" asked Henry. Steph hadn't noticed him, but he was suddenly there.

"Geno is an asshole," said Steph.

Henry nodded. "He's not pleasant to work with."

"Could you make sure only dudes assist him?" asked Steph.

"I can't make any promises," said Henry.

"I—"

Henry only nodded again. "I've got to take care of this," he said, and then walked up to the front gate to greet the VIPs, along with Linda and the rest of the new workers.

The first shuttle stopped, and the VIPs piled out. The VIPs were all the other people staying at the compound over the duration of the festival. They had paid dearly for it, with most of their tickets costing north of $5,000. It included a room, food, and signings and pictures with the stars, and passes to all the films. These were the whales, and where a significant portion of the show's profits would come from.

As they stepped off the shuttle most of them were on their phones, recording their arrival. That it took place in an old cultist compound had its own kind of charm to some of them, Steph was sure. Most of them were dudes, but a few women got off the bus.

They began getting them situated, as they grabbed their bags, and the bus pulled off, giving room for the next. There would be five small shuttles full of VIPs, which would be the last of the arrivals for the day.

The VIPs were staying in the old dormitories, where the vast majority of the cultists used to live. Steph accompanied the swarm inside, helping people find their rooms, most of them lugging their own bags. She didn't know what to expect from the inside, but it didn't surprise her too much. It was cramped, with plain wood paneling covering the walls. The beds all had new mattresses and sheets, but the rooms were small. Most people shared them. Some complained.

"Five grand for this?"

"Man, this room is tiny."

"This better be worth it."

But most seemed just happy to be there. This was their vacation for the year, and they were the most dedicated of horror fiends. They'd see new movies early and meet their idols.

"This is awesome! I can't believe we're staying in the Kalman compound."

"God, I am so psyched for Midnight Star! And we get to see it here!"

"I can't wait to meet Nancy Slaughter! I had such a crush on her as a kid."

It took a while, but everyone eventually found their room and roommates. Some people cracked open some beers, before the night's party. A few of the workers stayed behind to provide any help needed, while everyone else retreated to get the party ready in the grand ballroom.

As Steph left the dorm, she noticed William, the caretaker, loitering against the side of a nearby building. He was spooling wire in a bundle, and layering other bundles, covered in cloth, in his ATV.

She thought back to his comments about visiting the compound. He had avoided the question about why he was there.

"Steph," said Gary, and she turned to him. "You there?"

"Sorry, I was gone for a second," she said.

"This place will do that to you," said Gary. "We need to get going. We have to set up the party. Or at least supervise."

"Is everyone going to be there? Or is just for the VIPs?" she asked, as they walked back toward the large ballroom with the rest of the workers.

"Everyone's going to be there. All the celebrities," said Gary. He chuckled. "It's in their contracts."

# 6

The party set-up went quickly, with the addition of the new workers. They placed tables with place settings. The DJ set up her own station, while everyone else laid out all the chairs necessary. The night would include dinner, and so a catering company had arrived, laying out all the food.

It was a lot of planning, and a lot of prep, and it was running Gary ragged already. He hustled from place to place, making sure everything was working well. He could have hired someone to take care of all of this for him, but Gary wouldn't spend money on something he could do himself. And every dollar he didn't spend went back into the video store. As the afternoon ended, the workers were let go, to either explore the compound or chill in their lodging until the party that night.

"So what exactly are we doing at this party?" asked Dan. They both sat in Steph's room, in the Clue mansion.

"Everyone keeps calling it a party," said Steph. "But it's more like dinner and drinks, and talking. I highly doubt anyone will even dance."

"But I mean, the celebrities will all be there," said Dan.

"Yes," said Steph. "They'll technically be there. But they'll each sit at a table with a handful of the VIPs. They'll make small talk. And after they finish dinner, they'll probably leave."

"That doesn't sound like much of a party," said Dan. "I thought it'd be a little more loose than that."

"The celebs would be swarmed all night."

"You could ask people to respect them."

"Ha," said Steph. "They paid thousands of dollars to be here. Do you think they'll just be nice?"

"Hmm," said Dan. "Probably not."

"Maybe some of them," said Steph. "But some won't. And does Frank Buchanon need that in his life. Or Mary Jo Carter? No. They'll be nice, they'll shake hands and make small talk. But this is a novelty. It's not supposed to be 'become friends with celebrities' time."

"Then why go at all?"

"I mean, if I could afford a dinner with Frank Buchanon, you'd better believe I'd be spending that money," said Steph. "Even if was just small talk. And it's free food and an open bar."

"Free food," said Dan, with air quotes. "They're paying for it with their ticket."

"True, but what else are they going to eat?" asked Steph. "It's not like they can drive down to the grocery store. It's an hour away."

"I think the kitchens have the basics."

"You know what I mean," said Steph. "They paid for it. Might as well take advantage. As for our duties, I think we're largely there to keep the peace."

"Between who?"

"Between the celebs and the VIPs," said Steph. "Just to make sure no one gets swarmed."

"We're not bodyguards."

"No," said Steph, "but I doubt we'll have to be. Most people will stop when asked. And there'll be more than you and me if need be. Why did you ask between who?"

"Because it seems some stars don't like each other very much. Nancy gave Mary a death stare as I was bringing Mary in. I thought she was going to launch herself at her."

"Doesn't seem like most of them are too friendly," said Steph. "You should have heard Steven Hellman. He hates everyone."

"I mean, when was the last time you saw him in a movie?"

"I don't know," said Steph. "He was in that weird slasher vs slasher flick twenty years ago."

"Yeah, twenty years ago," said Dan. "He wants to work, but the world has changed. His world has changed. I'd be upset too."

"Doesn't need to be an asshole about it. You should have heard him talk about Joe Banshee."

"What'd he say?" asked Dan. "Joe was nice to me. Him and Abel both."

"I mean, Frank mentioned it too," said Steph. "Joe didn't cast them. Didn't call Hellman when he rebooted Sleep Terror."

"There's only so many parts," said Dan.

"Like you said, it's a different world," said Steph. "They're old Hollywood, in a weird way. They didn't adapt."

"God, I haven't mentioned Levi Stark," said Dan.

"I didn't realize he was coming."

"He's showing his next film."

"I didn't know he *had* a new one."

"Don't worry. If you step within five feet of Levi, he'll be happy to tell you about it. Jesus, he wouldn't stop talking about how great it was, and how it deserved more attention than Midnight Star."

"Didn't he make the Terminal Conclusion movies?"

"Yeah," said Dan. "All six of them."

"He made six?" asked Steph. "I think I've seen three of them?"

"You're not missing much," said Dan. "But he seems to think Joe's a hack. Not just Joe. Everyone but him."

"Lovely," said Steph. "The weekend's already shaping up great."

"But you got to talk to Frank, right?" asked Dan. "How was it?"

"It was good," said Steph, smiling.

"Oh, come on," said Dan. "Spill."

"It was great!" said Steph, letting her excitement out. "He talked about trying to find parts, and them probably recasting Axl in the Vile Buried reboot—"

"They can't do that!" said Dan.

"That's what I said," said Steph. "And—"

"And?"

"And he seemed unhappy that his room was between

Nancy and Mary."

"Hmm," said Dan. "Maybe that's the source of the death glare."

"She protected me today," said Steph.

"Who? Mary?"

"Yeah."

"From who?"

"Geno."

"What'd he do?" asked Dan.

"He came on to me," said Steph.

"Gross," said Dan. "That motherfucker. Have you told anyone?"

"I told Henry," said Steph. "He said he'd try and only send guys to help him from now on. That probably means you."

"Well, shit," said Dan. "Still."

"Mary stepped in and got me out of the situation," said Stephanie. "What an asshole."

"No one likes him," said Dan. "Even Joe. His movie would haven't happened without Geno, and he *still* doesn't like him."

"Working with him probably makes Joe like him less," said Steph. "Being around him for ten minutes made me never want to see him again."

"He's got us over a barrel," said Dan. "Splatterfest isn't this size without him."

"But does it need to be this big?" asked Steph. "I always loved going when it was out of the store, and Gary would show movies on a projector in the parking lot."

"It needs to be this size if he wants to make any money," said Dan. "If we want to keep the store alive."

"He seemed so frazzled while we were setting up," said

Steph.

"I imagine he's stressed out of his mind," said Dan. "This kind of event planning is juggling a hundred balls at once, and all of them are glass. Drop any of them, and there's no picking it back up."

"Why doesn't he ask for help?" asked Steph.

"You know Gary better than most people," said Dan. "He doesn't ask for help. Hell, him asking us to volunteer was more than I expected."

"But to get in bed with Geno?" asked Steph.

"Gary doesn't like him," said Dan. "He said so himself. But there was no one else who would float him the money. How long has it been since Blockbuster went out of business?"

"Over a decade."

"And when was the last time you bought a DVD?"

"I got a used copy of Kiki's Delivery Service three weeks ago," said Steph.

"You know what I mean," said Dan. "No one goes to video stores anymore. Everyone streams everything. If it's not included on a streaming platform, it might as well not exist. Only weirdos and collectors visit the store."

"I'm very aware of our clientele," said Steph. Her mind cycled through all the regulars. Terry, who only bought Italian giallo films on Blu-Ray. Janine, who wanted all the John Ford westerns, but only on VHS. It reminded her of her dad, she had said. John, who collected parody films, the more obscure the better. There was a laundry list of them, collectors in the truest sense of the word. They would go anywhere to add to their collection. Thrift stores, eBay, The Video Store. Anywhere. But with all their purchases, they didn't keep the store in business. Not anymore.

Gary had always run events out of the store, even from the very beginning. He would show bad movies in the back room to an audience of a dozen people, everyone sitting on top of each other, everyone sweating, but everyone having fun heckling the movie, drinking beer and wine.

Then they got too big for the back room, and they moved to the front. And then to the parking lot. And as they grew, Gary never charged much for the tickets, or for anything else he sold. He only wanted to make people happy. He preferred to foster a sense of community. And he did.

"And real estate prices keep going up," said Dan.

The video store sat on a desirable block. Back when Austin was just the weird liberal outpost of Texas, that didn't mean much. Rent was cheap. But now two hundred people moved there a day, and the legacy stores and restaurants were closing every day, being pushed out by corporate interests with deeper pockets. Community didn't matter. Only money did.

"It's not fair," said Steph. "They'd kick out Gary and put in some chain."

"They don't care about fair," said Dan. "And what else does Gary have?"

"Not much," said Steph. He had never married, or had kids. The Video Store *was* his kid. He had nurtured it, and taken care of it, and built a village of people around it. But it couldn't survive without more support. Splatterfest would have to be the thing.

"He's got the store," said Dan. "He's in his fifties. This is his legacy. And I know you'll say that he doesn't care about stuff like that. I think he does. He cares a lot. He keeps getting wistful around me, and it scares me. Like the video store is almost over, and after that, there's nothing else. I'm worried about him."

"You don't have to convince me that Gary cares," said Steph. "That's what I like about him the most." He was always willing to listen, to anyone. The growing number of homeless could count on Gary to invite them in during the winter, or during long storms. Gary wanted the store to be an extension of him, and it was.

"That's why he's working with Geno," said Dan. "There's no other way. And he probably thinks it's a necessary corporate evil. Anything, if it will keep the store alive."

"At a certain point, is Splatterfest the same, though?" asked Steph.

"I don't know," said Dan. "I've only been a couple times. Most of the people traveling in over the next few days aren't regulars. They're horror fans from around the world with a lot of money. The little indie place is going the way of the dodo. Maybe if he bought the land, he could manage. But it would cost millions now. Gary eats hot dogs for dinner."

Steph sighed. "All we can do is help," she said.

"You're right," said Dan.

"I need to get ready for tonight," said Steph. "So scram."

"What's there to get ready for?" asked Dan. "It takes ten minutes to take a shower."

"Maybe I want to do more than just take a shower," said Steph.

"Ooooh, are you getting yourself pretty for Frank Buchanon?" asked Dan.

"Oh, come on. I love Frank, but he's in his sixties," said Steph. "Can't I just look pretty for my own sake?"

"I mean, you can," said Dan. "But that's not you." He narrowed his eyes at her. "Henry."

"What does that mean?" asked Steph.

"I saw the way you looked at him," said Dan. "I mean, I don't blame you. He's got that Dorito shoulder to waist ratio."

"You are unbelievable," said Steph.

"So you're not denying it," he said, smiling. He got up from the chair and walked out, making kissy noises.

"You're such a child."

"Just teasing," said Dan. "You're a bombshell. You'll knock him dead." Dan closed the door behind him.

She glanced at the mirror. Her clothes were half covered in dust, and she looked tired. She had planned on looking nice for tonight, and she had to admit a part of it was because of Henry being there. He was cute. Maybe he was single.

Perhaps it was ridiculous. Maybe she should be sensible.

She looked at herself a minute longer.

*Fuck it. I'm getting dressed up.*

# 7

"How's it looking so far?" asked Gary, as he wandered to where Stephanie and Dan were standing, near the bartender.

"Seems fine," said Steph. She looked over the ballroom, filled with round tables covered with white tablecloths and a horror themed centerpiece, themed appropriately for the celebrity that sat there. Steven had a clawed glove, Frank a chainsaw, Nancy a pick axe. The celeb at each table sat with a handful of VIPs, all randomly distributed. The room was filled with chatter, more than Stephanie expected. It seemed like an awkward situation for the celebrities, but she guessed that after enough time of being famous, you were familiar with the song and dance of people being impressed by you.

Everyone had already grabbed their food, and they ate,

everybody talking to the celebrity, with no real conflict as far as she could tell. She had walked around, trying to make sure no one needed any help, but it was all smooth sailing. She eyed Geno, who sat next to Nancy, his beady eyes focused only on her. Steph was anxious for her, but Nancy didn't betray any discomfort. She mostly seemed bored.

"Great," said Gary. Gary wore a button-down shirt, still with suspenders, but he had traded in his old pair for new ones, the metal fittings bright and shiny. "You look very nice, by the way."

"Thank you," said Steph. She had finally settled on a classic rose print dress, one that hugged her curves, and had put on some make-up. Henry had been in and out throughout the dinner so far, but she had dropped any charade. She wanted to catch his eye. She assumed he'd come back at some point. God knows how much he had on his plate, having to handle the whims of a handful of celebrities.

Gary wandered away, and Steph grabbed another drink from the bartender before doing a circuit of all the tables, checking that everyone was doing okay. Dinner was almost over, and then they were giving a last call for food. This was also a signal to the celebs that they could dip out at this moment if they felt like it. A few did, as soon as they could extract themselves from any conversation they were embroiled in. Mary Jo Carter left, winking at Stephanie as she passed. A fleet of golf carts with volunteer drivers were waiting to take them back to the lodge.

Abel also dipped out, after a brief whisper into the ear of Joe Banshee. Abel was in every one of Joe's movies, and now he starred in Midnight Star after a long career of playing bit parts and monsters.

But the rest of the celebrities stayed, surprisingly. Not too surprisingly, they all drank heavily, taking advantage of the open bar. There were no drinks back at the lodge, which might explain why some of them remained.

The party got a little looser after the caterers put the food away. Some VIPs left, but a lot of them stayed. Some danced, enjoying the horror themed tunes the DJ pumped out.

Steph stopped drinking after her second, switching over to water. Gary had given them permission to drink, as long as they remained in control. Steph wandered through the ballroom, absorbing everything, serving as a chaperone of sorts.

She found herself near Frank Buchanan, unsurprisingly. She was a little surprised to find him talking to Steven Hellman at the most secluded table. Stephanie stood nearby, close enough to listen in. It was technically eavesdropping, but her curiosity outweighed her guilt.

"I feel the same way," said Frank. "I don't think you're out of line."

"Not even a phone call!" said Steven, his voice raising above the din of the music. "Reboots the franchise that was built upon my back, and can't even give me a phone call. I understand that they're not going to build the franchise around me, not at my age, but they could throw me a bone, you know?"

"I understand," said Frank. "They use us to make money, to raise up an empire, and what do they do after?"

"They toss us out with the trash!" yelled Steven. A few people glanced over at him. Steph could hear it now, clearly. Steven was drunk as a skunk.

"Exactly," said Frank. "You should say something, you

know."

"I should?" asked Steven.

"You should," said Frank. "If I had Sam in the room with me, I'd talk to him."

"I just want a little respect," said Steven, anger in his voice.

"Sometimes, you've got to put the fear of God in them," said Frank. "Summon the sturm und drang, you know what I mean?"

And Steven answered, but Stephanie's attention was diverted, as she saw Henry come in from outside. His face was harried, and he walked over to the bar and ordered something. The conversation between Frank and Steven was interesting, but she hadn't dressed up for nothing, and she might as well talk to him while the last vestiges of liquid courage still flowed through her.

"Hi," she said, as Henry sipped on his drink. He jumped at her voice.

"Hello," he said. His eyes danced over her and then returned to his drink.

"How's it going?" asked Steph.

"Oh, you know," said Henry. "Just monitoring everything." His voice stayed flat, and he looked out over the tables and the dance floor. He took another swallow.

"Ever been to Texas before?" asked Steph, doing her best to draw his attention.

"It's been a long time," said Henry, but he still didn't look at her. He sipped his drink again.

*Oh, come on. I got dressed up and everything.*

She strolled over in front of his eyes. She'd make him see her.

"What are you drinking?" asked Steph, smiling as genuinely as she could.

"I'm sorry—was it Stephanie? I don't mean to be rude but I've got to make sure—"

"You bastard!" yelled a voice, and everyone stopped and looked to the source. It was Steven again, but this time he stood over Joe, who was sitting down and chatting with a few of the VIPs.

"Come on, Steve, we can talk about this some other time—"

"No, I've waited long enough!" he yelled. "I've been pushed off by too many people, too many times. How many times have you ignored my phone calls? How many goddamned times?"

The DJ had turned off the music, and only Steven's voice filled the ballroom.

"That's right, too many goddamned times! You couldn't even give me a goddamned courtesy call, after I spent thirty years of my life building a franchise! My name, my face, my ability created something, and you came along, climbed up on my shoulders, and you didn't even ask for my permission before you did it! You couldn't even throw me a goddamn bone!" Steven's hands were balled into fists at his side. They shook with anger.

"Steve," said Joe. "Please calm down."

"No! Not anymore! Tell me why! I want an answer!"

"The studio told me you weren't interested. That you had disavowed the production. And we thought it was best, with the reboot, to you know, try a new thing. We wanted to establish a fresh face for the franchise, and you know, having you around would just remind them of the old movies."

"Remind them of the old movies?" asked Steven, his face confused.

"Yeah," said Joe, his voice level. "We wanted a clean break."

"What did you say?" asked Steven. He knelt down closer to Joe.

"We wanted a clean break," said Joe.

"I'll give you a clean break!" yelled Steven, and he punched Joe with his right hand, his fist connecting with Joe's eye. Joe fell backwards in his chair, onto the ground, and Steven was on top of him, trying to hit him again, but Joe was much younger and in better shape, and quickly tied up Steven. Everyone in the vicinity descended on them, pulling Steven off of Joe, helping Joe to his feet. Steven struggled in their grasp in his anger, but then pulled himself back and away. He gave one last look full of venom at Joe and then marched toward the exit.

Stephanie watched all of this agape, not expecting an explosion like this on the first night. Half the VIPs stood similarly. Some recorded it with their phones.

Geno emerged from the bystanders and tried to walk with Steven, saying something to him in a hushed tone.

Steven stopped, and turned toward Geno. "Go fuck yourself, Geno!" he yelled, leaning over the shorter man. His finger hovered inches away from Geno's face. "At least Joe is an artist. He *makes* things. You're just a boil on the ass of the industry, a slimy asshole who can't do anything but be a parasite!"

And in a flash, he was moving again toward the exit, leaving Geno sputtering, his face turning red. Steph couldn't help but smile at Geno being so publicly embarrassed.

Steven left, and then Nancy jogged after him, her clutch in hand. Geno grabbed at her wrist as she passed him.

"Get your fucking hands off me," she said, acid in her throat, and pulled her hand away, and was out the door.

The room stood frozen for a few moments, and then Gary ran to the DJ, and soon music filled the space. Everyone exchanged a few glances, and then the party started anew.

Steph turned to look, but Geno was already gone.

Henry went after him without a glance back. Steph sighed.

*Welp, there goes that.*

The music had started again, and some tried to recapture the earlier fun, but it was too late. People left, back to the dorms to get a good night's sleep, or to more private festivities. Frank, Joe, and Bill were soon gone, and Gary cleared out the few stragglers.

"I wasn't expecting that," said Dan. "That was crazy."

"I had overheard Frank talking to him," said Steph.

"Talking to who?"

"Steven," she said. "He was kind of egging him on."

"Well, it worked," said Dan. "He was pissed."

"Yeah, it worked alright," said Steph. She couldn't help but feel disappointed in her idol. Frank had always seemed so cool, so above it all. But she saw him down in the mire and her stomach soured.

"Gary said we could go back," said Dan. "I'm going to get some sleep."

"I think I'll help clean up," said Steph. "Keep my mind off things."

"Suit yourself," said Dan, and he was gone. Catering had

already begun putting what remained away, with the volunteers folding up tables and chairs. They would be up again early tomorrow, getting things set up for the first official day of the con.

"You don't need to be here," said Gary. "You've had a long day."

"I might as well be useful," she said.

"You're allowed to rest, Steph," he said. "Plus, you shouldn't ruin that beautiful dress. Go get some sleep. That's an order. Tomorrow's going to be even longer."

Steph grabbed one of the carts and drove back herself. It was her first time out in the dark on the compound, and alone to boot. She hadn't thought about it before she left the ballroom. The sky was full of stars. It was beautiful, the quiet interrupted by the wheels underneath her crunching through the rocky dirt. It was easy to be tricked by the peacefulness. It was easy to forget the horrors that had once happened here.

She continued, trying to keep the unease out of her mind. Soon she was at the lodge, pulling the golf cart nearby. She went to the front door when she caught sight of an ember flaring in her peripheral vision. It was Bill, smoking in the shadows.

"Would you like some now?" he asked.

"No, I'm okay," she said. "But thanks for the offer."

"Keep me company then?" he asked.

"Sure," she said. The late spring night was pleasant, and how many chances did you get to hang out with a legendary horror director?

"That was quite a show, wasn't it?" he asked.

"You could say that," she said.

"Steven really got himself into it tonight," said Bill. "But try not to hold it against him. He's had a rough time lately."

"You've worked with him, haven't you?"

"Yeah, both our last major movie," he said. "God, what a piece of crap. I'm not surprised the studios won't have anything to do with me after that."

"What was it called?" asked Steph.

"I wish I could forget," said Bill. "Alien Spectre. It made no goddamn sense. We had no budget, and half the stars didn't want to be there. It was doomed to fail, no matter how hard Steven and I fought for it."

"Sorry," said Stephanie.

"Oh, don't be," said Bill. "Shit happens. It's the only attitude you can have working in Hollywood. Sometimes shit happens. You can work hard, do your best, and it still won't work out. I wanted to direct other stuff, you know? Not just horror movies. But I got trapped by the money they made."

"Would you change anything, if you could?"

"Probably not," said Bill. "Because what I got others would literally kill for. I should be thankful. I *try* and be thankful. Steven's the same. He was always a little more wild than me."

"He showed it tonight," said Steph.

"At least he blew up at Geno too," said Bill. "That prick."

Steph laughed at that. He elbowed her. "Thanks for keeping me company." He threw the remnants of the joint down, and squashed it with his heel. "This old man is going to bed."

"Good idea," said Stephanie.

He held the door for her, and they went inside.

Steph retreated to her room on the first floor and sunk into the bed, managing to slip out of her dress before falling dead asleep.

# 8

Steven rushed out of the ballroom and climbed into the first golf cart he saw, a young man idly sitting behind the wheel.

"Please, take me back, before I do anything else too stupid," he said, struggling with his words. The kid flicked on the motor, and was about to go, when Nancy's voice stopped him.

"Wait," she said. "Let me ride with you."

Before either could stop her, she jumped on board and sat next to Steven, the three of them tight together.

"We good now?" asked the young man.

"Yes, please," said Steven. "Before anyone else wants to tag along."

They silently rode. Steven tried to calm himself down. He couldn't believe he had shown his ass like that. Over decades, he had never been one of those stars. He'd never yelled on set, or been rude to anybody, either a subordinate or a boss. But he had found himself surly this weekend. Worse, he had found himself *mean*. And no matter what he had done, he hadn't been able to exorcise those feelings. The meanness wouldn't go away.

It wasn't there anymore, now. Maybe it just needed to be unleashed. He had let it build up inside for so long, and it had come out, all at once.

"Yeah, it came out. Came out in front of fifty people," he muttered. A melancholy, a desperate melancholy had replaced the meanness.

"What did you say?" asked Nancy.

"Nothing," he said. "I'm sorry."

"It's okay," she said. She grabbed his hand and squeezed it. It felt nice. If he had any shot at salvaging his career, he had flushed that down the toilet. Maybe not by punching Joe, but certainly by yelling at Geno. Geno would tell all his producer friends, and even if they hated him, they wouldn't give him a chance on principle alone. Thick as thieves, they were.

The driver pulled up to the lodge, and they both got off the vehicle, before the young man sped away, back to the hub.

Nancy still held his hand. They stood in front of the mansion.

"Let's go for a walk," she said. "Cool off for a bit."

"I don't know how easy that will be," said Steven. "Some feelings just don't vanish."

"I'm well aware," she said. She pulled him along, and they walked in the dark, lit only by the stars and a sliver of moon. Soon their eyes adjusted and they could see well enough not to stumble on the rocks.

Within a minute they were clear of everything, all the buildings distant in the darkness.

"I hope we can find our way back," said Steven.

"I have a good sense of direction," said Nancy. "Plus the outside light on the lodge is the only one aside from the sky. I think we'll be fine."

"Fair enough," he said. "I made a proper ass of myself back there."

"You sure did," said Nancy. "Impressive, really."

"It doesn't feel impressive," said Steven. The night air felt good, and he felt the drunk wearing off just enough. He could handle his thoughts again. "It feels like I lost control."

"Sometimes it's hard," she said. "I'll smooth things over with Joe."

"You don't have to—"

"Oh, shut up, Steven," she said. "Let me help you, for once. Joe will listen to me. He still has a crush on me, even though he's twenty years younger than me."

"Is that why he casts you?" asked Steven.

"You don't think it's because of my talent?" asked Nancy.

"I didn't mean—"

She squeezed his hand. "I'm just fucking with you. Yes, that's why he casts me. But whatever. Work is work."

"I wish I could be that pragmatic," he said.

"Well, when you've had to scrounge for every part you've ever had, including the ones you're famous for, it shapes your worldview a little differently," she said. The rocky sand crunched underneath their feet.

"I tried to help," said Steven. "But they never listened to

me, anyway. I was just a monster to them."

"I needed help from someone outside, not in," she said. "Somebody outside of the pigeonhole I've lived in my entire career. The same one you were in."

Steven nodded.

"You can't smooth things over with Geno, though," said Steven.

"No," said Nancy. "And even if I could, I wouldn't."

"Who would?" asked Steven. "And it'd be worse for you."

"Eh, fuck him," said Nancy. "We're not dead yet. We've got time left. There's still hope for us geezers."

"You're still a young whippersnapper," said Steven. Nancy was at least fifteen years his junior.

"It doesn't feel that way sometime," she said. "Feels like I only play grandmothers. I'm not that old."

"We were young once," he said.

"Yeah, once," she said. "Not anymore."

"Better than the alternative."

"I guess that's true."

They faded away into silence, and continued to walk, enjoying the peace.

"God, this place is truly hellish," said Steven.

"It's peaceful," said Nancy.

"I can't shake the feeling," said Steven. "Of what happened here. It's looming over me."

"It's all in the long, forgotten past," said Nancy. "No ghosts here. Not even the dead."

"The past is never dead. It's not even past."

"Mr. Smarty Pants."

"It's Faulkner," said Steven. "I don't even like him that much, but I still quote him." He sighed. "Do you think they'll quote us after we're gone?"

"I mostly just screamed," said Nancy. "So I don't think so. You had a couple good ones."

"It was all camp," said Steven. "Not bad, but still camp. Puns about sleep and nightmares, stolen from old pulp magazines. The writers didn't need to dig down deep to write Johnny."

"You're not dead yet," said Nancy. "And when you are, you won't have to worry about this petty bullshit, anyway. You'll be dead."

Steven laughed at that, a dark laugh, but a laugh.

"Let's go back," said Steven. "I'm tired, and we have to still face the actual festival. I should apologize to Joe."

"I'll talk to him first," said Nancy. "As for Geno, well, fuck him."

They returned to the lodge, following the light. The night was quiet. It seemed everyone had settled down while they were gone. They walked upstairs, the massive house silent.

"Do you want to—you know, stay with me tonight?" asked Steven. Nancy squeezed his hand once and then let go.

"I'm too old for that," said Nancy, with a small smile.

Steven could only maintain eye contact for a moment, before breaking it, looking down at his hands. Liver spots and beat up fingernails. He nodded.

"I understand," he said. "Goodnight."

"Goodnight, Steven," said Nancy, and she went into her room without a glance backwards. Steven stood there for a second, still looking at his hands. He exhaled deeply and went to his bedroom, closing the door behind him. He sat down on the bed and pulled off his boots.

*Made a fool out of myself twice tonight. Why did I ask her to stay with me?*

"Because you're lonely, you old clown," he said. He undressed and slipped on pajamas. His room, despite his earlier complaints, was huge, his bed comfortable. He'd been an utter asshole. He laid back, his eyes closed.

Maybe that was the problem all along. He needed to rebuild relationships. Foster growth in himself again. He had been trying so hard for so long to reclaim something that was already gone.

He needed to make something new. He'd had that idea for a screenplay. He had written half of it, long ago, and then got frustrated, and thrown it aside, because he realized he was much too old for the main character. He wanted to star.

But it was still a good idea. And he was perfect for the older mentor figure. A strong supporting role. And it would sell, he just knew it. The reemergence of the eighties aesthetic had made it more likely than ever.

He could ask Bill to direct. Bill understood, and he had the talent, if he would stop smoking weed for more than ten minutes. They could finish the screenplay and shop it around. They could find someone to give them the money. Maybe even do it for Netflix, or Amazon. They were throwing money at washed up stars like him all the time.

He had a sudden burst of energy. He felt alive again, like he could break down the door.

Maybe the outburst had been for the best. It was embarrassing, but getting it out of his system let him get past the resentment and the bitterness. He still had a future. He knew it.

He wanted to do it all now, tonight. But everyone was

asleep. He would face tomorrow. He'd make amends. He wasn't too old. The past *wasn't* past.

Steven's ears perked at a creaking noise from the bathroom. He raised his eyebrows. He had left the door unlocked. He hoped a fan wasn't camped out in there. He'd had enough drama for the day.

Still, he grabbed a candlestick from a nearby table and poked his head into the expansive bathroom, flipping on the light. He found nothing. The room was empty. The place was old, and the shifting Texas temperatures probably just made it creak.

Steven heard a noise behind him this time, a quick shuffling. He turned, raising the candlestick, turning back into the bedroom, but there was nothing again. He was imagining things. He was tired, half-drunk, and full of emotion. He needed sleep.

Tomorrow, though. He would make up for his explosion at dinner. He would take the first steps to the beginning of a career renaissance.

He dug through his overnight bag. Where were his pills? He couldn't sleep without them.

*The goddamn TSA. They always did this shit. Rifled through my luggage like I'm a drug mule.*

He found them. As he'd aged, rest had been harder and harder to come by. He finally went to the doctor and got the pills. He hated them, but he needed the sleep, no matter how reliant on them he became. They had been a problem, at first. But he'd gotten better with them. He slipped one under his tongue and put the bottle at his bedside.

Steven flipped off the lamp, casting the room into darkness. He closed his eyes and focused on nothing. The pill would do its work in a moment.

Within a couple minutes it kicked in, his body growing warm and sluggish. He shouldn't have taken it after drinking, but oh well. He'd be fine. Sleep overtook him.

Then the light kicked on again, and a hand clamped down over his mouth. He tried to struggle, but his arms and legs were slow to respond. Then he felt the prick of a needle in his neck, and he opened his eyes to see someone injecting him with something.

"Wha—why?" he got out. His tongue wouldn't respond. The figure held his hand over Steven's mouth still, even as Steven went limp.

Steven recognized the last words he heard. They were from the first Sleep Terror movie. He had said it to all of his victims.

"Sweet dreams."

9

The buses pulled up at 8 AM to mark the first official day of Splatterfest. More volunteers had arrived early that morning, before Steph was even awake, working the Friday or Saturday, and in return, getting access for free on another day.

These weren't a few shuttles filled with VIPs. These were the general admission buses, dropping off attendees from a dozen different hotels all within an hour of the compound. It was a logistical nightmare, one of the few Gary wasn't in charge of. And as soon as one was empty, it departed to pick up more people, and another would pull up, unloading dozens more. Within a few minutes, hundreds and then thousands of fans wandered the grounds. They would only be there for the day, before departing again for the night. Some would come back every day, others cherry picking the days they would visit.

They stared agog, taking pictures of everything. Within half an hour the wi-fi was nearly unusable, clogged with people throwing pictures up on Instagram. The buses would come throughout the day, dropping off more and more guests.

Still, the compound was expansive, and the layout of events kept the public spread out throughout the area. Gary had programmed a wide range of things. He had always wanted Splatterfest to be a variety show of sorts, and although there were signings, photo-ops, and screenings with the celebrities, there were also plenty of things that were just celebrations of classic genre movies, trivia events, cosplay contests, and much more.

As soon as the buses unloaded, there were dozens of people in costume, some as horror icons, but even more as superheroes and anime characters. Stephanie considered herself well versed in pop culture, but even she couldn't recognize some of them. Steph watched them arrive and then hustled to the ballroom where she helped Dan finish setting up the signings and photo-ops area. The celebrities would cycle through throughout the event, signing autographs, selling merch, and taking pictures with fans, all for a fee.

"How's everything looking?" asked Steph.

Dan breathed hard, wiping sweat off his brow.

"It seems alright," he said, as he smoothed out a red tablecloth, and then laid down white masking tape on the floor, marking the waiting area for the fans. Linda informed nearby volunteers about etiquette and procedures for signings and photo-ops. They would have the hard work of corralling guests and keeping everyone behaved. A security guard hovered by the door, hired to work the event, in case anyone got out of hand.

"Have you seen Gary at all this morning?" asked Steph.

"Very briefly," said Dan. "He was running around like a chicken with its head cut off. He must be slammed packed with everything going on."

"There's so much happening," said Steph.

"Whatever happened with you and Henry last night?" asked Dan. "I saw you talking before Steven blew up."

"Oh, nothing," said Steph. "He barely even looked at me. He's a cute boy, but he isn't interested."

"I mean, he has a job to do," said Dan. "Might just be more concerned with that."

"I guess," said Steph. "Still doesn't feel great, being ignored, after I dressed up and everything."

"There's always Ted," said Dan, raising an eyebrow.

"Okay, well maybe it's okay being ignored," she said.

Linda paused in front of them, watching over the different teams of volunteers. Steph wandered over to her.

"Hi. Linda, right?" asked Steph. Linda jumped.

"Hi," said Linda. "Yes, that's me."

"Sorry. I'm Stephanie, if you don't remember from yesterday," said Steph. "Just thought a proper introduction was in order."

"Nice to meet you," said Linda. "You work for Gary, correct?"

"Yeah," said Steph. "You're Henry's assistant?"

"Yes," said Linda.

"How long have you worked with him?"

"Not too long," said Linda. "Just over a year."

"Is he—is he single?"

"We don't talk about our private lives too often. Mr. Lindew likes to keep things strictly professional."

"Oh. Of course," said Steph.

"He's never really shown any—"

"Um, ma'am?" asked a volunteer, jogging up to her. "Where exactly do the markers go for the general admission crowd?"

Linda smiled at Steph. "Excuse me, but I have to go take care of this." And she was gone, following the worker off to one of the other signing areas.

"What was that about?" asked Dan.

"Just curious about Henry," said Steph.

"Probably would be better to forget about him at this point."

Steph sighed. "You're probably right."

A little old lady walked up, wearing her Sunday's best. Her gray-blue hair was done up in a huge beehive. The gaudy VIP badge hung from a lanyard around her neck. She smiled as she approached Steph.

"Can I help you?" asked Steph.

"Is this the line for Frank Buchanon?" asked the woman.

"Oh, yes, ma'am, it is."

"How long until he arrives?" she asked. "I've been waiting my whole life for this."

"Probably just a few minutes," said Steph. "I didn't know they were letting the VIPs in yet."

"I sweet-talked the man at the door," said the woman. "My age has a few benefits."

"I bet," said Steph.

"What's your name?" asked the woman.

"Stephanie."

"Nice to meet you, Stephanie. My name is Velma. Yes, like Scooby Doo." She extended a hand and Steph shook it softly, her skin cool.

"Nice to meet you," said Steph. "Are you enjoying the festival so far?"

"Oh yes," said Velma. "My husband died last year, and I decided to treat myself for our anniversary. I've wanted to meet Frank since 1981 when the first Vile Buried came out."

"I'm sorry to hear about your husband," said Steph.

"Oh, it's okay," she said. "He had a good run. He was always jealous of my feelings about Frank, anyway. I'll see him again when it's my time. Until then, I plan on enjoying myself." She laughed, and Steph joined her. It was infectious. It cheered her up for a moment. "Will you do me a favor?"

"I can try," said Steph.

"I want to stand in line for Frank, but I have trouble staying on my feet for too long. Do you think you could steal me a chair, and I could use it while I wait?"

Steph looked around. She didn't know the rules, but Velma was a VIP anyway, and Gary had said do anything within reason.

"Sure," she said. "I think that's okay. I'll grab one for you." Steph grabbed one from a stack along the wall and put it down in the front of the VIP line.

"You'll be the first to meet Frank today," said Steph.

"Oh, you are too sweet," said Velma. "I can't wait!"

Frank Buchanon appeared before long, in a baby blue suit, edged with black, wearing dark sunglasses. His hair was curled in a perfect pompadour. Before the festival began, she had seen that Gary had assigned her to Frank's first signing session, and she had been thrilled, knowing she'd get to spend time with her favorite star. But the course of a single day had soured her on it. She remembered his whispers to Steven the night before. He had instigated the fight.

"Make sure the prices are marked clearly," said Frank, helping Steph lay out his merch on a long table that preceded fans meeting him. "It makes everything go faster if they don't have to ask how much things cost."

Steph labeled all the items, most of them headshots and stills from movies to be autographed. A few toys were there, along with a few big movie posters, for the whales.

"That looks good, kid," said Frank. He sat back. In a couple minutes, the signing would begin. Steph looked out and saw the line already hundreds deep. The VIPs lined up separately, and the general admission fans eyed them with a mixture of jealousy and resentment. They would get first dibs on all the signings and photo ops. If she was spending a few thousand dollars on a ticket, she'd want preferential treatment too.

She glanced at Frank, who stared at his phone, his face blank. If he felt any remorse for his actions the night before, he didn't show it.

"What did you say to him last night?" asked Steph.

"What?" asked Frank. "What are you talking about, kid?"

"Steven Hellman," she said. "You talked to him last night, and then he got into a fight with Joe Banshee."

Frank looked at her for a second, before turning back to his phone. "Don't know what you mean."

"I heard you," said Steph. "Both of you were drinking. You were riling him up. You were antagonizing him. And then he went and punched Joe in the face."

Frank glanced up at her again, his eyes hidden behind his sunglasses. "And?"

"Don't you care? You took advantage of him. He was drunk, and upset, and then he made a scene in front of everyone. Won't that hurt him? Or his career? I thought you were better than that." Steph had to fight to keep her voice down. The lines of fans were only a few dozen feet away. She wanted to yell, but she wanted to avoid the same scene she was criticizing Frank for.

"What did I tell him?" asked Frank. "I told him the truth."

"The truth?" asked Steph.

"Yeah, kid," said Frank. "You're young. And I know you've been told that your entire life whenever you questioned someone older than you, but it's true. You're young. Got your whole life ahead of you. And some things only come with experience. Experiences like seeing cast members of a TV show based on things you built get paid millions and millions of dollars, time after time, for a show that doesn't even scratch at the surface of the thing you made. Of seeing people you thought were friends suddenly forget about you when times are tough. Of sitting at a table for a few hours in the middle of nowhere signing autographs for twenty bucks a pop when everyone else is happy at home. After you're fed shit for a while, you're gonna get sick."

"So you get him angry instead of doing anything yourself?" asked Steph.

"Hey, Steve is the one who started the conversation, not me. If you expect me to guard my words around him, you've got another thing coming. I told Steven the truth, but I didn't tell him to go fight anyone. He did that all on his own. Lecture him, not me."

"I—"

"If you really want someone to talk to, find Joe. He's the problem, not me or Steve. We're just washed up old actors. He's the young gun who came in here, without a lick of talent or experience, a rock star handed the keys to the kingdom. Every producer crawling hands over feet to work with him. All he's done is make gory crap without any sense of art or depth. It's sold well, so I guess that doesn't matter. And they hand him remake after remake, and he pleads ignorance, and uses words like respect and honor, but none of that means shit, kid. He's erasing our legacies, one frame at a time, even if he says he isn't. You'd be angry too, if you were watching yourself be forgotten."

"They've been remaking movies since there's been movies," said Steph.

"It doesn't make it right," said Frank. "Joe doesn't care about us. Neither does the industry. Thank God these people are here, or I'd have no one. Poor Steve is the same way."

"I'm—I'm sorry," said Steph, taken aback.

Frank held his gaze for a second longer and then looked away and then back. The scowl on his face disappeared. "Don't worry about it, kid," said Frank, waving her off. "I know it's not great seeing all this bullshit up close, but now you now how I feel. I've lived in it for years and years. I can't help but get worked up about it. I shouldn't be attacking you. You couldn't understand."

The crowd roared in front of them, as the first people were let through. Velma waved from her chair in line. Steph waved back.

"Looks like they're unleashing the beast," said Frank. "Don't let them through unless they've paid."

# 10

The next couple hours flew by, with Stephanie taking money from hundreds who wanted to meet Frank and get something signed. As soon as the signing was over he disappeared, off to do photo-ops, staged somewhere else in the compound.

Steph worried that she'd judged him too harshly about his words to Steven. Nothing he had said was wrong. But she barely had time to think about it, because she had to be over at the legacy screening area, to assist Nancy Slaughter with the screening and her Q&A.

Steph hopped into a golf cart and hauled ass over there, dodging con-goers as they loitered in the compound. She honked her horn aggressively, and they eventually moved out of the way. It was only Friday. There'd be even more people there over the weekend.

She got there just in time to formally meet Nancy and to get seated. A few hundred fans had gathered in the impromptu theater. Nancy stood up in front of them.

"Hi," she said. "We're about to watch The Butcher Shop. It came out in 1985. This was the one that put me on the map." The crowd applauded, and Nancy paused, waiting for them to finish. She half-smiled. "Thank you. We'll watch the movie, and then we'll have a Q&A afterward."

Nancy walked to the back and sat next to Steph. The room darkened, and the projector started playing, throwing the film onto a massive screen. The hard rock started playing, and then the opening credits rolled. The film started with the slasher villain John Butcher killing his first victim. Steph had seen the movie once and had never thought much of it. She glanced at Nancy. Nancy clearly didn't want to be there. She rubbed the bridge of her nose, her eyes closed.

Stephanie tried to focus on watching the movie. Might as well try to enjoy it. They'd be there for another ninety minutes. Just as The Butcher killed his second victim, Steph felt a touch on her arm. It was Nancy. Nancy leaned over.

"Follow me," she whispered into Steph's ear, and then she slowly got out of her chair and sneaked to the edge of the room and out through a side door. Steph followed her, trying to remain quiet. It led out into a small room, adjoined by a bathroom. Nancy looked back to make sure Steph was with her and then locked the door.

"I can't watch that shit again," said Nancy, grabbing two chairs from the stack next to the wall.

"Won't we get in trouble?" asked Steph. "What if they notice you're gone?"

"I got sick," said Nancy. "And you wanted to make sure I was alright."

Steph shrugged and nodded. She was here to help Nancy, and if that meant helping Nancy shirk watching The Butcher Shop, then so be it.

"You don't like The Butcher Shop?" asked Steph.

"Are you kidding me? It's total garbage," she said. "I had rented an apartment in LA that was way too expensive. I needed to make rent. So I did that damn movie. I was working in theater. I didn't realize that I would be a scream queen for the rest of my life."

"It's not that bad," said Steph. "The movie, I mean."

"It's another generic slasher," said Nancy. "Nothing special. But do you know how many times in my life I've been stopped and asked about it? How many times people have talked about my kill scene? Fucking weirdos. They stop me on the street and all they want to talk about is how gruesome my death was."

"I can see how that'd get annoying," said Steph.

"Well, it used to be," said Nancy. "Turns out what's even more frustrating is no one recognizing you at all anymore, because you've gotten old."

"You look great."

"Thanks," said Nancy. "But in this industry, women aren't allowed to age."

"There's hundreds of people out there who wanted to see the movie with you," said Steph. "It could be worse."

"It could be," said Nancy. "I—I wanted to be more than this, you know. And I blinked, and everything flew by. All the opportunities, gone. In the blink of an eye. It feels empty."

"Is that what you told Steven?" asked Steph.

Nancy rolled her eyes. "No," she said. "I told him we still had time left. And I'm lucky that Joe casts me in stuff. Steven doesn't have that. But it doesn't mean I don't understand him."

"What about Frank?"

"What about him?"

"He was telling me the same stuff this morning," said Steph. "He had gotten Steven all fired up last night."

"I knew it," said Nancy. "Steven's not the guy to make waves."

"But Frank is?"

"You could say that."

"He mentioned something about you."

"Oh yeah? What was that?" asked Nancy.

"He saw that he was rooming between you and Mary, and he seemed anxious about it," said Steph. "But he wouldn't go into any more detail."

"I forget how young you are," said Nancy. "We used to be an item. It got serious. I thought we were going to get married. Fangoria called us the 'First Couple of Horror'. Instead, he dumped me."

"Oh," said Steph. "I'm sorry."

"It's fine," said Nancy. "I'd say it's water under the bridge, but it's not. No amount of therapy has gotten it out of me."

"But Mary?"

"Who do you think he left me for?"

"For Mary?" asked Steph. "Really?"

"Yeah," said Nancy. "She left his ass not six months later. The prick deserved it. I was never good enough for him. He had to try and move up in the world, you know? And it had to be her. I could have forgiven him if it hadn't been her."

"What's wrong with Mary?" asked Steph. She remembered her pulling Steph away from Geno the day before.

"Oh nothing," said Nancy. "Aside from the fact that she only ever looked out for herself, and didn't give two shits about her friends as soon as it didn't directly benefit her."

"You were friends?" asked Steph.

"For a while," said Nancy. "It seemed like a small world back then. There weren't many scream queens then, so we got along. We watched each other's backs. You've met Geno, I assume?"

Steph nodded, but the look on her face must have given her feelings away.

"Yeah, exactly," said Nancy. "Well, there were a lot more Geno types then, and it was constant work to protect yourself. We kept each other as safe as we could."

"What happened?" asked Steph.

"Imagine you and all your friends are in a pit," said Nancy. "You're surviving down there, but you all want out. And every day, you try and do your best to get everyone out of that pit. Every day. You chisel away at the walls, you boost people up, you do whatever you can to escape. And one day, all your friends and you make a human ladder, so that just one of you can get out. And that person, as they're climbing, all they're doing is making promises. The whole time. About how they'll come back with rope and pull everyone out. All of you. They'll get you all out."

"But they didn't come back," said Steph.

"No," said Nancy. "They got out, and everyone was happy. But they never came back. And worse, they did it all so you could see. Big movies. Awards. Even goddamn yogurt commercials for a quick buck. But they never came back with that rope. And if you ask them about it? Their answer? 'What rope? We were always on our own.'"

"That's hard," said Stephanie.

"She was our friend, and she forgot about us. She was *my* friend, and she forgot about *me*."

"That sucks," said Steph.

"Yeah, well, that's life," said Nancy. Nancy looked at Steph. "Sorry to dump this all on you. You're getting it from all angles, aren't you?"

"I did volunteer," said Steph.

"You're funny," said Nancy, chuckling. "Let's go back out there for the end of the movie. I'll answer some terrible questions and we can move onto the next thing that will try our patience."

They slipped back out into the darkened room, and it seemed no one noticed. Everyone still watched the movie, their eyes watching as The Butcher chopped up another victim. Soon the movie ended, the lights turned back on, and Nancy went to the front to speak. She stood in front of a microphone, with another microphone placed in front of the crowd. People lined up to ask questions.

"Why did you change your name?"

"It just made sense at the time. Nancy Slater isn't the name for a scream queen. Nancy Slaughter is. It got me more attention, and more jobs. I never really liked my last name, anyway."

"Which of your movies is the favorite?"

"I think The Deep Place. It's not very well known, but it gave me a chance to play something very different from usual."

Steph had never seen it. She would need to. There were still a dozen more people in line, and they came up in order. The crowd was getting a little antsy, but Nancy was doing her best to keep them entertained.

"Who's your favorite co-star?"

"Can you give us any secrets about Midnight Star before the premiere?"

"God, I'm such a huge fan, I've seen all your movies. You're a huge inspiration to me, I want to be an actress when I grow up. What kind of advice would you give to an aspiring actress?"

Nancy answered all of them, trying to remain patient with questions she'd probably heard over and over again. Nancy was a common guest at conventions. Being able to entertain fans like this consistently must be difficult.

"Did you ever think about branching out from horror movies? When you see the career of Mary Jo Carter, who transitioned into comedies and dramas, do you wish you could have done the same?"

Steph's stomach sank. Nancy's frustration bubbled up to the surface. She heard a noise from behind her, and she turned to see the door open, and someone sneak in. It was Henry, and his face was full of worry. He made his way to the front of the room, toward Nancy.

"No, I never thought about it all. I was quite happy toiling away in crappy slasher after crappy slasher. All I wanted from my career was working in bad movies so that some forgotten monster could kill me with a machete or a chainsaw—"

Henry walked up to her and whispered in her ear. A look of sheer sadness and horror crossed Nancy's face, and she looked to Henry with confusion and doubt. He nodded again, and she burst into tears, covering her face and then running off, out through a back entrance. Henry spoke into the microphone.

"I'm sorry folks, we're going to have to end the Q&A a little early. Please exit the ballroom slowly and safely." He turned off the mic. The crowd murmured in confusion, but then slowly stood up, working their way toward the exit.

*What was happening? Why is Nancy upset?*

Steph got up, navigating her way through the crowd toward Henry, who now studied his phone while the crowd cleared out.

"Stephanie," he said as she approached. "I was looking for you."

"What happened? What's going on?"

"I—I don't know how else to tell you," said Henry. "But Steven was late for his signing, so we went to his room. We found him there. He's gone."

"What?" asked Steph.

"He died last night."

# 11

Stephanie hurried over to the lodge. A crowd had already assembled as the news disseminated throughout the festival. A sheriff's vehicle and an ambulance were parked outside. Fans murmured behind caution tape as a policeman held the cordon.

Within moments the door to the mansion opened, and two EMTs came out, holding a gurney between them. A body lay on it, covered in a white sheet. The crowd's murmur got louder, the body all the confirmation they would ever need. Stephanie gasped at the sight of it. It was pulled from her, against her will.

The EMTs carried the corpse over to the ambulance, and slid it inside, out of sight. They drove off right after. They had no more business here, and the morgue was a long drive.

The crowd started dispersing then, with no more sights to see. They wouldn't be allowed in. They all were on their phones, using the wi-fi to spread the news of a sudden celebrity death. Steph wanted to go inside, but didn't know if the cop would let her pass.

Before she could press him for entry, Gary came out, ducking under the caution tape. His face was white and bloodless, deep bags under his eyes. He couldn't hide the stress, but there was more than that, something Steph didn't recognize. Maybe it was just him being overwhelmed.

"Stephanie," he said, seeing her. He hugged her, and she returned it. Gary was never the most affectionate person, and the hug said a lot.

"What happened?" asked Steph.

"The cops are still in there," said Gary. "Looking at everything, you know. But they seemed to lean toward suicide. There was a bottle of sleeping pills by the bed. It was empty. A fifth of vodka, too. So, maybe it was an accident. But it's hard to take a whole bottle of sleeping pills accidentally."

"Oh no," said Steph.

"You saw him last night," said Gary. "He wasn't thinking straight."

"Yeah, but he was angry," said Steph. "He wasn't sad. He didn't seem suicidal."

"Sometimes anger can be just as self-destructive," said Gary. "We don't know what was going on inside his mind."

"Nancy told me she was with him afterward, and that he seemed to have calmed down," said Steph.

"Who knows," said Gary. "They'll do blood work on him, but it might take a week to get the results back," said Gary. He looked around at the dispersing crowd, and then bent over, breathing deeply.

"Are you okay?" asked Steph.

"I'll be fine," he said. "I didn't really sleep last night, and now, with all this—it's a lot."

"Do you want to lie down?" asked Steph.

"I can't," said Gary. "There's too much to do."

"What are we going to do?" asked Steph.

"I don't know," said Gary. "A part of me says that we should cancel the rest of the weekend. I know a lot of people have invested time and money into this, but someone dying?" He sighed again and looked out over the compound. "God, it was hard enough without it."

"What will Geno think about that?" asked Steph.

"He would probably hate the idea," said Gary. Steph heard a golf cart behind her, sliding to a stop. "Speak of the devil."

She turned to see Geno hopping out and marching toward them, a thin bead of sweat falling down one side of his face.

"What's going on, Gary?" asked Geno. "Don't tell me that Henry was right. Did Steven kill himself?"

"Please, Geno, keep your voice down," said Gary. Some fans still assembled looked over at them with wide eyes.

"Oh, whatever," said Geno. "It's not like we can keep the news quiet, anyway. Half the fucking world knows already. A picture of the body is floating around on Instagram."

"Oh God," said Gary. He doubled over again.

"Get yourself together," said Geno.

"A man died, Geno," said Steph. "Are you that heartless?"

"Who are you?" asked Geno.

Gary stood up, his face even whiter. "I think we should

cancel events for the day."

"What?" asked Geno.

"We shouldn't ask people to perform when they've just lost a colleague," said Gary.

"Perform? They're signing autographs and answering questions," said Geno. "They're not performing."

"I don't care," said Gary. "We should be human."

"Fucking Jesus Christ," said Geno. He squeezed the bridge of his nose. "My goddamn head won't stop hurting, and this is not helping. Listen to me, Gary. We are not shutting down, and certainly not over this."

"Over this? Steven is dead!"

"And?" asked Geno. "Do you know how much money we'll have to refund? How many sponsors we'll upset? What if half the VIPs want to back out? We could lose a hundred grand, easily. *I* could lose a hundred grand."

"But—"

"No buts," said Geno. "Whose money is funding this thing? Oh right, it's mine! It's my money, it's my festival, and I decide what to do, and we're sure as hell not shutting down for the day. If it upsets people, they can leave without a refund. But that's on them, not on us. You understand? Tell me you understand me."

Gary stood there, his face pale, his lips squeezed together. "I understand."

"Good," said Geno. "Here, I have the perfect solution. This place has a PA, right? Centralized broadcast?"

"Yes," said Gary. There were speakers laid out throughout the grounds, still there from years ago, when John Kalman would say prayers for the entire compound, all at once.

"In a few minutes you're going to make an announcement about the unfortunate passing of Steven. We'll have a moment of silence and offer a quiet area for anyone who wants to mourn. There's so many goddamn empty buildings here, I'm sure we can open one up for them. How's that for humanity?"

"Okay," said Gary, still tight-lipped.

"Great," said Geno. "Good thing I'm here Gary, or this whole goddamned thing would fall apart." He got back into his golf cart and the driver sped away.

"What an asshole," said Stephanie.

"But he's right," said Gary. "We can't afford to shut down the festival, not even for the day."

"We can't let money drive all of our decisions," said Stephanie.

Gary looked at her and then away.

"It's not always that easy, Steph," he said. "Sometimes you have to do things you don't like to protect what you love. I've poured too many years into the store for it to collapse now."

Steph had nothing to say to that. She couldn't argue with Gary's feelings about his legacy.

"Would you write the announcement?" asked Gary. "You're a better writer than me."

"Sure. How long do I have?" asked Steph.

"An hour," said Gary, looking at his watch. "Is that enough time?"

"I think so," said Steph. "Will they let me inside?"

"Yeah, if I tell them to," said Gary. "I would steer clear of Steven's room, but you should be fine. E-mail me it when you're done. I've got to go. This has set me back even more. Thank you for your help, I couldn't do this without you."

He hustled off, grabbing one of the golf carts and driving

off toward the central area. Steph went inside, ducking underneath the caution tape. She thought to go to her room, but went upstairs instead. The police were still in Steven's room talking in hushed tones. She glanced over before knocking on Nancy's door. She didn't know if Nancy was there. Or if she would answer.

But she did, her makeup caked around her eyes.

"How are you doing?" asked Steph.

"I've been better," said Nancy. She looked over Nancy's shoulders to the cops still in Steven's room. "I've been waiting for them to leave, but they're still over there. Come in, I can't stand looking at them."

Nancy opened the door wider and Steph went in. The room was nice, bigger than hers. Nancy's luggage was strewn all over, with dresses, blouses, and pants hanging from every available spot.

"This huge ornate building and not one goddamn closet," said Nancy.

"I could try and help with that," said Steph.

"Oh, don't worry about it," said Nancy. "It's not like I'm moving in." She grabbed a bag and threw it on the floor with a thump. "Sit here."

Steph sat down on the corner of the bed.

"Sorry I ran off on you," said Nancy.

"It's okay," said Steph. "I understand."

"I know what they're saying over there," said Nancy, motioning with her head toward Steven's bedroom. "That he killed himself with sleeping pills."

"It's sad," said Steph.

"I don't believe it for a second," said Nancy. "You should have heard him last night."

"I mean, we all did," said Steph.

"No, after," said Nancy. "He seemed calmer than he'd been in a long time. He seemed hopeful."

"Then what was it? An accident?" asked Steph.

"I don't think so," said Nancy. "Steven was particular with his pills. He never took too many. He had problems in the past. He hated them anyway."

"Then what could it be?" asked Steph.

Nancy looked at her. "You heard him yelling last night. You saw him punch Joe. *You* got him settled, didn't you?"

"Yeah," said Steph.

"Well, then you know that he wasn't the easiest to get along with. Maybe someone got tired of him."

"You're saying someone killed him?" asked Steph.

"I'm saying that I don't buy for a second that he committed suicide, or that it was an accidental OD. So what's left?"

"That seems a little crazy," said Steph. "Did you tell the cops?"

"Yes," said Nancy. "But they looked at me cross-eyed. They trust what's in front of their face." She sat down on top of her own clothes. "Maybe I should do the same. He always kept things to himself. Maybe he was struggling more than I thought."

Steph got up and walked over to her. "Gary's going to do an announcement over the PA and have a moment of silence. I'm going to write the announcement now. Is there anything you want me to add, anything to say about Steven? You were the last person to see him alive."

"He asked me to spend the night with him," said Nancy, tears flowing down her cheeks. "I thought about it. Steven was always nice to me, and he wasn't a bad-looking guy. But

I said no. It wasn't—wasn't my fault, do you think?"

Steph hugged her then, holding her as Nancy sobbed.

"No, of course not," said Steph. "Whatever reason he did it, it wasn't because of you. It felt like his problems were a lot bigger than any one person."

Nancy cried, and then let go of Stephanie, wiping away her tears, running black. "I hope I didn't stain your shirt," said Nancy.

"I think I'm good," said Steph. "I was going to change, anyway. I need to go write the announcement. I'm almost out of time."

"Good luck," said Nancy. Steph went to leave. "Stephanie." Steph paused and turned back to Nancy.

"You can write the normal sad goodbye," said Nancy. "Just say that he was more than just a movie monster. That's all he ever wanted."

# 12

"Hello, Splatterfest attendees. This is Gary Morton, founder of Splatterfest. I have some sad news to report, if you haven't heard already. Steven Hellman, star of the Sleep Terror series, was found dead this morning in his room. Cause of death is still unknown. But we will not remember Steven for his death, but for his life. For his contributions to film, and to horror in general. In the thousands of hours we collectively have sat down and enjoyed his films. Not just for Johnny, whose cultural impact is immeasurable, but for all of his work, great and small. Steven was a good man. He was more than a movie monster. He was an actor. We will have an area for grieving set aside throughout the weekend. Ask a Splatterfest worker and they will guide you to it. For now, I'd like to take a moment of silence to recognize the life of

Steven Hellman."

Gary's words echoed through the compound. Steph listened to them as she waited for a panel to start, an "Icons of Horror" panel which would have featured Steven among the stars on it. She sat silently, the gathering crowd out in the seats. Some took off their hats. A couple wiped away tears, but it was news to very few. Word had traveled quickly, and the raucous energy that had filled the grounds just hours ago was now gone.

The moment of silence passed, and a soft murmur filled the space again. Steph sat nearby, offstage, waiting around in case somebody needed something. As the crowd packed in, the doors shut and the panel began.

Four chairs sat on stage, with two of them occupied by Frank Buchanon and Abel Goffin. Frank was famous for playing Axl in three different movies plus the television show, while Abel had played multiple hulking slasher monsters in five—or was it six—separate films, until transitioning from out from behind the mask to star in Joe Banshee's Hell trilogy. And now he was playing John Kalman in Midnight Star. A moderator sat in the third chair, a YouTube personality that Stephanie didn't know named Kyle Palmer. He wore a vintage *Halloween* t-shirt and looked happy to be there. She supposed that was his job. The fourth chair was empty. Steven's.

His absence loomed over them all. The panel started, and the moderator did his best to keep the topic off of Steven, and to keep everything moving. He bounced between the two of them.

"Abel, I'll begin with you," said Kyle. "And I'll start with where we are, the Kalman compound, and its connection to your new movie, Midnight Star. You play John Kalman, the man who started the Midnight Star cult, built this compound, and was ultimately responsible for the death of hundreds. How does it feel to actually be sitting here, inside the compound?"

Abel raised the microphone to his mouth. He wore designer jeans and a plain black t-shirt, his hair trimmed into a buzz cut. His muscles strained at the fabric of his shirt. Even in his fifties, Abel was in terrific shape. Standing at six foot five, he looked massive in the chair. He dwarfed both Kyle and Frank.

"It's kind of crazy, you know," he said. "I spent a couple months playing this absolute maniac, and now I'm visiting the place where he died. Where he killed so many people." Abel's voice was deep, but quiet.

"Do you feel connected to him?" asked Kyle.

"Yeah, Abel, do you feel connected to the mass murderer?" asked Frank, his voice snide. The audience laughed. Steph did too. Frank's wit hadn't dulled over the years.

Abel chuckled himself. "I mean, yeah, I guess I do. I don't like him, you know. He was a killer. Led a bunch of people out here, and then killed them all. But I inhabited him for months, so I still feel him, y'know? I learned a lot about him, and despite everything, I still feel empathy for the guy. But that comes with the territory. When you play a monster, sometimes people are going to associate you with real ones."

"Frank—"

"Yeeeess, Kyle?" asked Frank. The crowd laughed again. Frank smiled cleverly.

"How do you feel being here?"

"It's a little creepy, you know?" said Frank, giving an exaggerated shudder. The crowd laughed again. "Not that I can't handle it. But still, man. Thinking about all those people that died here." Frank paused then, and Steph saw his facade drop for just a moment. He had inadvertently referenced Steven, and he had realized. But he slipped his mask of confidence back on.

If Kyle noticed, he said nothing, moving right through into another question. The panel continued that way, with Kyle doing a good job of bouncing between the two stars, keeping the crowd engaged, and keeping the mood light, even with the news of Steven's death hanging over everything.

"My last question," said Kyle. "Abel. How do you feel about your legacy? You've been known for some time as the big slasher villain, invincible and invulnerable. But, and it is a big but, is that you wore the mask, and only the most well-educated horror fans knew the man behind the mask. But with the Hell trilogy and Midnight Star, you and your face have become well known."

"Well, you said it," said Abel. "I'm still building my legacy. I'm not as young as I used to be, but I'm using the opportunities I've gotten and building upon them. I'm more than just another movie monster."

"Frank, how about you? Do you ever think about your legacy?" asked Kyle.

"I think we all do," said Frank. "Not to get too serious, you know, but it's kind of the human condition. We aren't here for very long, and most of us want to leave something that outlives us. So yes, I think about it. I try not to obsess over it, but it's hard sometimes. A lot of the time I'm happy that I'm leaving behind a character like Axl, who I think is a lot of people's favorite—"

The crowd interrupted him with a loud cheer. He smiled and nodded to them.

"—but other times, I wish I could have done more. But I don't have a pet director to keep me employed, not anymore." Abel glanced at him then, the soft face turning hard in an instant. If looks could kill, that glare would have done it. But then Abel's eyes cut back forward, realizing himself. If Frank noticed, he didn't show it.

"I think me playing the leading role is behind me, sorry to say. I don't need to work, but I do enjoy it. Does that answer your question?"

"I think so," said Kyle, smiling. "Thank you, gentlemen, for your thoughts and time." Everyone stood and applauded, while Kyle shook both their hands. Steph noticed that Frank and Abel didn't shake, didn't even look at each other. Did no one like each other?

They walked off stage. Kyle ignored her, immediately on his phone. Abel strode off outside. Steph was about to leave to help somewhere else in the compound when Frank's voice stopped her.

"Hey, kid," he said. "Let's get lunch."

"I should help," said Steph.

"Blow it off," said Frank. "Tell them I'm being a diva. They'll believe it."

Lunch was salad in the green room set aside for the talent. They sat alone.

"I bet everyone else is just eating in their rooms," said Frank. "Chow here isn't half bad, though."

"Yeah, it's alright."

"You doing okay, kid?"

"Yeah, I guess," said Steph. "It's still hard to believe."

"You're telling me," said Frank. "I was one of the last people to speak to him. I still don't believe it."

"Were you friends?"

"No, not really," said Frank. "It's hard to have friends in this business. Or maybe it's hard for guys like me and Steve. Some people, they got a lot of give to them, you know? They can absorb a lot, and nothing reflects out. I'm not one of those people, and Steve wasn't either. I was usually just a smart-ass. Some people liked it. Most people didn't. Steve just got prickly. And people definitely didn't like that. But I think we understood each other, even if we weren't close. We'd seen each other enough at things like this."

"How many conventions do you do a year?" asked Steph.

"Oh, I don't know," said Frank. "I used to tell my manager to keep it to one a month, but now I take as many of them that will pay my fee. I don't really need the money. It's just something to stay busy. It's still performing, sorta."

"What was the deal between you and Abel back at the panel?"

"You noticed that, huh?"

"He looked like he wanted to kill you for a second."

"I don't know why."

"I mean, you called Joe Banshee his 'pet director,'" said Steph.

"Well, yeah, but it's true," said Frank. "Look at Joe's last six movies. Abel has been in all of them, getting increasingly bigger and bigger parts. And let me tell you, it's not because of his acting."

"Then what is it?"

Frank looked around the room. "Do you really not

know? I thought you kids were smart these days."

"I haven't seen anything about it," said Steph.

"I guess that's a good thing," said Frank. "You could say that Abel and Joe's relationship is a bit deeper than just collaborators."

"What does that mean?" asked Steph.

Frank rolled his eyes. "Jeez, kid. They're a couple. They're dating. Pretty serious, too."

"What?!? They're gay?" asked Steph.

"I would assume so," said Frank. "They're together, and that's why Joe casts him in all his movies. The budgets are low, and he has his dedicated fans, and so they make money, so most studios let him do what he wants."

"I would have never guessed," said Steph. "They must want it kept a secret, right?"

"Yeah, even though half of Hollywood knows," said Frank. "It's 2020. They'd probably be more popular than ever if they came out. Maybe they will, when the time is right."

"Did Steven know?" asked Steph.

Frank laughed at that. "He didn't, for a while. Then at a convention last year he walked into Joe's room, while they were, you know. He figured it out real quick."

"Oh my god," said Steph, laughing.

"I'm gonna miss him," said Frank. "I hope I didn't drive him to it."

"Nancy said he seemed hopeful before he went to his room," said Steph. "About the future. Said she didn't believe he'd kill himself."

"How did she take the news?" asked Frank.

"Not well," said Steph. "She was still crying when I left her."

"She always cared too much," said Frank. "It was a blessing and a curse."

"She…" started Steph, but then trailed off.

"She hates me," said Frank. "It's okay, you can say it."

"I was going to say that she didn't have anything nice to say about you. Said you left her for Mary."

"That's not what happened," said Frank. "I mean, I don't blame her for hating me. I deserve it. I was a total asshole at the end. But I didn't leave her for Mary. Mary just happened to be there. I left her because I panicked."

"About what?" asked Steph.

"Marriage, kid," said Frank. "I never envisioned myself as the settling down type, and then guess what. Boom, it's about to happen, and I freaked the hell out. Became impossible to live with. So I did the thing that made sense. I got out of there. It wasn't the right thing to do, but I was young and stupid."

"Have you ever apologized to her?"

"I tried, once," said Frank. "But she blew up at me, and I gave up."

"You should try again," said Steph. "Want me to talk to her?"

"You're a good person, kid, but no," said Frank. "I'm a grown-up. You've got enough on your plate with all of us fuck-ups. But you're not wrong. Maybe I can try again tonight, at the party."

"Oh god," said Steph. "I forgot that there's another one."

"There's three more," said Frank. "Believe me, I'm keeping track. I have a legacy screening to attend before dinner, and then I have to get ready. Thanks for eating lunch with me."

"You're welcome," said Steph. "No one will believe that I got to eat lunch with Frank Buchanon."

"I'll see you at dinner, kid," said Frank. "Don't worry. It can't be worse than last night."

# 13

Steph wanted to go back to her room and take a nap before she had to help with the directing panel, but her phone buzzed with a message from Henry.

*Could you go pick up Joe and Abel and provide them a tour of the mine?*

Steph sighed. She messaged back.

*Can't William do it? I don't really know it very well.*

A moment passed, and then a reply.

*He's busy. You don't have to give them history, you just have to drive them, they're waiting at the mansion.*

Steph sighed again. She was already exhausted, and the day was only half over. They still had the party tonight. She grabbed her cart and drove it over to the lodge, where Joe and Abel stood outside, both vaping while they waited in the shade. Abel was dressed the same as in his panel, while Joe wore a band t-shirt for someone she'd never heard of, but also in a pair of tight designer jeans. His long dread-locked hair hung nearly to his waist. They spoke quietly between puffs on their vape pens. Steph stopped the golf cart in front of them.

"Your chariot, gentlemen," she said, with a half-smile.

"Awesome," said Joe, and they climbed in next to her, all sitting in a row. She could feel the cart tilt slightly to the right as Abel sat down.

"You guys want to go to the mine?" asked Steph.

"Yeah, absolutely," said Joe.

"You sure?" asked Steph. "It's not that exciting."

"Definitely, man," said Joe. "To actually see the place? Yeah, we got to." Abel said nothing.

"Alright," said Steph, and sped away, the electric motor of the vehicle softly whirring. They sat in silence as she drove past a few loitering attendees, who goggled at Joe and Abel as they passed. She didn't expect to find any out much farther. The rocky dirt crunched underneath the tires, and she wondered if she should bring up Steven's death. She heard Abel murmur something in Joe's ear, and she opted for silence.

"How far out is it?" asked Joe, breaking it instead.

"A few more minutes," said Steph. "It's separate from the rest of the compound. Is it—is it in your movie? The mine, I mean."

"Oh yeah," said Joe. "It's part of the climactic showdown. It's fucking awesome, if I do say so myself."

"Showdown?" asked Steph. "A showdown between who?"

"Between John and Susie," said Joe. "After John has poisoned everyone, and she discovers all the bodies. She tries to hide in the mine, but John corners her and they have a bloody fight. She eventually kills him with—what was it, Abe?"

"A pick-axe, right in the head."

"A pick-axe! It's gnarly."

"Did—did that actually happen?" asked Steph. "I thought everyone drank the poison and then Kalman committed suicide in the church."

"I mean, no, of course not," said Joe. "Susie isn't a real person. I made her up for the movie. You have to have a starlet, y'know?"

"But I thought it was based on true events," said Steph.

"It is based on true events," said Joe. "A lot of stuff in the movie happened, but we're not in the documentary business. We have to tell a story. So we livened it up a little. Susie doesn't drink the poison, and we have a climactic battle at the end. Not a big deal. We there yet?"

"It's right ahead," said Steph. Abel's eyes stared straight ahead, fixed on the entrance to the mine.

"This is it," he said, with his same quiet tone.

Steph piloted around the chain-link fence and up to the gate, stopping the cart. Joe stretched, his arms fully sleeved in tattoos reaching to the sky.

"Do you have flashlights?" asked Abel.

"I think there's some in the storage on the back of the cart," said Steph. She fished around inside and found two.

"Only two of them," she said.

"You keep one," said Abel, taking the other from her.

"Just the chain-link fence protecting it," said Joe.

"It's just a hole in the ground," said Steph. "There's nothing of value here."

Abel muttered something, but Steph couldn't hear him.

"What?" she asked.

"That's not true," he said, wandering toward the entrance. "There's history here."

"I suppose that's true," said Steph, following him, with Joe right behind her. "But it's just misery. William told me that this was a mine just to keep people busy. Kalman promised his followers salvation if they did more work, but they were digging toward nothing."

"Memories of pain still have value," said Abel. His fingers slid over the rough wood supports at the entrance.

"I suppose that's also true," said Steph. Abel flipped on his light and walked into it. She had hoped they wouldn't go in, but she exhaled and followed. Joe moved past her, walking right behind Abel.

"What else did William tell you?" asked Abel. "About the mine." They wandered deeper, and soon the only illumination was from their flashlights.

"Nothing else," said Steph. "Sorry I don't have more info for you."

"No problem," said Joe. "Abel did all the research for playing Kalman. He probably knows more than anyone on Earth. Isn't that true, Abe?"

"I know a lot," said Abel. "Kalman was an interesting man. Seeing all his work, in the flesh—it's something."

"But he was a murderer," said Steph, reflexively.

"Undoubtedly," said Abel. "But still, he had force of will. He made this place out of nothing."

"The compound?" asked Steph. "He had hundreds of followers who did all the work."

"Exactly," said Abel. "They were an extension of him."

They walked deeper in the darkness, and Steph's stomach ached. She felt the walls close, the rough limestone within reach on both sides. She wasn't claustrophobic, but this was no normal cave.

"It's incredible," said Abel, running his hands over the stone.

"Is it?" asked Steph. Abel continued to walk. William had said it was over a mile deep. Were they going all the way to the bottom?

"Of course it is," said Abel. Joe followed behind him. "People did this. Chasing their belief, following their faith. There was nothing here, and through sheer force, they carved a path into the Earth."

"But it was for nothing," said Steph. "It was an exercise in futility. In emptiness. It was a tragedy."

"There can be beauty in that," said Abel. "That's what this represents."

"How far down do you want to go, Abe?" asked Joe. Steph heard the anxiety in his voice.

"A little farther," said Abel. They passed a small alcove, with crates stacked up.

"I wonder what they're keeping down here," said Steph.

"Probably just storage," said Joe. "Although it's not like it's easily accessible."

Abel stopped his forward progress, finally. He peered deeper into the mine with his light, the tunnel continuing downward.

"I think we did a good job emulating it," said Abel. "But there's nothing like the real thing."

"We did a good job," said Joe. "But this thing is crazy. If I close my eyes, I can hear the pick axes plinking away. Tink, tink, tink."

Steph closed her eyes, and Joe was right, she could hear them too.

*Tink tink tink*

She imagined them, groups of men and women sweating down in the dark, smashing away stone, digging deeper and deeper to please their master. Kalman would visit, and encourage them, and once in a while, take someone aside, and reward them for their service, for their belief, for their faith. The others would work even harder, knowing that salvation could be earned through their dedication and toil.

She opened her eyes. The three of them were the only ones inside the mine, and all those memories of tragedy were just that. The ache in her guts hadn't gone away. Steph wanted to be back on the surface, under the hot Texas sun.

"I think it's about time to get back," said Steph. "You have a panel in a little while, Joe."

"Oh shit, you're right," he said. "We better get going, Abe."

Abel still peered deeper into the mine, particles of dust floating through the beam of his flashlight.

"Yeah," he said, finally, and turned, his enormous frame filling the small space. Steph immediately felt better. They walked back toward the entrance. They had only walked for ten minutes, but the trip back to ground level felt like it took a million years.

Soon light filtered down and they switched off their flashlights. Steph breathed a sigh of relief. She knew the mine was safe, but the same unease from earlier was still there, even as they climbed out of the darkness and into the sunlight. They returned to the cart, and Steph closed the gate behind them. Abel lingered, staring into the dark void.

"Playing Kalman affected you, huh?" asked Steph.

"Abe went full method while on set," said Joe. "It was amazing to see. It was like he was a whole different person. He transformed himself for it. This movie is going to blow people away. He should get awards consideration. I'm serious, it's incredible."

Abe turned away from the mine, sitting in the golf cart again.

"That's nice of you to say," said Abel, cracking a small smile. "But it was nice to just have a role to play that wasn't some silent monster. I couldn't have done that without you, Joe."

"Ready to go?" asked Steph.

"Yeah, let's head back," said Abel.

Steph goosed the accelerator away from the mine. It felt good to leave it behind. Even in this cursed place, it emanated dread and despair.

Abel and Joe sat mute for the whole ride back, but Steph only thought of Abel's words inside the mine. Of the beauty in the tragedy of this place. And maybe he was right. Maybe there was value in the sadness and murder, lost in the people who had died tragically. Steven's death had only made it worse. It felt like an affirmation of that sorrow, of that curse. Regardless of what Abel or Joe said, she couldn't see any merit here, no matter how hard she looked.

When she reached out, she only found darkness.

# 14

Kyle moderated the panel again in front of a crowd packed full of people. Steph didn't blame them. Sitting before them were legends of horror directing, the best, and most famous directors of the past and present. Oh, and also Ted Nowakowski.

Steph didn't know what Ted had told Gary to convince him to be a part of this panel, but he stood out like a sore thumb. She knew him because he was an Austin local, and a Splatterfest regular, but he was unknown to the average person, and to even the more hardcore horror fan. And now he sat next to some of the most famous horror directors alive. Steph stood near Abel on the sidelines, watching as they started.

Kyle tapped on his microphone a couple times.

"Alright, let's get this panel started," said Kyle, and the crowd quieted down, ready to hear the discussion.

"We've got quite a group of here today," said Kyle. "We have Bill Chancellor, the legend himself." Applause. "We have Joe Banshee, director and rock star." Applause. "The Gore Auteur, Levi Stark." Applause. "And, Ted Nowa—Nowakowski. Did I say that right, Ted?" Ted nodded with a wide smile as a few people clapped out of politeness. Ted smiled and waved to the crowd, but Steph didn't blame them for not clapping.

"Let's start this off with you, Joe," said Kyle. "You're premiering Midnight Star this weekend, after a controversial production and now, in an even more controversial premiere, debuting the film in the Kalman Compound, site of the Midnight Star massacre. How does it feel?"

"I mean, it feels good," he said, chuckling. The crowd laughed. "It didn't feel controversial. It felt natural, honestly. It's a heavy story, for sure, but I don't think it should be off limits just because of that."

"There have been critics—"

"Oh, whatever," said Joe. "There's a reason they're critics and not directors themselves. Made nothing their entire lives, only tearing down the work other people have made. The film doesn't glorify John Kalman, it merely tells his story, and it's damn entertaining, if I do say so myself."

"Fair enough," said Kyle. "Levi, you yourself are premiering a picture here as well. Death Destiny."

"That is correct, Kyle," said Levi, sitting up, plastering a big grin on his face.

"Feel any pressure? Or feeling overshadowed at all?" asked Kyle.

"Pressure?" asked Levi. "Never. I'm confident in what I made. Frankly, it's a modern masterpiece. A suitable successor to Argento and Cronenberg. If anything, my film will loom over everything else this weekend." The crowd ooohed. Bill raised his eyebrows in doubt.

"Hear that, Joe?" asked Kyle.

"I'm not overly concerned," said Joe.

"I—" started Levi, but Kyle cut him off.

"Bill," said Kyle. "How are you doing?"

"Oh, I'm alright," said Bill. "Trying not to sweat my balls off whenever I step outside." The fans laughed, and Steph smiled. He truly didn't give two shits. Kyle laughed alongside them.

"Are you showing any new projects here?" asked Kyle. "I know you've been working on some new music."

"Oh, always," said Bill. "An old man has got to keep busy. But nothing ready yet. Maybe next year."

"Any film projects coming up?"

"Kyle, you're cute," said Bill, and the crowd laughed again. His thin frame was engulfed in the chair. "No studio trusts me. I don't blame them. I'd probably just spend all the money on dope." The attendees cheered, with several whoops.

Kyle smiled. "Joe, you said that you don't feel the film is controversial. Has visiting the compound affected you at all? Had you been here before you made the film?"

"No, no I hadn't," said Joe. "Not exactly on the way to the grocery store, you could say. I'd seen the documentaries, you know, and I did my research before I wrote the screenplay, and I think I captured it pretty well, along with my cast and crew. But being here, man, it's a whole different thing."

"How so?"

"I mean, like, I just went out to the mine, right? Have you heard about that?" asked Joe.

"I'm not familiar," said Kyle.

"It's way out on the property. I sure as hell wouldn't walk there, you'd fry. But we went out there earlier today, me and Abe, and went down inside. It's a mine, but it's a mine to nowhere, man."

"What do you mean?" asked Kyle.

"Like—"

Levi interrupted him. "Kalman used it as a trial for his followers. If they wanted favor, they would work in the mine, as a test of their faith. They weren't mining anything. They were only digging. But the truly faithful wouldn't question that fact. They would dig and dig for nothing as long as Kalman told them to," said Levi. "A better explanation."

Joe smiled at him. "Thanks, Levi. And yeah, we went down there, and you could feel it, man. Abe said it while we were down there, that it was a terrible tragedy, but there was beauty there too, and I think our movie really captures that."

It was Levi's turn to raise his eyebrows in doubt, but he said nothing. Steph spotted Ted sheepishly raising his hand, trying to get Kyle's attention, but Kyle ignored him.

"You seem to have done your homework, Levi," said Kyle.

"Some rudimentary research," he said. "It's not like I directed a movie about it or anything. But it is fascinating being here. And like Joe said, it feels haunted. An appropriate venue for a Splatterfest, and a great place to debut Death Destiny."

Steph caught some movement out of the corner of her eye and saw Henry, also watching the panel. How long had he been there? He seemed to always be everywhere. He ducked away.

Ted practically windmilled his arms to get Kyle's attention.

"Yes, Ted?" asked Kyle. "You have something to add?"

"I wanted to say that as a Texas native, the Kalman compound is a legendary place, and I think it adds ambiance to the festival. I am very excited to see Midnight Star and Death Destiny. Being here, in such a haunted location, adds a lot of weight to both the premieres."

"That sounds great—" started Kyle.

"And I'd like to add that I'm currently running a Kickstarter for my next film, Blood Possession. We're on pace to raise enough money, but with all of your help, we could easily meet the goal—"

Levi's voice cut him off. "Who are you?"

"I'm Ted Nowakowski. I've directed—"

"Yeah, I'm sure you've made a lot of movies. But why are you here?"

"I—"

"Because look who you're sitting next to. Why on Earth do you think you belong here?"

The room fell silent. Ted awkwardly stared at him, everyone waiting for something to break the silence.

"Surely, I'm not the only one thinking that," said Levi.

"Just because he's a nobody doesn't mean you have to say it, man," said Joe. "Just—"

"Oh please," said Levi. "That's rich coming from you."

"I'm sensing some hostility, brother," said Joe.

"Hostility? I think you mean someone isn't bowing down and worshiping you for making a mediocre movie about some cultist and then strong-arming some festival to make the whole thing about you—"

"Worshiping me? Dude's just been asking questions—"

"Yeah, about Midnight Star, over and over again. About Kalman. This isn't a history panel. Ask about film. But I guess nobody else cares about that except for me."

"Please, Levi—" started Kyle.

"Shut up," said Levi. "I don't even know who you are. You're doing a piss-poor job."

"You don't got to be an asshole, man," said Joe. Levi stood up and Abel tensed next to her. Joe and Levi were roughly the same size, and Steph had no idea who would win in a fight. But if Abel went in there, Levi would get his clock cleaned.

"Gentlemen, please, please," said Kyle. "Let's all calm down."

"Don't know if that's going to work, son," said Bill. He hadn't moved. Levi stared at Joe for a moment longer and then turned away from him.

"The Death Destiny premiere is tomorrow, and I hope to see you all there, and at the panel just before it. I won't have to battle for time there," said Levi, dropping the mic and storming off the stage.

The room was silent, all watching Levi walk away. Henry was suddenly there again, talking to Levi, but Levi blew him off, marching outside. Henry followed him. Steph couldn't imagine managing all these personalities.

"Well," said Kyle. "Let's get back to business."

The crowd stayed, and Kyle returned to his routine, but the awkwardness was still there, no matter how many smart-ass remarks Bill said. Steph felt the worst for Ted. He didn't say an entire word the rest of the panel, just sitting there, the microphone limp in his hand. She didn't like him, but he didn't deserve that.

The panel went by quickly, and Joe returned to Abel's side right after. Steph eyed Abel. The look of anger on his face hadn't disappeared after Levi had left. She didn't hear what they said as they walked away, but Joe was clearly trying to calm Abel down.

Bill was unaffected, walking back to a golf cart so he could return to his room. Ted looked morose.

"You okay?" asked Steph.

"Yeah, I'm fine," said Ted. "I thought—I thought this would be a difference maker for me."

"Don't let that asshole get you down," said Steph. "There's still a lot of weekend left."

"Yeah, you're right," said Ted, but he still looked upset. He'd been dressed down by one of the most popular horror directors in front of a crowd of hundreds. Ted had made a half dozen movies with almost no budget, but he had to want more.

"There's still opportunity," said Steph, trying to smile, and Ted returned it glumly, walking away. "See you at the party tonight?"

"Yeah, sure," he said, without glancing back.

The room emptied out. It was the last big panel of the day, and soon the buses would line up to take the general admin people away. Steph needed to go back and get ready for another party. She remembered the night before and wanted tonight to be a calmer affair. Frank had said it would be. She hoped he was right.

# 15

"Have you seen Nancy?" asked Steph. Dan sat in the kitchen in the mansion, eating a sandwich.

"I think she's in her room," said Dan. "At least, I haven't seen her leave. Why?"

"Just worried about her," said Steph. "She was so distraught about Steven."

Dan nodded. "Don't know if she's still up there, but it's worth checking."

Steph walked up to the third floor, her footsteps echoing in the mansion. Noises of shuffling, banging around, and running water filled the lodge, with different people getting ready for the party that night, or just resting after an exhausting day.

Nancy's door was closed, and Steph knocked. She waited a few moments, and heard no sound from inside. She knocked again.

"Nancy?" she asked. "Are you in there?"

Still no answer. She knocked one more time, not expecting much. She glanced backward, looking around the hall, but all the other doors were shut.

No, that wasn't true. One door was cracked open, some light escaping.

*Steven's room.*

The police had left the door open on their way out. Or someone else had. She remembered Nancy's suspicion about Steven's death. That somebody had killed him. It had seemed ridiculous at first. If someone wanted Steven dead, why would they do it here? But she thought to the argument with Joe the night before. The weird behavior of Abel in the mine.

Nancy still hadn't answered the door, and there was no crack of light underneath. Either she was out or she wasn't answering, and the slim glimpse of Steven's room beckoned. The police had come and gone and presumably collected all the evidence they needed. But there had been no word from them about a presumed killer. It was a suicide, surely.

But why the doubt from Nancy? It had crept into Steph, and she walked over to Steven's door and pushed it open, closing it behind her.

She was inside Steven's room, and she didn't know why. A sudden curiosity had seized her, and forced her through the door, and she now realized that she shouldn't be here, that this was forbidden, going through a dead man's things.

*You know why you're here. You're looking for something suspicious.*

The sudden guilt eased then. She was on a mission. The pain that had risen in her stomach fell to manageable levels and she looked around the room. It didn't look that much different from when she had brought Steven here, just yesterday. So much had happened in a day. Steven had been alive, and now he was dead, and she doubted he would have predicted that.

He had been an asshole, demanding better treatment, and nicer things. Bill had come in and distracted Steven, and she had gone on to her next assignment.

But his stuff was still here. The cops hadn't taken it, leaving someone else to collect it. She didn't know who. Steven's luggage was strewn everywhere, his closet filled with his clothes, collared shirts and slacks hung up inside. The bedding was pushed aside, probably when they had collected his body.

She looked through the room, forcing herself to slow down and pick through every item, looking for anything suspicious. She rifled through his luggage, but it was only more clothes, an assortment of stuff that would be of no use on the trip. She guessed Steven was an over-packer. She unzipped all the side pockets, and still nothing.

The room itself. She opened up all the drawers in the dresser, and in the side tables, but there was nothing there. She got down on the floor and looked under the bed, but nothing hid there except for some dust bunnies.

Maybe there was something in the bathroom, something the police had overlooked. She went in, the bathroom looking similar to hers. His toiletries were piled up on the sink and searching through them quickly revealed nothing sinister. The bathroom was empty otherwise. She walked back out into the bedroom.

There was nothing suspicious here. Her own instincts, Nancy's suspicions. They meant nothing. She looked to the bed again, where Steven had died not twelve hours earlier.

*They had discovered him here, lying in bed. He took too many sleeping pills, downed them with too much alcohol, and that was it for Steven. Intentional or not, he died.*

Steph sighed. Everything pointed to it. So why was Nancy so sure about the opposite? She couldn't ignore the feeling inside, the instinct that something was wrong.

*It's just this place. It's haunted, full of horror and death. It invites those feelings.*

Steph sat back on the bed and rubbed her eyes. She desperately wanted to sleep, to lay back in bed and read, but she couldn't. She had a party to go to tonight, to manage more idiot celebrities.

She should just leave. It was a mistake to come in here at all. All it had done was invite those bad feelings.

*Take one last look. Maybe you missed something.*

Steph got up and backed up against the door, taking in the room as a whole. *Think, think.* Remember how it looked when you brought Steven in. What had changed?

A lot had happened in the past day, and she had brought him in a flurry of activity, going through almost a half dozen rooms. Everything had blurred together and trying to recollect any details was tough. She put herself in her shoes the day before, thinking back to dragging Steven's unwieldy luggage up the stairs. He'd complained about everything. It was too hot, too far out. He wanted a mini-fridge and said he was going to die here.

*He'd been right.*

But nothing else was coming back. She'd gone to bring in both Ted and Levi, and then Geno, and all of it had smashed together into a mess of memories. She had been dead tired by the end, and then there was the disastrous party.

Steph closed her eyes, and then re-opened them, trying to take in the room all at once, instead of focusing on anything in particular. What else was there?

There was Steven's fit about the painting above his bed, the landscape watercolor that he detested, and needed out of his room. He had said that he couldn't sleep with it hanging above him. She had taken it downstairs, and—

*But there was something else there now.*

Steph hadn't noticed it, hadn't really looked to the walls at all, had been too focused on everything else, trying to find some other piece of evidence. A footprint, or a a fragment of fabric left behind by a killer.

But the cops would have found that. They wouldn't know to search for something different in the decorations. They would have assumed it was how it was supposed to look.

They wouldn't notice the Midnight Star hanging over the bed, placed there with purpose.

She had been too focused on finding something small to notice something so direct. It wasn't big, but it was noticeable, placed directly over the headboard, overlooking the bed. It definitely hadn't been there before.

Someone had put it there.

The *killer* had planted it there.

Nancy was right. There was a killer, and they had killed Steven. They had killed him in the night.

She reached up and pulled the star off the wall, hung there by the same nail that the painting had hung on. It was light, made of wood, a perfect duplicate of the massive star that stood atop the church in the compound. It was the midnight star, the representation of the cult. This wasn't an accident. Someone had killed Steven Hellman, and they had done it in the name of the Midnight Star. In the name of John Kalman.

But was she sure?

Could Steven have hung up the star, found somewhere in the room, or in the compound? Or someone else, entirely unrelated? It wasn't proof, wasn't proof of anything other than they had hung up a star. It wouldn't get the cops back out here.

But it was something. She would have to tell somebody. But who? She didn't know, but she hung up the star again, above the bed. Carrying it around would prove nothing.

She would tell Dan. He could keep a secret, and they could work on something together. Together, they could go to Gary, and maybe talk it out with him.

The grandfather clock rang out from the first floor, tolling loudly. She looked to her phone. *Shit.* She only had a half hour until the party tonight, and she had to be there to help. She still needed to shower and change.

She opened the door and stepped out to see Henry knocking on Nancy's door. Steph quietly gasped and gently shut the door behind her, hoping he wouldn't notice her.

She walked away, softly stepping, as Henry knocked again.

"Nancy?" he asked. Steph was almost to the stairs. She didn't want him seeing her up here—

"Stephanie?" he asked. She pivoted, grinning as wide as she could.

"Hi," she said.

"I didn't notice you up here," he said. "I was looking for Nancy. Have you seen her?"

"No," said Steph, still smiling. "I haven't seen her. I was searching for her too."

Henry smiled, and his face lit up. "I feel bad for delivering the news to her earlier. I should have probably waited for a better moment, but I've been so overwhelmed with everything."

"I get it," said Steph. "You've been busy."

"There's so much going on," he said. "And it's only gotten worse with Steven's death. To think, he was in there just a few hours ago." Henry nodded his head toward Steven's door.

"Ah. Yeah," said Steph. She inched toward the stairs. "I need to get going. To get ready for the party."

"So you'll be there?" asked Henry.

"Yes," said Steph. "I kinda have to."

"Great," said Henry. "I've been wanting to talk to you. Maybe I'll get a chance there."

"Oh, uh, sure," said Steph. He'd been so indifferent before. "I need to go, though."

"Sure," he said. "I don't think Nancy is in. Maybe she's already at the party. I'll see you there."

"Sounds good," said Steph. She smiled one more time and hurried down the stairs, into her room. She didn't think Henry realized that she'd been in Steven's room. She only had fifteen minutes now, she had to hurry. She could find Dan at the party and chew his ear. And talk to Henry, she guessed.

# 16

"We need to talk," said Steph. Dan nursed a beer, standing to the side of the party, observing the festivities. It wasn't very festive. The mood was somber after Steven's death, and everyone was in their cups. Everybody drank, even the celebs.

"Right now?" asked Dan.

"Yes," said Steph, keeping her voice low, already pulling him away from the main area, near the wall where the shadows hung heavier.

"Hey, watch it, I don't want to spill—"

"Shh," said Steph. "Remember how I said Nancy thought Steven was killed?"

"Yes," said Dan. "But it doesn't make any sense. Who would want to kill Steven? Sure, he may have rubbed some people the wrong way, but—"

"I went in his room," said Steph.

"What? What do you mean, you went in his room?"

"I went in his room. Earlier, when I went to check on Nancy, his door was ajar, and I slipped in, and I looked around."

"It's an active crime scene, Steph!" said Dan, his voice raising.

"Keep your voice down," said Steph. "And I thought you said he committed suicide."

"You know what I mean," said Dan. "The cops are still investigating. We should just let them do their job."

"How long do you think it'll take before we get any answer about his death?"

"I don't know," said Dan. "Gary said the hospital is a few hours away, and I assume they'll do a drug test or something—"

"So days to get the results back," said Steph. "In the meantime, we have a killer loose!"

"There's no killer, Steph."

"I found a midnight star in his room."

"And?" asked Dan. "If you haven't noticed, we're in the Kalman compound. Those things are everywhere."

"It wasn't there before," said Steph. "I moved Steven in, remember? There was a painting over his bed, and he wanted it removed, and I had to lug the damn thing downstairs."

"So?"

"So, there was nothing there. The wall above his head was bare. But I go back in and there's a star there?"

"He could have hung it up," said Dan. "It's not proof of anything."

"After he complained about a painting, he's going to hang

up a random midnight star above his bed? Why would he do that?"

"I don't know," said Dan. "But the star itself doesn't prove anything."

"It proves someone else was in his room," said Steph. "Someone killed him, Dan. Nancy is right."

Dan sighed. "Let's say she is right. That there is a killer here. Why on Earth would they hang up the midnight star?"

"Because they're a secret cultist," said Steph, quietly.

"I—" Dan started, but then stopped. "I find that hard to believe."

"Why else would they choose that? Why else unless they needed to prove a point? If they just wanted to get away with murder, they wouldn't do anything," said Steph.

"You're not wrong," said Dan. "But why Steven? Why now?"

"I don't know," said Steph. "We should tell Gary."

"Tell him what?" asked Dan. "That there's a secret cultist on the loose, and he's killing celebrities?"

"Yeah, I guess," said Steph.

"What is he going to do?" asked Dan.

"I don't know," said Steph. "He should know. Maybe he can keep people safer."

"Safe from what?"

"From the killer."

"Steph, Steven was killed in his bed, in the middle of the night," said Dan. "By someone who had access to the mansion. That whittles it down to the celebrities and to one of us."

"One of the VIPs could have sneaked in," said Steph.

"It's possible," said Dan. "But someone would have seen

them coming or going, right? One of the security guys would have seen, right?"

"Probably," said Steph.

"So you're going to tell Gary that because you found a midnight star hanging up on the wall, we should consider all of the celebs murder suspects?"

Steph sighed. "No, but you have to admit something is going on."

Dan stared at her. "I don't want to downplay your suspicion. Something's wrong. But we need evidence. You heard Geno earlier. He raised hell at the mere thought of ending the show. And it'll be the end of the store if we cancel, for any reason."

"Then what do we do?" asked Steph.

"We keep our eyes open," said Dan. "Now there's two of us. If anything else suspicious happens, we pay attention. But until we have something more concrete—"

"Yeah, I know," said Steph. "Have you noticed anything strange?"

"Nothing particularly," said Dan. "I've been babysitting Geno most of the day. What an asshole. Have you seen anything?"

"Um. Well, Frank told me that Abel and Joe are a couple."

"You didn't know?" asked Dan. "I thought everyone knew."

"No. I guess I didn't think about it," said Steph. "And I took them on a tour of the mine."

"God. Creepy. Did you go down inside?"

"Yes," said Steph. "I wouldn't call it a great time. But Abel kept talking about the beauty of everything. It was weird."

"I mean, he's playing Kalman in the movie," said Dan.

"You don't think…?"

"That portraying Kalman made him a secret cultist?" asked Steph. "I don't know."

"We can keep an eye on him."

"Keep an eye on everyone," said Steph. "Like it was hard to trust people before."

"We should get back to work," said Dan. "Gary is going to chew us out if he notices us slacking off."

"No, he won't," said Steph. "I doubt he'd even notice if we stood over here all night."

"Even so," said Dan. "We can't watch things from the outside."

They left the outskirts of the room, and stood near the food and bartender, watching all the action. Everyone behaved themselves, if not drinking more than the night before.

"How's it looking tonight?" asked Gary, walking up to them.

"Seems okay," said Dan, finishing his beer. "Everyone's drinking."

"I don't blame them," said Gary, guilt dripping off his words. "A man has died." Steph and Dan shared a small glance. "We should have canceled."

"It's not your fault," said Steph. They all looked at Geno, who sat next to Mary Jo, gesturing broadly, swinging his drink freely back and forth, liquid sloshing out from side to side. Mary smiled, apparently enjoying the conversation.

"I don't know how she's doing that," said Dan.

"She's a good actress," said Steph. "Because she doesn't like him any more than anyone else does."

"I shouldn't have gotten in bed with him," said Gary. "I

just wanted to keep the store going. This was the way to do it."

"It's not your fault Steven died, Gary," said Dan.

"I wish I could do more than a moment of silence," said Gary. "It's not right." He walked off to the bartender and ordered something.

"Gary's not a drinker," said Steph.

"I don't blame him tonight," said Dan. "And we're only getting started. We still have a couple more days of this. I'm going to get some meatballs." Dan walked toward the food, leaving Steph alone.

Steph breathed deeply and exhaled, trying to get rid of tension that had built up inside her, but it stayed put. She glanced over the crowd, all the celebrities in attendance, most of the VIPs here. One of them was a killer. She studied their faces, attempting to see behind their eyes. She wanted to eliminate most of them out of hand, but she couldn't. Any of them could harbor murder in their heart.

Joe walked past them, getting a drink, away from his table. Ted jumped up from across the room and moved quickly, standing in line behind Joe. The look on Ted's face as he crossed the room was one of opportunity.

Steph wandered closer, her back to them.

"Hi, Joe," said Ted. "I was wondering if you had time to talk right now. I know you said you were busy before—"

"I'm sorry, now's not a good time—"

"Please, Joe, it will only take a minute," said Ted. Steph heard the desperation in his voice.

"I—"

"The pitch is right up your alley. The story is of a hard rocker who finds himself on the outs with his record company, and desperate for fame, invokes an evil curse for happiness. He finds his success, but the price is much too high, and he has to fight the devil to win back his conscience! It's heavy metal horror meets satanic panic, and I would love for you to work on it with me. What do you say?"

A silence hung in the air, and Steph turned to see the conversation out of the corner of her eye. Ted was excited, his face full of the enthusiasm he was an unending font of, which at first was endearing and then quickly became exhausting. Joe stared at him, and she already knew his answer.

"Look, kid—"

"I—"

"You gotta stop interrupting people. Let me talk. You seem like a nice guy, and I'm sure your movies are fine, but you don't belong here. Just because you got into the festival doesn't make you one of us. I have a lot on my plate, and I can't be fielding elevator pitches from anybody with an IMDB profile. You want your big break? Talk to Geno."

And then he turned and ordered his drink, not looking back. The bartender handed over a beer, and then Joe walked away, still not looking at Ted. Ted stood there, silent. Joe sat next to Abel. People had finally started going out on the dance floor. The party was getting a little more raucous. Enough booze and people forgot their sorrow.

"You okay, Ted?" asked Steph, approaching him.

He breathed deeply. "No, not really," said Ted. "I need a drink." He went to the bartender and returned with a glass of something brown. "I assume you heard all of that."

"Yeah," said Steph.

"I don't know what to do," said Ted. "I thought this

would be it, you know? My big shot. Finally get some face time with some big names, and those opportunities would open up, right?"

He took a long drink.

"Maybe—" she started.

"But it's a joke. All those years of making no budget movies, of trying to build my name locally, to try and make something of myself, so I don't have to work at goddamn Petsmart anymore—it was stupid. All these assholes couldn't give a shit about making anything. They only care about profit. That's all this is." Ted waved his hand over the party. "I thought Gary was smart, you know, doing this. Making Splatterfest bigger. But I was wrong. This is just—"

"Excuse me," said Henry, appearing from nowhere. Steph jumped at his voice. "Ted, can I borrow Steph for a moment? I've got some business to talk to her about."

"Uh—" said Ted, but Henry had already led Steph away from the conversation.

"Hi," said Steph, stunned by his suddenness. Henry wore slacks and a button-down shirt, his sleeves rolled up. He looked sharp, and as handsome as ever. He smiled at her.

"Sorry about that," said Henry.

"I mean, it's okay. I was giving Ted a shoulder to cry on," said Steph. Henry smiled again.

"Will he be okay?" he asked. Steph looked over to Ted, and he was getting another drink. He'd be alright.

"I think so," said Steph. "He's a little fed-up with everything going on."

"This business will do that to you," said Henry. "It chews you up and spits you out if you're not careful. Big breaks aren't easy to come by."

"So—you wanted to talk?" asked Steph.

"Yes," said Henry. "Can we go outside? Away from all this noise?"

"I mean, I'm kinda on duty," said Steph.

"I wouldn't worry too much about that," said Henry. "I'll tell them I needed your help with something."

"Oh, um, sure," said Steph. Steph followed him as he exited the building. It was immediately quieter. Some people loitered there, smoking and drinking. Henry walked farther until they were out of earshot of everyone.

"I wanted to apologize to you," said Henry. "For last night. I was rude."

"It's okay," said Steph. "There was a lot going on."

"There was," said Henry. "But it doesn't make it okay. I—I was trying to be professional, you know. A pretty girl, trying to get my attention, and I blow her off, because I'm doing my job. But it takes no more work to just have a pleasant conversation with you. So I'm sorry."

She looked into Henry's eyes. He meant what he said. "Apology accepted," said Steph.

"Thank you," said Henry. "So—will you go on a walk with me?"

"What about the party?" asked Steph.

"The kids can take care of themselves for a few minutes," said Henry, dimples in his cheeks popping with his smile.

"Fair enough. Let's go."

# 17

"I want to apologize again," said Henry. "For acting so cold to you." They walked away from the main compound, leaving the thumping music behind them. The moon was bright, but they carried flashlights. They followed a well-worn path, over and through the rough terrain, scrub grass and brush growing on the side of them. Soon it was quiet, except for the rocky soil crunching beneath their feet.

"It's okay," said Steph. "It's been a stressful couple days."

"It's no excuse," said Henry.

"There has been a lot going on," said Steph. "And after Steven's death, I can't imagine the extra work you have."

"There has been a lot of pressure on me," he said.

"Forgive me for asking, but what exactly is your job? I know you handle the celebrities, but also Geno, but also seem to do some event planning."

"It's no problem, I sometimes don't know myself. I'm a jack of all trades, of a sort. I'm working for Geno on this project, but generally I'm a freelance producer and consultant for production companies. I get things done, so to speak. I connect people, get contracts signed, wrangle different businesses to do all the things necessary."

"You're a contractor," said Steph.

"That's not too far from the truth," said Henry.

"How did you get into the work?"

"I kind of fell into it. I found myself in Los Angeles, working for a producer, and realized that I could do what he was doing, and do it better. So I started my own company and built it up from the ground floor."

"Do you enjoy it?"

"Can I be honest with you?"

"I mean, sure."

"No, I don't enjoy it," said Henry. "I'm good at it, and I make excellent money, but I don't enjoy it. I manage personalities. Most of them aren't very nice. You don't get very far in Hollywood without being selfish, and that manifests in the people I work for and with."

"Just in the past two days I've gotten my fill," said Steph.

"That's a small taste," said Henry. "Imagine that every day."

"I don't think I could do it," said Steph. "Why keep doing it, then?"

"Mostly the money," said Henry. "I have a nest egg built up."

"Thinking of getting out?"

"Maybe," said Henry. "Depends on a lot of factors, obviously."

They continued to walk, the light from the main compound far behind them.

"Do you know where we're going?" asked Steph.

"Not really," said Henry. "I wanted to get away from the noise."

"I think we're headed toward the entrance and the highway."

"Do you want to go back?"

"No, it's okay," said Steph. "The quiet is nice."

"You work for Gary, right?"

"Yeah," said Steph. "At his video store."

"A video store? I didn't know they still made those."

"They do," said Steph. "But just barely."

"What do you do there?"

"A jack of all trades," Steph said with a smile. "I help run the store, and manage the inventory, and organize events."

"Then you understand," said Henry.

"Our events are usually nothing like this," said Steph. "I've helped with the past three Splatterfests, but we've run them out of the parking lot and the store itself. Super low budget, with some projectors."

"Why the big jump, then?" asked Henry. "Feels like a substantial gamble, to move from a parking lot to a place like this, doing a destination type show."

"We had to," said Steph. "Surprise surprise, a video store isn't doing too well in 2020. And Splatterfest is always our biggest event of the year, and we saw the opportunity, and we took it. Gary already regrets it."

"Because of Steven's death?"

"I think it's not having control," said Steph. "Geno has us

bent over a barrel, and Gary doesn't like his baby being in someone else's hands."

"Lie down with dogs, get up with fleas."

"But if it'll keep the video store open another year or two, I still think it's worth it," said Steph. "A few more days of Geno gets us out of debt. How long does this trail go?"

"I don't know," said Henry. "We're getting pretty far out." He was right. The lights from the main compound were only distantly visible. Soon they would be out of sight. Still, Steph enjoyed the walk and the company. The stress of the festival seemed a thousand miles away, and the worries about a secret cultist were forgotten.

"Holy shit," said Henry, and then Steph saw it. They had reached the canyon, the deep and narrow gorge they had passed over upon entering the compound, Steph remembering every movement of the van on the bridge sending butterflies into her stomach. "Didn't feel like we walked this far."

Henry stepped closer, his light disappearing into the chasm. Steph looked down to her left, and saw the bridge, illuminated by the moon. It was barely visible, a thin sliver of concrete at the edge of her vision.

"Be careful," said Steph.

"I'm always careful," he said, stepping a little closer, until his toes were only six inches from the precipice. He peered down into the darkness.

"You're making me nervous," said Steph.

"Afraid of heights?"

"Respectful of them, I'd say."

"Don't worry, I'm not getting any closer. I just wanted to see the bottom," he said. "Or at least try."

"Can you see it?"

"I'm not sure," he said. "I think so? Might be my eyes playing tricks on me." He tossed a rock over, and it was silent for a long time, before a small echo of splashing reached them. There was water down there, somewhere.

Steph slowly stepped to the edge, peering carefully, her flashlight dancing over solid ground and then disappearing into the void. Her heart beat hard in her chest, and the backs of her knees ached as she approached. She felt the earth tilt beneath her, trying to upend her, even though it remained flat. But still the desperate curiosity persisted. She wanted to look down into the dark and find out if she could see the bottom. She got closer and closer, inch by inch. Soon she was there. She peered out, craning her head and neck, looking over the end of the white rock, into the darkness.

She looked down, and Henry was right. The moon's light reflected off the thin stream of water at the bottom of the canyon, and the shining skein reached them, hundreds of feet higher. The anxiety and fear of looking down disappeared for a moment, as she focused on the sight, but then it all came flooding back in an instant, and Steph froze, realizing her vulnerability, a brief vision of Henry standing behind her, able to kill her with a simple shove, falling down into that dark abyss, the small stream of sparkling water getting larger and larger until she hit it and she died. She felt him behind her, ready to push her, and she gasped, turning suddenly.

But he wasn't. He had moved back from the edge, and was looking over at the bridge, across the landscape, and she realized how stupid that sudden fear was.

"Did you see it?" he asked.

"Yeah, it's there," said Steph. "You're not seeing things."

"That's reassuring," he said, smiling again. Steph exhaled, and all the dread inside melted away. "We should probably head back."

"Yeah, probably," said Steph. "Party's over by now."

Henry pulled out his phone. "A few minutes ago," he said. He turned, and she followed, backs to the chasm, returning to the path toward the compound. "Thanks for walking with me."

"I'm glad I did," she said. "I feel a lot better, just with this break from everything."

"Back into the fire," he said.

Steph thought then, to tell Henry about the secret cultist, about her suspicions about Steven's death. Would he believe her? Maybe, and he knew the celebs better than anyone else. He could get into places she couldn't. He'd be a valuable ally.

But she had no proof, nothing concrete.

"What do you know about the Midnight Star?" asked Steph.

"The movie? Or the cult?"

"The cult."

"Oh, what everyone knows," said Henry. "I read some stuff while I was organizing the event."

"They believed in aliens, right?" asked Steph. "Coming to save us in a spaceship?"

Henry laughed. "That was Heaven's Gate. Midnight Star preceded them by a few years."

"Not aliens, then?"

"As far as I know, Kalman preached that a cosmic angel would come down and judge us. He was preparing for that. Or at least, that's what he said."

"How is that different from aliens?"

"What's the difference between Catholics and Protestants? They both believe in Christ, but there have been many wars fought between their differences."

"I guess you're right," said Steph. "What would Kalman have thought about all of this?"

"Oh, he would have hated it, I'm sure," said Henry. Steph saw the lights of the main compound again, twinkling in the distance.

"The excess of Hollywood?"

"He despised it," said Henry. "Having been deep inside of it, I halfway understand it. But he was a corrupt idiot."

"Dan said that it excused having the festival here, because of how Kalman felt."

"You don't agree?"

"I don't know," said Steph. "It's not really him. It's more all the people who died here. I can still feel them, sort of."

"There's a lot of terrible memories here."

"And now there's more. Have you heard about Steven's cause of death?" asked Steph.

"Nothing yet," said Henry. "Authorities said they'd let us know, but they said it would take a few days for a blood test. I don't think they'll find anything surprising."

"Yeah," said Steph. "Nancy thinks someone killed him."

"I heard."

"You don't believe her?"

"She's very upset about his death," said Henry. "And she wants it to be some big conspiracy. But the simplest explanation is usually the correct one. Unfortunately, in this case."

They were getting closer to the main compound area again. The thumping bass of the party had vanished. A few people still loitered there, but most had retreated to their rooms.

"Can I drive you back to your room?" he asked.

"Uh, sure. Where are you staying?"

"Oh, I've got a room in the dormitories."

"Couldn't find space for you in the mansion?"

"I opted for the dormitory," said Henry. "It's not as swanky, but it gives me a little distance from the celebrities. And Geno."

"Can't blame you for that," said Steph. They walked through the general area, and hopped into a golf cart, Henry jumping behind the wheel.

He piloted down the worn path, the cool night air whisking by them. She was going back into the lion's den. There was a killer somewhere in the mansion, and she didn't know who. She felt safe with Henry.

Soon they were at the lodge.

"Last stop," said Henry. "It was nice spending some time with you. Would you like to do it again tomorrow?"

"That'd be great," said Steph. Henry took her hand and lightly kissed it, his lips soft against her skin. Her stomach fluttered, despite herself.

"Goodnight," he said.

"Goodnight," said Steph, and went inside.

# 18

He'd leave. That's what he'd do. Why the hell was he here, anyway?

Ted watched as Steph walked away with Henry. Joe had gone back to his table. He'd already forgotten about Ted. Ted stared at him, but he didn't glance in his direction. Ted was a fly on his windshield.

Ted looked at his drink, what was left of it, but didn't bother finishing, putting it down on a nearby table. He didn't need anymore tonight. It wouldn't make anything better. He was only doing it at all so he could fit in. When you schmooze, you're supposed to carry around a drink. Those are the rules. Ted didn't make them, but he would follow them, if it meant that he'd get to talk to someone powerful, somebody who could help hoist him out of the rut he'd been in for—

*Seven years, buddy. It's been seven years.*

But that wasn't happening. The music thumped louder, as more and more people danced, and Ted looked out over the crowd. All the celebs nodded with tired eyes as the VIP fans talked to them, spending thousands of dollars to have "conversations" with their heroes.

Ted grabbed an egg roll from one of the food line-ups and then walked outside, eating it in two bites. It was quieter out here, and it suited the pain in his heart. A handful of people loitered out here in the courtyard, drinking and smoking, right where they found all those dead bodies a few decades back. Ted walked.

Seven years.

In seven years, he'd made six feature films. He'd self funded them, wrote, produced, directed, and acted in them. He'd gotten distribution for all of them and eventually made money on every single film. All while holding down a full-time job.

Were they all great films?

No. He wouldn't even defend some of them as *good*. Forest Trolls, his first feature, was a goddamn mess, filled with bad acting, poor editing, and shots that made him wince now, seeing them. But you had to crawl before you walked, walk before you ran. If he kept making movies and continued improving, eventually someone would take notice. He'd seen the success stories, the rags to riches. Making low budget horror flicks, now more than ever, was a recipe for success in Hollywood.

Or at least that's what he told himself after no one returned his calls, after dozens of pitch emails went unanswered. If he kept grinding, eventually he would break through. It was a matter of time. Someone would notice his ability, would appreciate his particular style, and he would catch a break.

But it never happened. He plugged away, but no one cared, except for a small batch of friends who encouraged him. That was nice and all, but it wasn't success. Success was measured in dollars and cents. When he could quit his job at the pet store and make movies full time. And that wasn't close.

He'd used all his vacation days in the year just to come out here. He'd gone to Splatterfest since before he made movies and been friends with Gary for longer. Gary was his biggest cheerleader, always encouraging him, first to make movies, and then to screen them at Splatterfest, and further and further. Gary had gotten him in and put him in panels with the biggest horror directors on the planet.

Where he had bombed horribly. They had all been assholes, and they had treated him like a nobody. But it wasn't the end of the world. He could still get face time. He could pitch something, to people who had power in the industry. People would kill for that opportunity.

And Joe Banshee was the last in a line of failures, each star or director ignoring him, insulting him, or acting condescending. This was a quick paycheck to them, and they didn't care about him or his movies.

They didn't care about movies at all. And that's what hurt the most.

Ted loved horror. He watched everything, from the lowest of the low-budget to arty stuff like The Witch, and he loved it all. But there was nothing he loved more than making movies. Even at its worst, creating film was exciting, and challenging, and fulfilling. Even when he had to go work at the pet store the next day with no sleep, because he'd been up all night editing. He didn't care. It was worth it.

But he wasn't a real director. Real directors didn't work at Petsmart.

Why was he here? He was wasting his time and getting insulted on top of it.

*Fuck this.*

Ted realized he'd walked quite a ways, and found himself among the various empty homes that the cultists had lived in, back in the day. It was quiet out here, the light of the moon the only thing lighting the area. He looked at his phone. The party would be winding down by now. He wanted to get back to his room before everyone else did. He didn't want to talk to anyone. He would pack and leave tomorrow. He'd apologize to Gary, but this wasn't fun anymore. This wasn't Splatterfest.

He got his bearings and returned to the mansion. Even staying at the lodge felt awkward, surrounded by all these stars in the lap of luxury. Well, one more night, and then he could go back to his bed. It wasn't fancy, but it was *his*.

He arrived, everything quiet. If anyone else had already gotten back, they weren't making a ruckus. He hurried to his room. He needed to be away from everyone.

Ted walked upstairs and found his bedroom, locking the door behind him. It would do as a sanctuary until tomorrow. His duffel bag was on a table, with clothes strewn around the room, but he didn't want to pack right now. He didn't want to do anything. He only wanted to surrender.

He'd sleep, get up early, and head out. He could think

straight when he got home again. This place wasn't conducive to thoughtfulness. He could make better decisions at home. He went to plug in his phone, and found an envelope, face up, his name on it in short, spiky script.

Someone had left him a note. Why? And how'd they get in his room?

His curiosity got the better of him, and he opened it, ripping open the envelope.

*Sorry about earlier, kid, I couldn't talk to you in front of Geno. I like your work. Come out to the mine and we can talk business.*

*Joe*

Ted's eyebrows furrowed. What did it mean? Joe couldn't talk to him in front of Geno? Did it have something to do with their business arrangement? Everyone talked about how shady Geno was. Maybe Joe just didn't want any more projects within reach of his greasy fingers.

The hope that had been extinguished before rose again from within him. But still, it felt too good to be true. And why the mine? Ted hadn't even visited it, only knew that it was out past all the old housing.

*Because it's isolated, you dope. Because Geno would never, ever go out there. Who cares? Joe Banshee said he likes your work.*

Ted looked in the envelope again, but there was nothing else. This was too good to be true, and he felt like there was something up, but what other purpose would Joe leave him a message? Someone could have faked it, he supposed, but why would they? Why would they target him? Get him out to the mine, for what, to belittle him some more?

More than that, he *wanted* it to be real. It all would be worth it. It would change his whole life around. He shoved the note in his pocket and left again, grabbing a golf cart from the pool, keys already in it. He didn't know exactly where the mine was, but it couldn't be that hard to find, right? He turned away from the main area of the compound, toward unknown territory. The headlights cut through the darkness, illuminating a carved dirt path. He followed it, looking out over the landscape, trying to figure out where it was. He remembered a conversation with Dan about it, about how creepy it was, seeing it up close. What had he said? It's way out there, past the houses, at the edge of the property. Surrounded by a chain-link fence.

He passed the motley assortment of housing on his left, and soon there was nothing. The mine had to be out here somewhere. How far out could it be?

Then he saw the fence, the worn trail turning left, and Ted turned and followed it, the fence on his right. Eventually he came to the gate, a chain and lock hanging loose and open in the night. Well, *someone* was here. He parked next to the other cart that sat there.

*Explains how he got out here, at least.*

He thumbed off the power to the cart and got out, the night suddenly silent. He flipped on the flashlight on his phone, and walked through the gate, seeing only a few feet in front of him, the light blowing out his night vision. As he approached the entrance to the mine, he passed a sign warning him off, and then he saw the threshold itself, a dark hole opening up out of the ground, surrounded by a rocky outcropping. He panned around, suddenly expecting Joe to be standing there, but there was nothing, no one.

"Joe?" he asked, testing, but only silence answered him. The darkness of the mine's entrance stood there, his phone's light not penetrating its gloom. That void dampened his excitement.

He didn't want to go down there.

But still, his career was down in that mine, and for that, he'd do anything.

He stepped forward into the darkness. The light from his phone illuminated a few feet in front of him, the dark inside the mine oppressive, choking. Ten feet down, he could barely see the entrance behind him. The light from the moon provided only a slim margin of difference between the black of the mine and outside.

"Joe?" he called down into the darkness. His voice echoed back at him, but after a few moments, there was no answer.

*This is all a trick. Get out of here. Go home.*

But he couldn't turn back now. Success was down here. A real career and respect. All the people who had doubted him, questioned his decisions, they would eat their shame. He would force feed it to them, and he could taste it. All he had to do was continue down and find Joe.

He continued down into the darkness. The entrance was gone behind him, and his footsteps were all he heard.

At first, because then he could hear his heartbeat in his ears, and no matter how he tried to ignore it, it only got louder.

He walked for five minutes, and still no sign of Joe.

Had he lured him down here just to humiliate him?

Someone was down here. The other golf cart hadn't materialized out of nowhere.

"Joe? What the hell's going on, man?" asked Ted. "Or whoever wrote that note."

Then, a noise from deeper in the mine. Metal scraping on metal. Ted jumped.

"Hello?" he asked again, nearly shouting now. "What the fuck is going on?"

But there was no answer, and he heard the same grinding noise. He followed it. He wanted answers. He needed to know who brought him down here. If they would humiliate him, he would at least see their face.

"I'm tired of this shit," he said, finally, his anger rising to the surface. "Who the hell is down here? Levi? Joe? Abel? Who the fuck thought this would be funny? Let's lure the nobody down to the mine and scare the crap out of him. Did you dream this up while you were drinking at the party? While you were counting your money?" The noise happened again, and it was close now, but it was hard to tell from where. All the noise down here echoed around him, surrounding him.

He continued down, deep inside. The weight of the stone above him pressed down on him, and he felt the dead cultists, mining down here for nothing.

"Fucking hell," he said. "This is bullshit."

Still no answer. The metal scraping noise had stopped, and he was alone with his heartbeat again. He wouldn't spend the whole night here. All they were doing was wasting his time.

"Okay, fucko," he said. "I may not be famous, but my time is worth more than this. *I'm* worth more than this."

Ted said it, and he believed it. He felt better than he had in days, the anger solidifying his confidence again. He'd go home, and he'd do what he always did. He'd try again. He'd make another movie, and this time, this would be the one that would break through, and make him a name. It'd make him successful.

Then something sharp and heavy hit him in the back, and something inside him broke with a heavy CRACK. He fell, his lower half suddenly not responding to him. It hurt, everything hurt, his body filled with agony. He tried to speak.

"I—"

"Shh," said a voice from behind him, coming from the dark, and then the sharp heaviness hit him again, and this was higher up, in his back, and he could feel it inside him. He couldn't breathe. It moved inside his chest, and he realized it was a pick-axe embedded inside. It was through his lungs. He couldn't breathe.

"You wanted a big break. Here it is."

Ted tried to speak, but nothing came out. He heard the metal scraping noise, the pick-axe dragging on the ground, and then it whistled, moving through the air. He felt a momentary impact on the back of his skull, and then nothing.

# 19

Steph woke up, her eyes snapping to her cell phone. She'd slept through three alarms. She blinked, forcing them to focus on the time. She was running late. She scrambled out of bed and threw on clothes, scrambling out the door. The mansion was quiet.

She got to the main demonstration space a minute early, her heart beating hard. She hustled in, finding William already working on setting up the area, a team of volunteers unfolding hundreds of chairs. He watched from the side, silently observing.

"Hi," said Steph. "I'm here to help."

William nodded at her. "Well, right now I'm making sure the engineer dude that Mr. Stark brought in doesn't kill himself or someone else while he's planning the stunt, or whatever."

"What?" asked Steph. "What stunt?"

William pointed behind the stage, and a man stood on a ladder, working on some rigging, attaching lines and rope to the massive midnight star attached to the wall.

"Something to do with Mr. Stark's panel. Don't ask me. I just work here," said William. Bags hung under his eyes.

"So what should I do?" asked Steph.

"Stand next to me and look like you're supervising," said William. "Make sure that idiot doesn't kill someone." Steph stood next to William, following orders. The chairs were nearly set up, the volunteers working through stacks and stacks. After finishing here, they'd move on and help the first general admission guests of the day check in at the entrance to the compound.

"Hey!" yelled the man standing on the ladder.

Steph looked. He was trying to get their attention, gesturing at the two of them. William ignored him.

"William, I think—" said Steph.

William didn't look. "He doesn't remember my name. Let him dance for a few more seconds." Steph glanced at him. He shouted again.

"Can I get some help?" he asked, and William noticed him now, looking to him and walking over at a leisurely pace. Steph followed.

"Yes?" asked William, staring up.

"Could you grab me another spool of wire? I've used up what I had."

"You had a hundred feet," said William. "You've used all that?"

"I got some distances wrong, okay?" asked the man.

"Come on, dude. The panel starts in a half hour. I don't have much time, Levi will ream my ass if I don't get this right."

William held a stare for a moment, silent, and then blinked hard.

"Alright," he said, looking off. "Give me a few minutes, I'll grab some." He walked off, and Steph followed.

"Let's go for a ride," he said, and they went outside, jumping into his ATV. William turned the key and revved it up before flying off.

"We're going to get wire?" asked Steph.

"I asked him," said William. "I asked him how much he would need, and he told me a hundred feet."

"How much more is there?" asked Steph.

"Oh, plenty," said William. "It's not about that. No one thinks anymore. They just do. And all these Hollywood people. Just expect me to drop everything and help them."

"Well, isn't that your job?" asked Steph.

"My job is to take care of this place, and facilitate its use," said William.

"That doesn't include running gopher missions?"

"I mean, I don't know," said William. "I would like some politeness, some respect. Is that too much to ask?"

"No, I don't think so," said Steph. "I understand. They've been jerks to me too."

William steered the ATV away from the central area of the compound, past the church.

"I can handle people being mean," said William. "Doesn't do much to me. It's the disrespect that bothers me. On top of them coming here, with that movie—"

He stopped himself then, and Steph didn't know to ask for more info or not. She remembered William being here for the massacre. And lurking underneath was the suspicion about Steven's death. William had access to everything and knew the compound like the back of his hand. He'd been here. He could have done it. He could have returned here because he worships the Midnight Star.

Steph studied his face, and there wasn't anger there. Only sadness, his plain expression holding back something.

"We're here," he said, pulling the ATV down a side trail, and into a fenced off area, dominated by a big barn, with a few smaller sheds around it. He parked next to one of the sheds and jumped out.

"Do you need my help?" asked Steph.

"I wouldn't turn it down," he said, and Steph hopped off and followed him inside. It was filled with stuff, odds and ends of materials, lumber, pipes, rope, and tubes of caulk hung from all the walls.

"Could you grab the other end of this?" he asked, kneeling down next to a coil of metal wire. "It's not heavy, but a little help makes it easy." Steph kneeled and slid her fingers underneath the other side.

"1, 2, 3," and they lifted, and William was right, it wasn't that heavy, but Steph could see how hard it would be alone. They walked it out of the shed and loaded it into the back of the ATV.

"Let's head back," said William. "I'm sure that dude is getting antsy."

"Did Levi bring him along?" asked Steph.

"I'm not entirely sure," said William. "Might be best asking Mr. Lindew about that. They don't tell me a lot." William wheeled the ATV around and headed toward the hub. She glanced at her phone. General admission would enter within five minutes and then head toward the first panels of the day. They didn't have much more time.

They rode in silence, and the suspicion still hung inside her. She needed answers.

"Is it true that you were here when—when everything happened?" she asked, the ATV's tires cutting through the gravel.

William glanced at her quickly, and then his eyes cut back to the road.

"Sorry, you don't have to—"

"No, it's okay," he said. "Yeah, it's true."

"I thought everyone died," said Steph.

"Most did," he said. "A few kids got out. I was one of 'em."

"I'm sorry," she said.

"It's not your fault," he said. "My parents got duped. They thought this new religion was a way out from their lives. But Kalman tricked them. But I can't dwell on it. I was a kid."

"Can I ask—why did you come back and work here?" asked Steph.

"Most of the other kids were lucky, had family some-where," said William. "I didn't. My parents were all I had, so they put me in an orphanage. Not too far from here. And I was too old to get adopted. I grew up in the system. Didn't really have any prospects of a career. Working odd jobs to pay bills, but didn't have a direction. Then the people who bought this place from the government contacted me. Said they had looked into the survivors and wanted to give me a job here."

"And you said yes," said Steph.

"Not right away, but yeah," said William. "I don't know. I wasn't doing anything else, and the pay is decent for what mostly amounts to doing some odd chores and handyman type stuff. There's been a few events here, and that gets a little stressful, but nothing crazy. At least not until this. They provide my room and board for free. Gives me a chance to figure things out, y'know? Never got the chance when I was younger."

"Being here doesn't bother you?" asked Steph.

"It did at first," he said. "But I was here alone for a while. And I've kinda claimed it as my own, y'know? It's not Kalman's compound anymore. It's mine. It doesn't—it doesn't have that power over me anymore."

"Have you talked to the new owners?" asked Steph.

"Yeah," said William. He paused. "He's a nice guy. Seems like he wants to do the right thing."

"It doesn't bother you he let the movie premiere here?" asked Steph.

William said nothing at first, his brow furrowing. "I don't know. I don't like it. As much as I've gotten over everything, using it to sell a movie seems cheap. I knew those people. My parents were here. And I've seen Joe's movies. I doubt it'll be too respectful."

"I'm sorry," said Steph. "It's kinda our fault it's all happening."

"You didn't make the decision," said William. "It was the suits. The carrot and the stick. They use their money as the carrot at first, and then they use it as a stick, to beat you with it. They only care about the money—"

He stopped and took a deep breath.

"Sorry, I shouldn't talk so much. I'm just the help," said William.

"Only a couple more days," said Steph. "Then we'll be out

of your hair."

"That's true," said William. "Two more days."

William expertly came to a halt right next to the door, and they carried the wire inside past a line of attendees waiting for Levi's panel about his new movie. Levi stood there now, talking to the engineer who sat on top of the ladder.

"Finally," said Levi. "What took you so long?"

"Don't ask me," said William. "Your boy is the one who said he only needed one spool." Levi stared.

"Will this be enough, Jonah?" asked Levi, as Jonah climbed down, pulling a set of snips out of his tool belt and cutting more wire. "We've only got fifteen minutes until the masses pour in here."

"Shouldn't take me long, Mr. Stark," said Jonah. "Only a couple more line, and then I can wire the trigger. Ten minutes."

William stood there for a moment, and then returned to where Steph had found him this morning. She followed him, standing next to him.

"You're learning," he said, and he cracked a smile for the first time since she'd arrived. They watched as Jonah finished stringing wires from the midnight star to the ceiling, and then to the wall.

"What exactly is the plan?" asked Steph.

"I believe that Mr. Stark wants the midnight star to swing down and narrowly miss him, to stun the audience."

"That sounds dangerous," said Steph.

"It is," said William. "I told 'em it was a bad idea. But he and Geno insisted. We're getting extra security in here, apparently, just to make sure it's safe. But it's out of my hands."

Levi wasn't the only celeb in here, with both Joe and Abel

showing up, both talking to Henry as they walked in. Henry winked at her, and she could feel herself blush. Linda trailed behind him. Steph spied Bill and Frank chatting by a side door. They must have caught wind of the stunt.

Jonah the engineer had taken down his ladder, and held a tiny electronic remote in his hand, with a big red button on it. He had taped a blue X on the stage, small, but visible, and had led Levi over to it, pointing at it emphatically, and then at the button. Levi was getting instructions. Steph hoped he was paying attention, looking at the size of the star.

"Will the wire hold that thing?" asked Steph.

"That cable is stronger than it looks," said William. "The walls will collapse before it snaps."

"Alright, let's test it," said Levi. Jonah put a mic stand on the blue X and then backed away. They cleared away everyone from the area. Levi looked around, making sure no one was in the line of fire, and pushed the button. There was a small click heard from above them, and Steph watched the massive star swing downward, the nearly invisible guide wires holding it. Her eyes went to the mic stand, and the star swung down toward it. It looked to be in the wrong position.

The star swung down, massive and heavy, but fell right behind the mic stand, missing it by about five feet. If Levi stood on the blue X, he'd be fine. The star swayed back and forth, eventually slowing and stopping. Jonah called people over, and using the guide wire, winched it into place, snapping it right back where it used to be. The illusion was complete.

Levi nodded at Jonah and waved him off. Steph glanced at her phone again. Five minutes and the crowd would fill the space, and Levi would start his panel. The same You-Tube personality was there, talking to Levi, followed by Joe and Abel, all of them looking up at the midnight star and Levi showing them the remote. Everyone wanted to see the show.

Suddenly, the power flickered off, back on, and then off again.

"What the fuck?" asked Levi loudly.

"Goddamnit," said William. The room was dark, and several voices yelled out, and then phone flashlights turned on in the dark. William was one of them, and he used it to guide himself out the back door, with Levi following him. A few minutes later, the lights flickered on. Everyone else still stood around, waiting. Some idle murmurs and shuffling could be heard, but Steph stayed put.

William returned a minute later. They were late to let in the crowd, and Levi was letting him know it. William absorbed his complaints, and whatever he said worked, because Levi went backstage, and soon people were flooding in. William returned next to her.

"It's the damn circuit breakers in this building," said William. "Thought I had fixed them."

The fans filled out the seats, buzzing with anticipation. The Youtuber climbed up on the stage after a few minutes, to scattered applause.

"Who's ready to start the show?"

# 20

"Without further ado, the famed director of the Terminal Conclusion series, and both Murder Island One and Two, Levi Stark!"

The crowd cheered as Levi walked onto the stage, applause filling the space. Levi smiled widely, waving to the fans, and then shaking Kyle's hand. Kyle gestured to a chair opposite him, and Levi took a seat, followed by Kyle. The cheers slowly died down. The Midnight Star hung from the sky, ready for release. If anyone noticed the wires securing it, no one called attention to it.

"Mr. Stark," said Kyle. "This is your first Splatterfest, correct?"

"Yes," said Levi, straightening his tie, and then his watch. He wore numerous props to keep his hands busy.

"It's quite a way to make your debut here," said Kyle. "Having it here at the Kalman compound. In the shadow of the Midnight Star."

"I suppose that's true," said Levi. "But I'm not one to back away from a challenge. And this place has a dark history, but it doesn't do much to intimidate me. Despite what my films portray, I don't believe in ghosts."

"You've been staying here the past couple nights, along with a few of our select guests," said Kyle. "You haven't heard or felt anything strange?"

"Not at all," said Levi. "It's been peaceful. Aside from maybe some arguments or squabbles from my associates. Why? Do you think this place is haunted?"

"I don't know," said Kyle. "Sometimes it feels that way. It feels like there's a legacy of death here."

"Oh, well, that's a different story altogether," said Levi. "And something that is cogent. Ghosts are one thing, and legacies are another. And believe me, you won't find anyone who thinks about the impact of death, mourning, grief, as much as me." Levi counted off on his fingers as he spoke.

"Really?" asked Kyle.

"Of course," said Levi. "You've seen my work, right?"

"Absolutely," said Kyle. "Multiple times. I'm a big fan."

"Well, I interweave death through all my films. It's something you don't see from other horror directors. Real meaning and thought put into the theme, so it interacts, coalesces with all parts of the film. So many filmmakers just have non-stop gore-fests, without regard to what it all *means*. Like sure, I love bloody deaths. They're impactful, they're shocking, and they keep your audience engaged. But if they mean nothing, then what is it all for? It's something that I'm involved with at every level of creation."

"Wow," said Kyle. "I've never really thought about it."

"Many people don't," said Levi, still smiling. Steph had seen all his movies. They were entertaining, but she didn't know what Levi was talking about. There was no depth to any of them. It was a bunch of teenagers getting chopped in half in silly ways. Joe and Abel watched with Henry, and Joe's brow was furrowed, his eyes narrowed. Steph didn't know why he was here, but he didn't like what he heard. Abel stood silently behind him, his arms crossed, his face like stone. She tried to catch Henry's eye, but he only stared at the panel. How many of these had he sat through? A lot, she imagined.

"Are you excited for your premiere?" asked Kyle. "It's tonight, correct?"

"Yes," said Levi. "And I'm thrilled. I can't wait to show the world what I've made. It's a landmark achievement in modern horror. It will leave everyone gasping for breath."

"You're not worried about it being overshadowed?" asked Kyle.

"Overshadowed?" asked Levi. "By what?"

"By the premiere of Midnight Star," said Kyle. "I mean, it's sponsoring the festival, and the film itself is about John Kalman and the cult, set in the very place we're sitting. It has a large spotlight on it."

Levi's face froze in a rictus grin, his eyes staring at Kyle. He paused for a moment, and then answered, his smirk dropping. "My entire career I've had to overcome obstacles, Kyle. And this is no different. Every opportunity I've been given, I've taken advantage of. I've won every single box office weekend, even against much heralded competition. The spotlight will be large, but I'm positive it will only illuminate the flaws. I am confident that my film will steal that spotlight."

"Why so bold?" asked Kyle.

"To not put too fine a point on it, I've seen Joe's other films," said Levi, smiling again. "And none of them even approach Death's Destiny. And I doubt Midnight Star will do any better."

The crowd oohed in response, like tabloid television, which made Levi smile even broader. He fed off the audience, positive or negative reaction. Joe's face showed only anger now.

"You've prepared a presentation, correct?" asked Kyle.

"That's right, Kyle," said Levi. "You mentioned death hanging over us all, and I've geared the show around that. A little of how each of my films has touched on that theme, and I'll give the audience a preview of tonight, with an exclusive clip ahead of the premiere. Please, the first clip."

The large screen suspended behind them on the stage played a clip that Steph recognized from the original Terminal Conclusion.

"This is from Terminal Conclusion, my first feature," he said. "Now, most of you probably know that all of those films are about the prospects of cheating death. Tackling issues of mortality, and the inevitability of dying."

The video played, with the main character, a handsome actor, facing a death trap situation. The camera panned around, showing all the different threats that faced him, any number of things that could kill him. Finally, all of them in concert acted like a Rube Goldberg device, cutting off his head. The crowd cheered. The clip ended.

"In the first film, it was a horrific plane crash that our protagonists avoided, and then we saw them picked off, one by one, including Billy here, decapitated by a low hanging wire. Death would hunt them down, killing them all before the end of the movie. Now the crash would prove prescient, as 9/11 would happen only a few months later, spiking interest in the film after I released it on video." Kyle said nothing, but Steph wondered why he didn't try to push Levi on that. The plane accident was a pure coincidence. Levi hadn't predicted the future.

*Because this is all fluff, Steph. All of this is scripted.*

Steph knew it, but still resented Levi lying right to their faces.

"Death hangs over all of us. But the first film was only introducing the language, so to speak. One that I would play with as we moved through more of the other films. Setting up the cast of characters each time, the disaster they avoid, and then knocking them off, one by one, as I played the role of Death, making sure the characters paid the price for trying to escape their ultimate fate. Next clip, please."

It played, from the second film, with one of the female characters running through a warehouse. The camera cut quickly between all the dangerous items that filled the space. Loose planks of wood balanced precariously. Heavy blocks of metal. A puddle of water, and a sparking wire. Any of which could spell the end. But this time it's none of those things, the camera focused on another figure, trying to save her. In a forklift, he carefully placed the wood back on its shelf, the metal bars back in their place. But as he reversed, he loses control, and the forklift goes haywire, levers jammed, and one of the prongs rams forward, straight through the female character's head. Her brains burst out the back of her skull. The crowd cheered, and then again as the forklift continued, knocking a sequence of things off of shelves, a thin pipe eventually falling and impaling the male character.

"You can't avoid Death. Trying to prevent disaster will only create more chaos. The language changes, the films becoming a game with the audience, as I try and navigate their expectations, each kill a clever system of misdirects and ruses. You notice how the crowd has cheered, Kyle?"

"Yes," said Kyle. "I cheered too. That one is my favorite death in all your films."

"Thank you," said Levi. "But make no mistake, these characters dying are protagonists. Not heroes, but protagonists. And yet you cheer their deaths. You cheer literally, for Death. For me, frankly, as I play the role, as the creator and arbiter of these character's lives."

"You said it yourself," said Kyle. "You can't escape Death."

"And no one should," said Levi. "We all have our time. The next clip, please. This one is from Murder Island."

The video played. The main character ran through the jungle, trying to escape the team of killers hunting him down. He was bloody, his face dirty, breathing hard as he sprinted. A knife flew by his head, slicing open his cheek, but not killing him. He gasped, and fell, and then the killer was on him, another dagger grasped in his hand. They struggled, back and forth, but the main character saw a jagged tree branch and pushed the killer back into it, impaling them. He watched the killer struggle on the branch, not dead yet. He finished him off with a quick swipe of the killer's own knife, across his neck. The crowd didn't cheer, now.

"Murder Island inverted everything," said Levi. "I was weary of Terminal Conclusion. I was bored of playing Death. I was tired of Death winning, frankly. The team of hunters on Murder Island fulfill that role for me, and let me explore completely the themes of accepting mortality, while also exploring that maybe you might not cheat Death—but you can bargain with him, from time to time. Now. Who's ready for a little tease of tonight's premiere?"

The crowd roared and applauded.

"That's what I like to hear," said Levi. He sat back down, and the lights dimmed, as the final clip played, from the premiere of Death's Destiny. Steph didn't know what to expect. She knew the actor playing the main character, but she hadn't even seen the trailer, so she was cold going in. The video started, a close-up of the actor, zooming out to reveal a showdown with a dark hooded figure, both perched on a cliffside, the ocean roaring below them and a cloudy sky above, blotting out the sun.

The hooded figure flipped back his hood, revealing a bleached skull.

"There is no more dancing around it, Gavin," said the skull. "There is only the end."

Gavin grimaced at him and charged, pulling out a sword from a sheath. Death pulled his own sword out, massive, held in two bony hands.

*A fantasy film? Someone literally fighting Death?*

Steph rolled her eyes. Levi had disappeared up his own ass with this one. She was glad she hadn't planned on attending the premiere, if this is what the movie was filled with.

Just as the two swords clashed, the clip ended, and the

lights came back up. Applause filled the room, but even Steph sensed the lack of enthusiasm. She couldn't be the only person who thought it was corny.

"Just a tease, as promised," he said. "Tonight, in Death's Destiny, we finally confront Death. I hope to see you there. Now, Kyle, if you'd clear the stage. There's one last thing to attend to." Levi nodded at Kyle, and Kyle returned it, disappearing off the stage, and then walking far, far off to the side. He didn't want to be present for what Steph assumed would be the stunt.

"Now, Kyle asked me if I was afraid that I'd be overshadowed by the Midnight Star. Here, in the Kalman compound, it's difficult to avoid. It hangs over everything." He looked up at the large star that dangled over him. "But let me make this clear. Nothing overshadows Levi Stark. The Midnight Star is nothing, and I am not afraid."

Steph watched him take a small step. Now he stood on the blue X, exactly where it was in the rehearsal. He reached into a pocket, and there was a slight movement, and Steph heard a quick whirring noise from above, as guide wires let loose.

Steph looked up, as did most of the audience. The huge midnight star swung down in a wide arc, almost in slow motion. Steph remembered the practice from less than an hour earlier, as it swung right behind the mic stand, a Charlie Chaplin bit in real life, Levi avoiding catastrophe. Narrowly avoiding Death.

They watched the star fall, everyone together. Levi smiled, confidently, knowing it would miss him, and leave a perfect punctuation on his presentation, one that would be watched repeatedly on YouTube, sealing his legend as a horror director.

The star fell, picking up speed, the jagged point swinging through the air, the wires holding it true, right on course.

Steph looked to Levi, watching him, seeing the illusion come true, as it would miss him.

But it didn't.

The jagged point of the star swung down, finishing its downward arc, the heavy wooden tip striking Levi right in the neck, not so much cutting but knocking his head off his shoulders with a terrible thunk, still smiling as it tumbled to the ground. His body collapsed, the star swinging. Blood poured out of his stump, gushing onto the stage and floor.

The crowd gasped, silent for a long moment, waiting for someone to tell them it was fake. For someone to tell them it was a trick.

But it was no trick, and then they screamed.

# 21

Everyone screamed, watching Levi's blood pool on the floor. His head came to rest at the foot of the front row. The midnight star hung from its guide wire, exactly as it should have.

The crowd ran outside, after the initial shock wore off, the double doors thrown open. Henry ushered people away, trying to clear the area.

"Holy fuck," said William, standing next to her.

Steph's stomach lurched, and she swallowed down bile, turning away from the body. She glanced to the tech who had set up the stunt, who stood frozen on the side of the room, his eyes wide, staring. He ran to a trash can and threw up. Steph averted her eyes. Joe and Abel both looked stunned.

"What do we do?" asked Steph.

"Call the cops again," said William, his voice tired. "I'll go do it." He marched through a side door.

Another death. The tech, Jonah, had curled up against the wall, his head in his hands.

Steph walked over to him.

"Are you okay?" asked Steph.

"It shouldn't—it shouldn't have happened," said Jonah. "He stood on the blue tape."

Henry was there, the crowd gone now. Joe and Abel had disappeared.

"William went to call the police," said Steph. Henry nodded, but all his focus was on Jonah.

"What happened?" he asked.

"I don't think he's in the best state of mind," said Steph.

"He stood on the blue tape. It should have been fine! We tested it. You saw it, you both did."

He was right. They had both seen the test, with the massive star swinging down, and missing the blue tape. Levi should have been fine. But now his head was gone.

"What could have happened?" asked Henry, and Steph left them, steeling herself, walking toward the corpse. Two deaths now. Steven was no longer an isolated case, and the midnight star left over his corpse wasn't an outlier. The massive star had stopped swinging, finally, and now hung directly over the headless body of Levi Stark. An enormous amount of already drying blood pooled around it. His toes still touched the edge of the X created by the blue tape, the safe spot where the midnight star couldn't touch.

She looked back to the tech. Steph didn't know when he had arrived, but either he was the world's best actor, or he was genuinely horrified at the thought of being responsible for another man's death. Henry kneeled next to him, try-ing to talk, but only sputtered words came from the tech's mouth. His eyes were already vacant. Steph wasn't an ex-pert, but he didn't look like a killer.

Something was wrong here. The star hanging over his corpse couldn't be a coincidence.

She approached the body, her eyes avoiding the horrible stump where Levi's head used to be. Instead, she looked at the blue X. X marks the spot. Levi had followed directions, his feet squarely on the tape where he was safe. He was an egomaniac, but he wasn't an idiot, and he knew the dangers of the stunt. But the X was in the wrong place.

What were the options here?

*One. The tech had made an error with the placement of the spot, or the rigging of the wires.*

Steph thought back to the test, as the huge star swung through the air. The practice swing hadn't hurt anyone, and had borne out the X was safe. Could the star have swung differently with Levi? She didn't know the science, but the guide wires all looked the same.

*Two. Levi stepped off the blue tape.*

She had watched his feet as he pressed the button and released the star. He had stood on the tape, and it had killed him.

*Three—*

She stared at the tape. What else could it be? But then she looked past it, next to Levi's body. There was something on the floor, next to his pants leg. It was blue, a small shred of blue. The same tape.

*Three. Someone had moved the tape, during the blackout.*

It was obvious, now. Someone had scrambled in the

dark, had found the tape, and had moved it, and had left a piece behind. It looked the same to Levi, in the rush to start the show. It looked the same to them all. No one had noticed, and Levi had gotten his head taken off, standing right in the star's path. This was proof. They had killed Levi, just like Steven. There was no doubt in her mind.

She went back to Henry, who still spoke to Jonah. William stood there with him now.

"Cops are on the way," said William. "Along with an EMT. Doubt they'll be able to do a whole lot for Levi."

"Someone moved the X," said Steph. The tech looked up, his eyes alert again.

"What?" asked Henry.

"There's a shred of tape left from where the original X was put down. Someone, during the blackout, moved the tape. They moved it directly in the star's path. They wanted Levi dead and made it look like an accident."

"Are you sure?" asked Henry. "That's—that's murder, if that's true."

"I know," said Steph. "But the power was out for five minutes, give or take. It gave them plenty of time to move the X in the dark, during the confusion, and return to where they were, with no one the wiser."

The tech looked up at her, his eyes hopeful. "That has to be it. I didn't check the tape after the blackout. Someone must have moved it."

Henry stared at her. "I—I don't think I'm ready to call anything a murder just yet. Let's get the police here and see what they say."

Gary and Geno were there quickly, both looking haggard.

"Jesus Christ," said Gary, seeing Levi's head. "Oh, Jesus Christ, Jesus Christ." He started pacing, walking past everyone, muttering to himself.

"What the fuck happened?" asked Geno.

Henry told him, including Steph's idea about how someone moved the tape, causing Levi's death. He looked at her pointedly after it was brought up.

"Are you kidding me? Are you fucking kidding me?" he asked. He marched off to Gary, who now sat against the wall, his head in his hands. It was killing him. Splatterfest had killed two people. Steph knew him and knew the guilt would eat him alive.

Steph followed Geno. She wouldn't leave Gary to the sharks.

"We have to cancel, Geno," said Gary. "This is unconscionable."

"It was an accident, Gar," said Geno. "You heard the tech guy. It could have happened anytime."

"But it didn't, Geno. It happened here. On my watch. And now a man is dead. Levi Stark is dead," said Gary. His voice cracked.

"Levi stood in the wrong place," said Geno.

"Someone killed him," said Steph. "Someone sabotaged the stunt. They moved the tape."

"You don't have any proof," said Geno. "And you shouldn't be saying that stuff too loudly."

"I know what I saw," said Steph.

"We have to cancel, Geno," said Gary.

"Are you kidding me?" asked Geno.

"That's two dead," said Steph.

"I can count," said Geno. "Apparently you can't. I wasn't

bluffing yesterday. If you pull out, our contract is void, and I'm taking you down. I will pull every single penny I can out of you, and your precious video store is done for."

"Someone is killing people," said Steph.

"You have no idea what you're talking about," said Geno. "Steven Hellman was a drug addict, who couldn't wake up or fall asleep without taking a pill. Either he miscalculated his dose or he decided he didn't want to wake up again. Either way, that's not on me. And Levi? Levi is a fucking idiot who thought he was invincible. This isn't the first of his little stunts, and this time, he just happened to pay the piper. Celebrities dying isn't a national emergency. It happens every day. Most of these people ride the high wire their entire lives, and sometimes, they just fall off. I didn't cancel a premiere when Heath Ledger died. Do you think I'm going to do it when Levi Stark does?"

Gary stared at him. Steph's stomach fell. She clenched her fist. She wanted to hit him, but it wouldn't do anything.

"My money is on the line here," said Geno. "And if we cancel, we can wave goodbye to all of it. And that means no more precious video store, no more Splatterfest. I don't care what you have to tell yourself, but we are not canceling, not on my watch. I've been planning this shit for a year, and I'm not calling it off because of fuck-up celebrities. Capische?"

Gary stared, and Steph had never seen his eyes so dark, so full of rage. Gary didn't answer.

"Do you understand, Gary?" asked Geno. "Say yes, I understand."

"Yes, I understand," said Gary, finally.

"Good," said Geno. "And you." Geno looked to Steph. "Keep your mouth shut about murderers. You're going to start a panic, and believe me, it's not something you want with thousands of people on the property."

Geno walked off to talk to Henry, pulling him away from William. What was he saying? Reading Henry the riot act, most likely. Steph's eyes went back to the corpse, still there, waiting to be pulled away.

The EMTs and cops arrived over an hour later, making the long drive out to the compound once again. The EMTs bagged up his body with his head, while the police took statements from them. They talked to Jonah extensively, and he walked them through the stunt, and what happened. Geno took the cops aside and gestured broadly, but Steph couldn't hear anything they said.

"I think someone moved the X, that marked the safe spot," said Steph, to the female cop she spoke to. "There was a blackout for about five minutes, and someone moved it. The piece of tape—"

"Yes, miss," said the cop. "That's what the tech said, too. But there was no shred of tape left. The spot was bare. Impossible to tell if the tape was moved or not."

"There was a shred there—"

"Not anymore, miss," she said. "Did you take a picture?"

"No," said Steph. "I didn't think to. The EMTs! The EMTs must have accidentally removed it when they took the body."

"If they did, we'll find it at the morgue," said the cop. "But it just looks like an accident."

"Are you arresting the tech?" asked Steph.

"No," said the cop. "Considering Mr. Stark pushed the button himself, it's a civil matter. Anything else to add?"

"No," said Steph, looking over to Geno, who watched as William scrubbed the blood away. They would use this space a few more times during the festival. They needed it clean. William's thick forearms tensed as Geno spoke to him, pointing out the spots on the floor.

"If there's anything else, call us," said the cop, handing Steph a card. She pocketed it. Then the cops left, the EMTs too, driving away with a second body. Somebody had taken the shred of tape, the evidence that someone had moved the X, and had arranged the murder of Levi Stark. They had removed it while she wasn't looking. Or Geno had convinced the cops to not follow it.

It was barely evidence to begin with. But it was something, and it was too many coincidences. All doubt had left her. There was a killer among them. A secret cultist hiding in plain sight. Someone was a killer, and Steph would need to figure out who.

# 22

Steph found Gary outside, sitting on a box behind the central building. He looked beaten.

"You doing alright?" asked Steph.

"Ha," said Gary. "No. I am not doing alright."

"It's not your fault," said Steph.

"All over the internet is news of Levi's death. I saw someone captured the exact moment on their phone, and it's all over social media. They're treating it like it's a part of one of his movies."

"How awful."

"And now that's what they'll think of when they think of Splatterfest. Dead celebrities. That'll be my legacy."

"That's not true—"

"I should have pushed through with the cancellation after Steven died. Now there's two of them," said Gary. "On my watch. Two men dead."

"No one blames you for their deaths, Gary," said Steph. "Neither of them were due to negligence. Something is up around here, no matter how much people deny it."

"So there's a killer on the loose at Splatterfest?" asked Gary. "Is it bad that makes me feel better?"

"I don't think so," said Steph. "If someone's out there killing people, at least there's an adversary. An adversary that isn't you."

"Who's the killer, then?" asked Gary.

"I don't know," said Steph. "Someone was here at night, and also in the room earlier, who could switch the tape around in the dark."

"That's a long list."

"They're also a secret cultist."

"The Midnight Star is long dead."

"Might not be for long, after that movie comes out. Gives it some publicity," said Steph.

"Oh God," said Gary. "Another thing on my conscience."

"Maybe it's all in my head," said Steph.

"But you don't think so," said Gary.

"No," said Steph.

"Then what do I do?" asked Gary. "Cancel? Geno's right about one thing. If we cancel, Splatterfest is done for, and so is the store. I'll be ruined. I'll be a barista for the rest of my life."

Gary sat there, his eyes looking down into the Texas dirt, glancing up at her. Splatterfest was his child and it had given Steph a place to belong.

*She had just moved to Austin.*

She had always loved horror movies, but to everyone else, she was the weirdo, the gorehound. Nobody wanted to watch Nail Gun Massacre with her, or Friday the 13th Part VII. She had moved to Austin, and knew no one, and had no friends. And then she volunteered at Splatterfest. She saw The Video Store for the first time, a ramshackle building, the seams visible where additions had been thrown together, stepping up and down and through various parts of the store to get to different genres. She had been so nervous.

Steph had gotten there early, an hour early, but she couldn't have gone back to sleep with the raw nerves inside of her, and so she drove over there, and parked, and waited. She threw on some music and then sat there, in the morning dark, and the nerves wore off and her exhaustion returned, and she fell asleep. A tapping on her window woke her up.

"Excuse me," said the man. She didn't know him yet, but it was Gary, who had been there all night, getting ready for Splatterfest. "Could you move your car? We need this area for the film festival."

She moved it after a lot of apologizing, but then she helped Gary.

The sun rose, and more volunteers came, and Gary introduced her to everyone. Most of them were still her friends, some of her closest. At the end of the weekend, Gary hired her to help at The Video Store, and that became her life.

"Do you remember when you knocked on my window?" asked Steph. "When we first met? I was scared to death."

"I make an imposing figure in the dark," said Gary. "You were parked where the projector was going to get set up. I had considered letting you sleep longer, but there was really no more time for it."

"If it wasn't for you, Gary, I would still be that scared kid in the dark," said Steph. "With no friends."

"That's not true," said Gary. "You'd make friends, regardless of where you were."

"But I didn't have to," said Steph. "You helped me, and gave me a place to belong. That is The Video Store. That is Splatterfest. It's a place for outcasts and exiles and weirdos who don't belong anywhere else, and all that is possible because of you. Where we can bond and argue and enjoy all kinds of weird movies. Where we can feel safe."

Gary sighed. "That's very kind of you."

"It's the truth, Gary," said Steph. "We all feel that way. You've given us a second home, a refuge, a sanctuary. What was Dan doing before he started working for you?"

"I know he had trouble with his parents—"

"They kicked him out of the house, Gary. He was living on the street, and you let him sleep in the storage space until he got back on his feet," said Steph.

"It was the decent thing to do."

"It was, but it was also not a thing most business owners would do," said Steph. "Or people. But you did, and I could name a dozen people, just off the top of my head, that you helped in similar ways. And Splatterfest is a part of that. It's a celebration of more than just horror movies. It's a celebration of us, and what we've built."

"It doesn't feel like it," said Gary. "Not this year."

"This—this isn't Splatterfest," said Steph. "You were trying to make our community larger. To effect change on a bigger scale. And trying to survive."

"It feels like a mistake."

"If it keeps us alive," said Steph. "Then it was worth it."

"If everything goes through, we should make enough money to keep the store going for another year, at least," said Gary. "Maybe two. But after that—"

"I've been meaning to talk to you about it," said Steph. "But we need to change the store."

"What do you mean, change the store?" asked Gary. "I love the store."

"It's obsolete," said Steph. "And it isn't 1991 anymore. You can't just keep trudging ahead and expect the place to stay in business out of inertia. You have a different business model than you did when you opened, and the store doesn't reflect that. In fact, a lot of people, when they come in—"

"When they come in—"

"When they come in, they're scared of the place," said Steph. "It's not inviting. It should be inviting."

"It's homey."

"It is," said Steph. "It's the home of your weird uncle who collects a lot of weird shit."

"That's our charm."

"We don't have to worry about it now," said Steph. "But I want you to think about it. As your assistant manager, I'm officially bringing it up. Okay?"

"Okay," said Gary. "I'll consider it. We still have tonight and tomorrow to get through."

"Try not to get overwhelmed," said Steph.

"But two people are dead," said Gary. "The only deaths we've had before were fictional."

"You didn't kill those men, Gary," said Steph. "And if you're asking if we should cancel it right now, send everyone home, and take the full force of Geno's spite? I don't think so. I think we do what we've always done, what you've always done, and that is to try our best. If there is a killer on the loose, the only thing we can do is keep our eyes open."

"I hope it's all coincidences," said Gary. "But I trust you. And I trust your instincts."

"They're all I have," said Steph. "But something is going on. And if we send everyone home, and there is a killer, we'll never catch them."

"Do you suspect anyone in particular?"

"It was someone who had access to the mansion," said Steph. "And someone who was in the main hall earlier."

"One of the celebrities," said Gary. "Or one of the support staff." He stopped and thought. "You said it's connected to the Midnight Star, right? And you said William grew up here—"

"He wasn't in the room when the tape was moved," said Steph. "He had to go turn the power back on. And, after talking to him—he just seems sad. Doesn't seem like much of a killer."

"Oh," said Gary. "Well, that's the extent of my sleuthing. I'm never good at figuring out who the killer is in murder mysteries. It always surprises me."

"You're too nice, Gary," said Steph. "You can't imagine killing anyone at all."

"Come on," said Gary. "There's some darkness in me, I'm sure of it."

"You wouldn't hurt a mouse," said Steph. "Literally, I had to get rid of the mice in the store."

"They were just trying to survive."

"What did I say?" asked Steph. "That's what I'm talking about. But no, you don't cancel and ruin everything we've built for decades. Splatterfest is special. The Video Store is special. You don't give up on it. You fight for it."

"I knew there was a reason I hired you."

"You hired me because I showed up early and know how to work Excel."

"You also have an incredible knowledge of Italian giallo," said Gary.

"And I'll say it again, Argento is not overrated," said Steph. "He's underrated, if anything."

"I want to know what's going on in a movie," said Gary. "That's all I said."

"It's a visual medium!" said Steph.

"Okay, okay," said Gary. "I'm just teasing. Thanks for the pep talk."

"Thank you for believing me," said Steph. "We have to keep our eyes open."

"I'll do my best," said Gary. "I just don't have the time. And that's without Geno breathing down my neck about every little detail. He's driving me insane about this premiere."

"It's tomorrow night, right?" asked Steph.

"Yes," said Gary. "And it can't come fast enough. I'm tired of all these personalities, and this drama, and this compound. I don't believe in ghosts, but this place—something's not right. Even without the deaths."

"After tomorrow, we'll never have to visit the Kalman compound, ever again," said Steph.

"I've got to get back to work," said Gary. "If a premiere is happening, I've got stuff to do. Thanks for listening."

Gary left, and Steph watched him, each footstep a labor. She wanted to do something, but Gary couldn't cancel without risking the wrath of Geno. But maybe she could talk Joe into postponing the premiere and do the work for Gary.

# 23

She found Abel and Joe eating lunch together in the mansion, both sitting in the lounge. They murmured to each other until they saw her enter the room. A few dry logs filled the cold fireplace.

"Stephanie, right?" asked Joe, setting his plate with a sandwich and chips down on the small coffee table. "Do you need something?"

"I needed to talk to you," said Steph.

"About what? Is there a panel I'm forgetting about? I'm sorry if there is, we've been so busy the last couple days—"

"No, it's not that," said Steph. "I wanted to talk to you about your premiere."

"What about it?" asked Joe. Abel eyed her silently. He took the last bite of his sandwich, setting his plate down, filling the leather chair he sat in. He wiped his mouth with his napkin and gave her his full attention.

"I was wondering if you'd consider canceling it," said Steph. She tried to project confidence, but her voice wavered, both of the men's eyes on her.

"Why would we do that?" asked Joe.

"After the deaths, I feel like it's the right thing to do," said Steph.

"The right thing?" asked Joe.

"Yes," said Steph. "After what happened to Levi, we should cancel—"

"This isn't our show," said Joe. "Your boss is in charge. If we have to cancel, he has to make the call, not us."

"He's tried to talk to Geno," said Steph. "But—"

"But if he cancels he'll be on the hook for all the costs and refunds," said Joe. "So instead, he'll kick the can down the road, and blame it on us? Point all the guilt at us, because we choose not to cancel our premiere?"

"I—"

"Do you know how long it's taken to get this movie made?"

"I'm guessing—"

"Ten years," said Joe. "I've been shopping this screenplay for ten years, doing reboots and remakes for the studios. No one wanted it. Told me it wouldn't sell, wouldn't sell, wouldn't sell. That I couldn't have Abel as a lead. He's only a monster, a glorified stuntman." Abel's eyes narrowed. "All of my movies have made money. All of them. How many other directors can you say that about? Poor Levi? Nope. The legend, Bill Chancellor? Hell no. Name me anyone else working today that has my track record. I've been trying to get this thing made for ten years, with me in control, with Abel playing the lead, and we finally got it done. I had to call in a dozen favors, but it happened. And we get to premiere here, at the Kalman compound. All the eyes in the world are on us, and now, even more so because of Steven's suicide, and Levi's death."

"You're going to use their deaths for publicity?" asked Steph.

"I didn't kill anyone," said Joe. "And believe me, far worse has happened at these things, and no one has batted an eye. Just because this is all new to you innocent little fans doesn't mean that I have to throw ten years of work down the drain."

Steph's guts boiled, and her breath burned. She had to tell them.

"The deaths weren't accidents, or suicide," said Steph. "Someone killed them."

"What?" asked Joe, his face confused. "We were there. Levi pushed the button. No one else."

"Someone moved the tape marking his spot while the lights were out," said Steph. "They moved it right into the path of the star."

"Is there proof?" asked Abel, staring at her.

"The police didn't find any, but I saw it—"

"So no proof," said Joe. "And Steven? He ODed. Accident or suicide, no one forced those drugs inside him."

"Somebody hung a midnight star above his bed. It was empty before," said Steph. "Someone drugged him, and we won't know what it was until the festival is already over."

Joe rolled his eyes. "Because someone decorated his room after he left, that's proof he was killed?"

"Something is going on," said Steph. "Please—"

"You didn't know Steven," said Joe.

"No, but—"

"Why do you think we never worked with him?" asked Joe.

Stephanie paused. "I don't know. He said that you didn't respect him."

"He was right," said Joe. "We didn't. Because he was an addict and never got help. And whenever we tried to help him, he pushed us away. I wanted him involved in the Sleep Terror remake, but he literally dozed off during the middle of our first meeting. Cold sweats. Why on Earth would I bring someone like that aboard? It'd be irresponsible. It was only a question of *when* with Steven, not if."

"Someone could be planning something at your premiere," said Steph. "Involving the Midnight Star."

"They're dead and gone," said Joe. "And of all the things I'm worried about with the premiere, cultists attacking are not one of them. This is Abel's big break. He finally gets to show what he can do as a leading man. He's toiled his whole life to get to this point, and you want to take his moment from him?" Abel's eyes burned, staring at her.

"I don't want anyone else to get hurt," said Steph.

"Then have your boss cancel the show," said Joe. "And accept the consequences. But we have worked much too hard for this to throw it all away. This is the hottest premiere we've had in our entire careers, and a couple of deaths will not stop us." Joe patted Abel on the knee. "Let's get out of here." They stood up and left, leaving Steph alone in the lounge.

Were they right? Were the two deaths accidents? Two men who thought they were invincible, and it ended up killing them?

No, someone was hiding something. This was on purpose. John Kalman preached about his hatred of Hollywood, about the excesses of fame. And now two stars were dead, because of those excesses. Both with the midnight star. It couldn't be a coincidence. It couldn't be.

The door opened and Steph turned to see and then Abel was there, marching right at her, huge, looming over her. She instinctively stepped back as he walked at her, and he didn't stop, and she backed up against the wall, his shape standing right in front of her, his face full of anger.

"What do you think you're doing?" asked Abel.

"I—"

"Joe is a nice guy," said Abel. "Too nice of a guy. You have no idea what he's had to go through to get to where he's at. What he's faced, and what he's beaten. And—and how hard he's worked to get this movie made. And what it means to me he chose me to play the lead."

"People are dead—"

"I don't care," said Abel, his voice flat. "I don't care about Steven Hellman, and I sure as shit don't care about Levi Stark. You want to hold their deaths on us, just because we want to show a movie? Because your boss doesn't have the balls to follow his convictions? How dare you?"

Abel's breath was hot in her face. She wanted to run, but Abel's rage froze her.

"Joe's a nice guy," said Abel. "But I'm not. Not really. I keep it together because of him. Because of us. But I'm not a nice person, and I won't put up with what Joe will. So listen up. You drop this idea of calling off the festival, or canceling our premiere. You let that go out of your pretty little head. No more talk of murders, or cults, or the Midnight Star coming back. Steven was an accident. Levi was an accident. We will open our movie tomorrow night, and I won't have one plucky fan with some stupid ideas destroying our dream."

Steph stared at him. Tears formed at the corner of her eyes.

"Do you understand? Tell me you understand," said Abel.

"I understand," said Steph.

"Good," said Abel. "Because if I hear you're trying to ruin our premiere, the next time we talk, I won't be so nice." And then he was gone, back out the door, Steph left alone again.

She took a deep breath, trying to slow down her breathing. Her heart raced, and she wiped away the tears from her eyes. She kept expecting Abel to come back through the door and threaten her some more, but it didn't happen. It stayed shut.

As her breathing slowed, and her thoughts returned to the surface, the momentary doubt that Joe had introduced was completely gone. Because she had a suspect, someone who had access to the mansion, was in the room with Levi, and was connected to the Midnight Star.

Abel.

24

"I think Abel did it," said Steph. She sat with Dan in his room. He laid on his bed, playing on his phone. The day was over, only a couple hours to go until that night's party.

"What?" asked Dan. "Abel, the big movie monster dude, Abel?"

"Yes," said Steph. "Who else would I be talking about?"

"Why on Earth would he do it?" asked Dan. "He's got too much to lose. He's a celebrity, a movie star, about to premiere his biggest role yet. Why would he kill anyone?"

"You should have heard him when I took them to the mine," said Steph. "It was creepy then, but in retrospect, it sounds so much worse."

"He's playing Kalman in the movie," said Dan. "I doubt it's more than that."

"He has access to the mansion. He was in the room when the tape was moved. He has a connection to the Midnight Star."

"Yeah, he made a movie about it," said Dan. "It is *a* connection, but not much of one."

"I can see it," said Steph. "He does research into the Midnight Star. He reads all the books, watches all the old video of John Kalman. He inhabits the role. He *becomes* John Kalman. And after filming has stopped, John Kalman is still inside, somewhere."

"We're talking about Abel Goffin, here, right?" asked Dan. "He's literally played killers his entire career. And yet he hasn't killed a single person."

"That's different."

"How?" asked Dan. "I believe you, something is up, but you can't accuse Abel just because he was mean to you."

"He wasn't just mean," said Steph. "He threatened me."

"It doesn't make him a killer. It could have been plenty of people. Hell, why Abel, when it could just as easily be Joe?"

"I don't know," said Steph. "But I don't see the rage in Joe's eyes like I do in Abel."

"Everyone gets angry once in a while."

"It's not anger," said Steph. "It's something more than that."

"Enough to kill?"

"Yes."

"I don't see it," said Dan. "What about William? Or Henry? They were both there, weren't they?"

"William left the room right when the lights went out. He had to go fix them."

"Well, all the guests and VIPs were outside the room

when Levi was killed, so it can't be them."

"I highly doubt it," said Steph. "Someone would have seen them prowling around."

"Then Henry," said Dan. "He has access to all the rooms in the mansion, right? He has to."

"But what's his connection to Midnight Star?" asked Steph. "He's from LA. He doesn't even want to be here."

"That's what he says," said Dan. "Sounds like a secret cultist to me."

"We went on a walk last night," said Steph. "If he wanted to kill someone, he had his chance."

"Ooooh," said Dan. "You just don't want to admit that your crush is a killer cultist."

"He's not a crush," said Steph. "I'm pretty sure he knows I like him."

"Ooh la la," said Dan. "Going to move to LA with Henry, the killer cultist?"

"No," said Steph. "It's just some fun. That's why we're here, right?"

"Well, we're also trying to catch a killer," said Dan. "But who else could it be? Nancy? Mary Jo? It's not Bill. Frank?"

"It's Abel," said Steph. "I'm telling you. We need to find some proof."

"That might be tricky," said Dan. "Because I don't think he'll leave it lying around."

Steph sat down on the foot of the bed, rubbing her eyes. She would smear her makeup, but whatever. She'd reapply before the party.

"You alright?" asked Dan.

"No," said Steph. "I'm tired. I wish I could just believe this was all a coincidence. That all these people were nice, and I didn't have to have their terrible behavior in their head for the rest of my life anytime I watch their movies. If I ever watch them again."

"Art versus artist, dude," said Dan. "A tale as old as time."

"I don't think that's true."

"Yeah, it's the opposite," said Dan. "I don't think anyone worried about how people acted behind the scenes until like three years ago. Kubrick and Hitchcock were tremendous assholes, bordering on abuse. But Psycho and The Shining are revered."

"But no one talks about that, because they're old and dead," said Steph. "These people are alive."

"Think about all the movies we've watched at Splatterfest," said Dan. "Over the years. Did you ever think about how they were made? How the directors or actors acted on set, or in general?"

"No, but that doesn't mean that I shouldn't," said Steph. "It's not like I didn't think about it, but now that we've had to deal with them for a couple days, and they've been so callous about Steven and Levi's deaths, and all they care about is their egos and their power and their credit—"

"Not to mention maaaybe one of them is a killer."

"Even without that, there's a difference between knowing something in your head, and seeing it directly in front of you. It's a lot easier to not think about it when you haven't had a movie star threaten you because you asked them to cancel their premiere."

"Movies are made by hundreds of people," said Dan. "Some of them are probably not great. But you can't let that make you hate all movies. Or hate Splatterfest, for that matter."

"I don't hate Splatterfest," said Steph. "I just don't recognize it. To me, it was always a bunch of people drinking beers, sitting in a parking lot, enjoying a schlocky movie together. It's as much about the community as it is about the movies."

"What about the movies brought the community together?" asked Dan.

"I mean, horror movies are weird. I feel like they bring people who don't belong together, together. But it's not just Splatterfest. It's The Video Store as a whole. This feels cold."

"Gary's only doing this because he wants to save the store and the community. You know that," said Dan. "It would have gone under without this propping it up."

"But is it sustainable?" asked Steph. "Are we going to do this every year?"

"I don't know," said Dan. "Did I ever tell you what Gary did for me?"

"I know he let you sleep in the store," said Steph. "After what happened with your folks."

"It was more than that," said Dan. He put his phone down, looking at Steph. "He let me sleep in the back of the store and gave me a job. But it's not like it pays enough to pay for a place to live. All the places need first month, last month, deposit—god, it never ends. It would have taken me a year to get that much money. So Gary told me to find a place to live and come to him with the upfront costs. And I did. I brought him a few options. Most were kind of crappy, but better than nothing. Gary barely glanced at them. He knows the city. I included one that was nicer, but the upfront costs were like five grand. He wrote me a check for the entire amount."

"Jesus," said Steph.

"I know!" said Dan. "I'd never held that much money in my hands. I thanked him, and told him I would pay him back, no matter how long it took. He said there was no rush, but just don't tell anyone about it. That was three years ago. And just having a place to stay made all the difference. Gave me the chance to save. Last year, I came to him with the cash. In the meantime, Gary never brought it up. Not once. I told him I had the money for him, to pay him back. He told me to keep it."

"Wow," said Steph.

"That's how I could afford classes," said Dan. "So I don't know how long the store can stay open the way it is, or if we can continue doing this kind of thing with Splatterfest. But I know that this keeps Gary going. There's nothing more important to him than his store, and what he's built up around it. And I'll do whatever it takes to help. If that means seeing the ugly side of things once a year, so be it."

"It still feels gross," said Steph. "Especially after what's happened."

"It will take a lot more to nullify all the good Gary has done. It's okay to think both things at once," said Dan. "Things are allowed to be complicated."

"I just don't want Splatterfest to become something different," said Steph. "I don't want it to be this."

"This is the first year where we've gone big," said Dan. "If it happens again, we'll be wiser. We just have to protect it. Secret cultist killer or no."

"I need to get into Abel and Joe's room."

"I don't think that's a good idea."

"If there's evidence they're involved, that's where it'll be," said Steph.

"So you want to snoop in the dude's room who just threatened you?"

"Yes."

"Might be a tough ask," said Dan. "I left all my lock-picking tools at home."

"We don't need to break in," said Steph. "We just need the key."

"And how the hell are you going to get that?"

"I mean, what did you say earlier about Henry?" asked Steph.

"What, that your dreamboat is a member of the Midnight Star?"

"No," said Steph. "You said that he had to have a copy of all the keys. I'm seeing him tonight."

"What are you going to do?" asked Dan. "Steal it from him?"

"No," said Steph. "I'll just ask."

# 25

After the somber mood of the previous night's party, the energy was up again, with the dance floor full and the drinks flowing.

"Two dead, and everyone's dancing," said Steph.

"I wouldn't say everyone's dancing," said Dan. "You shouldn't generalize."

"Okay, not everyone. But there's a significant portion of people dancing without a care in the world that a famous director got decapitated today," said Steph.

"I don't know," said Dan. "I don't think it's crazy of them. They spent a lot of money to be here."

"That's two people dead, Dan."

"Two famous people," said Dan. "None of those people were friends with them. Hell, I'm not sure Levi had any friends at all. Nancy still hasn't gotten over Steven. She's not even here."

Steph glanced over the tables, and Dan was right. She hadn't shown up for the party, even if it was in her contract. Steph's eyes stayed on Abel, who sat alone, nursing a beer. She searched for Joe and saw him sitting next to Frank. They both had drinks in front of them, and they were whispering, and Frank kept tapping the table.

"What do you think they're talking about?" asked Dan.

"I don't know," said Steph. Frank tapped the table one more time, and Joe said something else, and whatever it was, it pushed Frank away. His face flashed with anger, and he downed what remained of his drink. He marched to the bar where the bartender lined up two shots for him. Frank swallowed them quickly, and then he was gone, leaving the party.

"It wasn't good," said Steph.

"Joe doesn't seem to make many friends."

"You need to keep an eye on Abel."

"What do you mean, keep an eye on him?"

"I mean, watch him like a hawk. Follow him wherever he goes."

"I don't think he'll take kindly to me being his shadow."

"Don't let him see you, obviously," said Steph. "Don't be obvious. But monitor him. He can't kill anyone if you're watching him."

"I mean, he might still be able to," said Dan. "He's very big and strong."

"Steven died in his bed. He made Levi look like an accident. He doesn't want to be discovered. He won't do anything if someone is observing, if someone's nearby."

"I'm just supposed to watch him all night? What will you be doing?"

"I'll be talking to Hen—"

Gary approached them then, in the same outfit as the night before.

"How's everything going?" he asked.

"Everything's great," said Steph, giving Dan a look to shut him up. "Considering."

"Good," said Gary. His eyes carried dark bags underneath. He seemed to have aged a decade in the last day.

"Are you okay?" asked Steph.

"I will be," said Gary. "I've been running ragged today, with what happened. I think I've fielded about five hundred different calls from the media. Two celebrities dead. It's all over every website, on every channel."

"I haven't had time," said Steph.

"I mean, it's publicity, I guess," said Gary. "It's what Geno wanted. Splatterfest all over the news, and Midnight Star. But not the kind I wanted."

"There's no such thing as bad publicity," said Dan.

"I don't think that's true anymore," said Steph. "We don't want Splatterfest to get canceled, literally or figuratively."

"It hasn't come to that," said Gary. "Not yet, at least. It's mostly morbid chuckles at this point."

"So Geno was right?" asked Steph.

"Yes. Unfortunately," said Gary. "I'm going to go to sleep. You two are in charge."

"What?" asked Steph.

"No," said Dan, a quick exhalation of sound.

Gary laughed, a loud chortle that Steph hadn't heard since they'd gotten here. "I'm just teasing. If anything serious happens, wake me up. But I need to sleep tonight, or I won't make it through the final day. Thank you both for your help today."

"No problemo," said Dan.

"I mean it," said Gary. "I couldn't have done it without you. And here, have some good news to try and balance out the sour mood in here. With the cash receipts coming in, it's looking like we'll be stable for another year at the store."

"Yay!" shouted Steph, louder than she meant. A few people nearby looked to her. But she hugged Gary. "That lightens the stress a little, doesn't it?"

"Yeah, it's a load off," said Gary. "One more day, and then back to business as usual. Have either of you seen Ted? We had made plans to have lunch today, but he's vanished off the face of the Earth."

"I haven't seen him," said Steph.

"Me either," said Dan.

"He wasn't in his room earlier," said Gary. "Probably just missed him. I know he's been trying to network. I'll check again tomorrow. Goodnight, guys."

Gary left, and as soon as he was out the door Henry came in, adjusting his jacket.

"I'm going to talk to Henry. I'll tell him about Abel and ask him for a key to his room."

"You really think he's going to say yes to that? He could lose his job if someone finds out," said Dan.

"We need an ally," said Steph. "Geno would keep this thing running through the apocalypse, and Gary can't afford to cancel. If we don't catch Abel before tomorrow night, he'll be gone, back to LA, and nothing will ever happen. I can talk Henry into it."

"If you say so," said Dan.

"Like I said, keep an eye on Abel. Okay?"

"Okay, I will," said Dan.

"Do I look okay?" she asked Dan, as Henry approached. Dan gave the thumb to forefinger okay signal, and she smiled.

"Dan. Steph," he said, smiling. "Everything going well?"

"Yeah, I think so," said Dan. "I'm going to get a drink." Dan walked off, leaving them alone. Steph watched him stand in line, his eyes beaming at Abel. *Very subtle, Dan.*

"Considering the events of the day, I feel like everyone's rebounded pretty well," said Steph.

"It's in our nature," said Henry. "To avoid grief and loss. Plus, Levi wasn't well liked. Most of the headlines today have been various puns about death."

"That's awful."

"You reap what you sow."

"Pun intended?"

"Oh, uh, no," said Henry. "Sorry. I didn't realize."

"It's okay."

"Do you still want to go on another walk with me?" asked Henry. "I understand if you don't, you know, being there for Levi and everything—"

"No, I'd still like to," said Steph. "I need a break. If you can still swing being away from everything."

"It shouldn't be a problem," said Henry. "I've been on the phone with insurance companies for the past three hours. I'm ready for a breather. Let me make sure Geno sees me, and then we can go."

Henry walked away, walking directly through Geno's line of sight, pausing in front of Joe and Abel to check in with them.

"He's cute," said Mary, making Steph jump.

"Y—Yeah," said Steph.

"Sorry, didn't mean to scare you," said Mary. She had a martini in hand, and her cheeks were red, but she didn't slur her words.

"Managed to get away from Geno, huh?" asked Steph.

"I put in my time, so to speak," said Mary. "Maybe he'll keep me in mind for a future project."

"Ugh," said Steph.

"Nature of the business, honey," said Mary. "Especially at my age."

"I'm sorry," said Steph. "It must be hard to have to do this, you know, after someone dying. Putting on a brave face, or whatever."

Mary said nothing, only sipped at her drink. She finally broke her silence. "Nature of the business."

"People dying?" asked Steph.

"Putting on a brave face," said Mary. She met Steph's eyes. "I never worked with Steven or Levi. They seemed fine enough. But we weren't friends. But should I be heartbroken about it?"

Steph didn't answer, not knowing if she was supposed to.

"Because I'm not," said Mary. "It seems like it hurt Nancy, but she always was soft. She blames other people for her own problems. It makes sense that her and Steven were friends."

"I—"

"Have fun tonight," said Mary, walking back to the bar. Steph watched her go, confused by her sudden coldness. Linda appeared, striding toward Steph, her eyes looking side to side.

"Hi, Linda," said Steph.

"Hi," said Linda. "How are you doing?"

"I'm okay, I guess," said Steph. "Considering everything that's happened."

"Yeah, it's been rough," said Linda. Linda looked exhausted and tense, her shoulders tight. Her body seemed balled up, ready to explode. "About that, I've been meaning to talk to you."

"Really, about what?" asked Steph.

Henry returned then, having made the circuit and showing his face to the right people.

"Hello, Linda," said Henry.

"Hi, Mr. Lindew," said Linda.

"Shouldn't you be busy with your duties?"

"No, you're right," said Linda. "Sorry." She looked once at Steph, and then walked away, her eyes scanning the celebrities, seeing if they needed anything.

"What's that about?" asked Steph.

"I can't have Geno questioning our work," said Henry. "If he doesn't see either me or Linda attending to things, there'll be hell to pay. And I don't mean to be hard on her, but she doesn't have to answer to him. I do."

"Ah," said Steph. "He's such an asshole."

"You have no idea." Henry looked at Steph. "You ready to go?" he asked.

"Yeah, I'm ready," she said. They went outside, and Steph tried to push out all the unpleasantness in her mind.

26

Steph breathed in deeply, held it, and exhaled as they walked away from the party. There was an ache of discomfort in her gut, and it wouldn't dissipate. A dozen different things rattled in her mind, and she couldn't keep them all in focus. The deaths, Abel's threat, the worries about the video store.

"You alright?" asked Henry.

"Yeah," said Steph. They wandered down a dirt path, a small weaving trail that dug farther into the property, away from the entrance and the main area of the compound. They both carried flashlights. "Just a lot on my mind." Steph pushed it all away. She needed to get the key to Abel's room. Everything else could wait. She needed to convince Henry that it was worth it.

"You and me both," said Henry. "Getting away from the

people is nice. Sometimes it feels like I'm being suffocated in there." The noise from the party was far behind them now, their breath and the soil crunching beneath their feet the only sound.

"Are we just wandering again?" asked Steph.

"Actually, William told me about a lookout. Said it overlooked the whole compound. Thought we could check it out."

"Did you know that William was a kid here? When it all went down?"

"I didn't," said Henry. "Is that true?"

"That's what he told me," said Steph. "It seemed sad. He said that he's glad to be working here, but I don't think I could do it. Being surrounded by those memories all the time."

"I'm sure he has his reasons," said Henry. "He's an intense guy. But he knows what he's doing. He's done a good job this weekend."

"Yeah, that's true," said Steph. "There's been a lot of pressure."

"You've got that right," said Henry. "I'll be glad when this is over."

"Splatterfest?"

"The weekend," said Henry. "I'm ready for the end."

"I think I am too," said Steph. She could only picture Abel flying off to Hollywood, the two deaths behind him.

They continued to walk, the ground slowly rising, curving to the left, short scrub bushes scattered around. Small puffs of dust rose with every step.

"Have you spent much time with Joe and Abel?" asked Steph.

"Some," said Henry. "They've been clients a couple times. They work with Geno a lot, which is how I made the connection."

"Have you ever noticed something strange about them?"

"What do you mean?" asked Henry.

"I don't know," said Steph. "Anything weird."

"If this is about their relationship, yes, I'm aware," said Henry. "You'd have to have your head in the sand not to notice—"

"No, not that," said Steph. "Have they talked about John Kalman with you? Or about the Midnight Star?"

"About the movie?" asked Henry. "I mean, sure they have. It *is* the centerpiece of the weekend. I went to a screening before we left LA. And to not put too fine a point on it, woo boy, it was not good."

"Not the movie," said Steph. "The cult."

"The movie's about the cult," said Henry. "But only in passing."

"Has Abel ever been obsessed with it?"

The incline steepened, and Steph's ankles ached as she climbed. She wore flats, and they didn't have the best traction. She slipped, and Henry snaked an arm around her.

"Thanks," said Steph.

"No problem," said Henry. "And I don't know. I know he method acted on set, and sure, he's excited about the premiere. He's talked about Kalman a lot, but we are here, in Kalman's former home. It's a popular subject. Why do you ask?"

They climbed, and Steph saw the end of the path ahead. The ground leveled off, and they stood on a cliff that overlooked the compound. She saw everything, the vast expanse of what John Kalman once controlled. The wind rushed by them. Golf carts ferried the celebrities to the lodge, and the mass of VIPs walking toward the dormitories. The party had ended for the night. The canyon cut through the earth in the distance.

"Levi's death wasn't an accident," said Steph, looking back to Henry, who stared out over the compound.

Henry sighed. "I know you said that before, Steph, but there was no evidence—"

"Someone removed it," said Steph. "There were a dozen people around that body, and any one of them could have pulled up that tape for any number of reasons. You were there. You saw it. The stunt worked fine on the test run. The only explanation is that they moved the X."

"Or the engineer's rigging failed," said Henry. "I'm not an expert on it, but I'm also not going to say it definitively one way or the other."

"It's not just that," said Steph. "I went into Steven's room."

Henry stared at her. "You shouldn't have done that—"

"The cops missed something."

"What do you mean, they missed something?"

"There was a midnight star hung above his bed," said Steph. "Hung by someone else. Not Steven. By his killer."

"There are a lot of those symbols around—"

"Steven specifically asked for nothing hanging over his bed," said Steph. "I had to remove a painting. And the cops wouldn't have noticed something wrong."

"Stephanie, that's all well and good, but going into guest's rooms—"

"Abel threatened me."

"What?" asked Henry.

"He waited until I was alone, and then he backed me up against a wall and intimidated me. Made me promise not to bring up the deaths or canceling the premiere."

"Well, that's a different story," said Henry. "That's unacceptable. I'll speak to him myself—"

"Henry, he's trying to cover his tracks. He had Geno remove evidence under the guise of making money, but it has nothing to do with the money. He went method to become John Kalman, and John Kalman never left him."

"You think Abel believes in the Midnight Star?" asked Henry.

"Yes," said Steph. "Steven attacked Joe on Thursday night, and then he ended up dead, with a midnight star hung over his bed. Levi tried to upstage their premiere, and he was decapitated by a literal midnight star. And who knows who else might be a target, or what he has planned."

Henry looked out again, over the compound.

"And if we don't do anything about it, he'll go back to LA, and never be punished," said Henry.

"At best," said Steph. "At worst, more people die."

"I had dismissed it," said Henry. "All his talk about the cult. About Kalman. I thought it was all to hype up the movie."

"See?" asked Steph. "Something is up, and he's behind it."

"Do you think Joe is involved?" asked Henry.

"I don't know," said Steph. "Abel cares about him. We can't rule it out."

"But what can we do?" asked Henry. "I think you're on to something. Where there's smoke, there's fire. But we don't have enough proof."

"But we can get it."

"How?"

"I assume you have a key for all the rooms in the lodge."

"I could get one," said Henry. "If I need it."

"We need to get into Joe and Abel's rooms. If there is evidence, that's where it is."

"That's risky," said Henry. "If we get caught, that's it for me."

"You have plausible deniability," said Steph. "I took the keys from you, and searched the room myself."

"But still—"

"We have to do something," said Steph. "Everyone else wants this to just go away."

"Christ," said Henry. He sighed again. "You're right, though." The wind blew past them, and Steph swore she heard a distant noise, carried on the wind, high pitched and grinding. Like an engine, or the sound of metal on metal.

"You hear that?" asked Steph.

Henry stopped, his head cocked to the side, but the breeze slowed and there was nothing. Henry only looked at her with an eyebrow raised.

"Must have just been the wind," said Steph.

"I can get the key tomorrow," said Henry. "And give it to you. But wait until you're sure it's safe. If Abel is a killer, and he finds you in his room…"

Henry trailed off, but the look in his eyes flashed with danger and concern.

"I can wait until they walk the red carpet," said Steph. "Everyone will have cleared out."

"But what if he's planning something for the premiere?"

"You'll be there," said Steph. "You can watch him. You'll already be doing it, right?"

"That's true."

"Thank you for believing me."

"You make a compelling case," said Henry. "And after some of the things I've seen stars do—murder isn't that out of the question. They all think they're above the law, anyway."

"We can stop him," said Steph. "We *will* stop him."

"I thought we were just going on a nice walk," said Henry. "The view is incredible up here."

"It is great," said Steph, turning to see Henry only looking at her. She felt herself blush. "You charmer. I don't know how you got that line to work on me, but it did."

Henry smiled. "It's true, though." He reached out for her hand, his skin smooth, softly pulling her toward him. "May I kiss y—"

Steph interrupted him with a kiss, closing her eyes and tenderly pressing her lips against his. She was tired of egos and bullshit and death. She wanted something nice and sweet. He returned the kiss, and they kissed once, twice more, before she pulled away.

"I guess that answers my question," he said.

We should get back," said Steph. "It's getting late.

"You're right," said Henry. They walked down the incline, still holding hands.

"Henry. About this—about us. After tomorrow, I don't—"

"How about we get through tomorrow first?" asked Henry.

Steph chuckled, despite herself. "Good plan."

# 27

"That damned son of a bitch," said Frank Buchanon to no one at all, as he lurched into his room. "That's what I get for trying to bury the goddamned hatchet, is some empty platitudes."

Frank swayed to the side, and grabbed onto the door handle before he fell, but then his hand slipped from the knob and he stumbled again, his foot twisting as he tumbled.

"Shit," he said, rolling over slowly. He was too old for this. He'd break a hip and then he'd never work again. He had to be Axl all the time, and Axl would never break his hip. Axl would do a pratfall, spout off a one liner, and then kill some monster.

Frank exhaled. The various aches from his fall faded

away, but the pain in his ankle remained. He rolled up his pants leg and slid down his sock, examining the injury. It ached. He had twisted the damn thing and it would hurt for weeks. He wondered if there was a doctor or somebody out here. Maybe they could give him a brace or something.

It could wait until tomorrow. One more day in this cursed place, and then he could go home, where there were no fans, no asshole producers, and no kiss-ass directors. Just some bourbon and his fireplace and his dog and his big TV.

He could sleep for now, deal with whatever came from tomorrow. He hadn't shown his whole ass like Steven had, even if it ended up not mattering for Steven. *Jesus, what a place to die.*

Frank picked himself up off the floor and stood up, testing his ankle. It still worked, even if it hurt like hell. It'd be swollen like crazy in the morning, though.

He'd worry about it tomorrow. Worry about everything tomorrow.

He laid back on his bed, and pulled his phone from his pocket, and went to plug it in.

*Wait a minute.*

Something sat on his nightstand. An envelope, one that wasn't there before. Somebody had been in his room. His bleary eyes focused on it. One word in elegant script on the front.

*Frank*

He looked around reflexively, even though he knew no one was in the room with him. He grabbed the envelope, pulled it open. A piece of paper sat inside, and he removed it, unfolding it.

*Meet me in the woods, past the dormitories.*
*Away from prying eyes.*


*MJ*


Mary Jo? His weariness didn't seem so overwhelming at the moment. She had given him the cold shoulder over the entire festival, but he guessed that was better than the outright hostility from Nancy. Maybe she had forgiven him. Or maybe she just felt lonely.

*Are you really going to go traipsing around in the woods, in the dark, because of some foggy memories of a dumb tryst thirty years ago?*

Frank slowly flexed his ankle. Some of the pain had worn off, and the rest was numb from the booze. He was too old for this.

But he stood up and tested his weight. He could walk, walk well enough. His curiosity itched away inside of him. Plus the gnawing feeling of potential romance with Mary. She still looked great, and what if it became something more than just a fling?

She could get him work. He had to try.

He had to try.

His phone was plugged into the wall, but was on low battery anyway. He left it. His frustration and anger had dissipated, and he exited, passing no one on the way out, locking his door behind him.

He slid back into the golf cart and steered it toward the general vicinity of the dormitories. It was dark, and the small headlights cut through the shadows.

Frank vaguely remembered seeing some scattered

woods near the dormitory as that girl drove him through the compound on the first day. He'd find the way. It couldn't be that hard.

He didn't pass anyone as he drove. Somehow he'd gotten behind the big cluster of buildings near the entrance of the grounds, the cart snaking down thin paths of dirt. Scattered trees were on his left, but nothing he would call "woods".

He continued to drive, the path meandering off to the left, which he thought was south.

*Maybe it was north?*

There was no other way to go, so he stayed the course. It couldn't be much farther. The booze wore off, bit by bit, and the pain in his ankle became a little sharper as he drove.

But soon the trees clustered closer together, and he came to a T-junction. Far down to his right he saw a small silhouette of the dormitories. Straight ahead, the woods grew tight together, and Frank drove off the road, swerving around trees, looking for any other sign of light in the darkness.

Mary would see the headlights. She'd have to. But then again—how deep were these woods?

He drove forward, going slower as the trees grew closer and closer together. The cart scraped over piles of dead brush and shrubs, broken branches scratching against the bottom of the vehicle. Frank wound his way through the underbrush when he found himself surrounded by trees, all too close for him to move but back.

The curiosity and thrill that had propelled him out into this late night adventure had quickly died away, as the effect of the booze wore off. He realized the predicament he was in. He would drive back and forget this whole thing. If Mary was out here, she'd have to deal with him no-showing.

Frank put the cart into reverse, but the tires spun, not finding any purchase. They didn't touch the ground, the undercarriage propped up on a stump, or brush, or something. Frank wasn't going to get down on his knees and look. He didn't even have a damn flashlight.

All he had were the headlights on the cart, and it wasn't going anywhere.

He looked back to the direction he came from, but he couldn't make out anything with the small amount of light that filtered down through the treetops.

*Dink dink dink*

What was that noise? A distant sound of hammering, filtering through to him from farther into the woods, past his golf cart. Could it be Mary? That made no sense, but going back wasn't possible. He'd be wandering through the darkness.

Frank walked forward, squeezing through the tightly packed trees, the headlights the only source of light. He could still hear the faint noise in the distance, deeper in the woods. His ankle throbbed now, and he limped as he trudged through the brush, trying to keep his weight off of it.

As he went farther from the cart, the light grew dimmer and dimmer, and he struggled to see as he pushed through. He chased the sound, but it had seemed to disappear. Just as he reached the very edges of the cart's light, he saw a glow in the distance, cutting around the trees.

The sound had disappeared, replaced by this light, and Frank pushed forward, even as his ankle throbbed. The trees were thick, and he had to step over and around brush and roots, the underbrush growing heavy. He didn't know where this light came from, but it had to be better than this.

He broke through the tree line, into a clearing, and saw the source of it.

*What the fuck?*

A shack stood in front of him, a ramshackle wooden building. A brilliant glow emanated from within, a bright, cascading light, pulsating.

This was impossible. It was straight out of The Vile Buried. They came across the shack in the woods. Axl returned to it, over and over again, always greeted by that terrible pulsating light. Axl would kill his friends, one by one, as the dreadful force possessed them.

Was this some practical joke? Or some publicity stunt by Geno?

The fear left Frank then, replaced by anger. He had been lured out here for a damn publicity stunt. Was Geno planning a reboot? He was, and he was going to make Frank look like a damned fool.

He marched toward the shack. He'd go inside, stop this nonsense. If Geno expected him to play along, he was in for a rude awakening. The pain in his ankle had faded, a surge of adrenaline hitting Frank. The light continued to pulsate, and he pushed open the thin door.

He didn't know what to expect inside, but what he found was mostly garbage. Old rusted equipment, rotting cardboard boxes, and piles of trash greeted Frank. There was nothing else in here but junk, with only a dim light bulb to light it. Frank spotted a flashlight, sitting on a decrepit shelf. He grabbed it, flicked it on. Light.

Then he heard a sound from outside, a different noise, a cackle. Distant again, but distinct.

"What the hell is going on?" he asked out loud. He barged outside, panning the flashlight back and forth, trying to see anything. The cackle rang out, deeper in the woods, past the shack, and he went toward it. He would get to the bottom of this bullshit.

He walked, his ankle still trailing slightly behind him. It swelled in his boot. Frank would worry about it tomorrow. He'd dealt with enough bullshit this weekend already. He limped through the woods, his flashlight searching for a sign of the laughter, which kept repeating, over and over again.

"I'm tired of this horseshit, Geno," he said aloud. "I don't know what the fuck is the deal with this shit, but you can cut the crap."

The cackle grew louder as he moved, and then he found the source.

A bluetooth speaker, tucked into the crux of a tree.

"They are fucking with me," he said, grabbing the speaker and smashing it against the rough bark until it was silent.

The creaking of the trees filled the woods, wind rushing through the leaves.

"This ain't funny," he said. "I swear to God, if I find out—"

A new sound, immediately recognizable, stopped Frank. It was the sound of a chainsaw. The shack, the witch's cackle, the chainsaw. All parts of his movies.

"Why are you doing this?" he yelled. He wheeled toward the new noise, advancing on it. He'd find the person responsible.

Frank swung the beam of light back and forth, trying to locate it as he got closer. Eventually this son of a bitch would run out of tricks.

It got louder and louder, the sound overwhelming everything else. Still, his flashlight couldn't find it. Another hidden speaker somewhere? He searched, forcing his way deeper into the woods.

Back and forth, and then his eye caught something. A glint of metal. It was so intense now, and he returned the light to the glint, hoping to identify it.

He quickly understood why the sound was so loud.

It was loud because it was an actual chainsaw, held by a shadowy figure dressed in black. All the anger, all the vitriol that Frank had summoned disappeared in a moment, replaced by sheer terror. He didn't know why this figure had done any of this, but all the questions and curiosity was driven from his mind. Only fear remained.

They revved the chainsaw then, and Frank turned and ran.

He had to get back to the compound. He dodged around trees, smashing through the underbrush as he sprinted, ignoring the terrible pain that pulsed through his twisted ankle. The chainsaw revved behind him, the mysterious person chasing him. Its volume got louder and louder every second, and it had to be on top of him, and then there was the shack, and Frank darted inside and slammed the door shut behind him. He locked the thin door, the revving chainsaw right outside, but it wouldn't hold for more than a few seconds against the saw.

Frank looked around the room, looking for anything to use as a weapon. He went to the pile of rusted equipment, digging through it. There was an old hatchet, the blade dark red, but it would do for now, and he grabbed it. The door was still intact, and the sound of the roaring saw surrounded the building. He tried to track it, but it seemed to be everywhere, and then it came through the wall, slicing right through the thin plywood, catching his arm and tearing a huge divot through his bicep.

Frank yelled in pain and pulled back. It came through again, and then there was a hole in the side of the building, the figure and chainsaw filling it. Frank held out the flashlight, trying to identify them, but their face was covered.

They charged, and Frank froze, but the blade didn't bite into him again. Instead, a heavy, sudden pain hit him in the head, and he was unconscious.

He woke up to the chainsaw revving again. He tried to move, but he was tied down. Chained down. The old table that had been up against a wall had been moved into the middle of the room, and he was chained to it.

*No no no no he knew this scene, Axl had chained down his girlfriend, and chopped off her limbs—*

The chainsaw moved then, and Frank felt the blade cut into his shoulder, chewing through flesh, sinew, muscle, and then bone, and then his arm was gone, and then he was unconscious, the pain too much. He didn't feel his other arm being removed, and by the time his second leg was gone, he was dead, the sudden shock and blood loss killing him.

The figure stood over him, revving the chainsaw.

"Hail to the king, baby."

# 28

Steph woke up before the sun rose. She had shared a final kiss with Henry before she had gone to her room, but the lingering feeling of pleasant romance hadn't made her rest any better. She had tossed and turned, waking up every couple hours, checking her phone, and going back to sleep. There was an anxiety in her she couldn't place.

By the time she showered and dressed, the sun had risen, dim light covering the compound and filtering into her window. Now that she was up, the bed called to her again, but she had bigger fish to fry. It was the last day of the festival, and she had more responsibilities.

The mansion was quiet as she left her room, heading toward the kitchen. She found Dan at the kitchen table, nursing a big mug of coffee, his eyes half-closed.

"Morning," said Dan, more than a grunt than a greeting.

"Morning, sunshine," said Steph, pouring herself a cup of coffee, and then sitting down next to Dan.

"You okay?" she asked.

"Hangover," he said.

"What do you mean, a hangover? I asked you to watch Abel."

"I was! But then Bill challenged me to a drinking contest," said Dan. "How could I deny our greatest living director?"

Steph sighed. "Did you win?"

"No. Turns out he's pretty good at drinking."

"I could have told you that," said Steph. "When did you stop watching Abel?"

"I saw him leave the party," said Dan. "And I was about to go after him when Bill caught me."

Bill walked in, dressed in all black, whistling, and grabbed a cup of coffee. He sat down next to Dan.

"How you doing, junior?" he asked.

"I'm okay," he said.

"You did a good job last night," said Bill. "Did I ever tell you when I outdrank Peckinpah? Now, it wasn't fair, he was practically dying—"

"I'll leave you two to it," said Steph. Abel could have gone anywhere after he left the party. Unfortunately, she had no time to shadow him.

She had a legacy screening first thing with Frank Buchanon, watching the first of the Vile Buried movies, the origin of Axl Johnson, the character Frank was most known for. She heard Bill keep talking about his exploits to Dan as she left. She found a golf cart and headed toward the legacy screening location, the old church where the Midnight Star would worship. She hoped to meet Henry afterward. She'd get the keys for Abel's room and investigate when she could.

A few die-hards already stood in line outside, gaming on a Switch or playing cards with one another.

Steph went inside, where rows and rows of chairs had been set up, a huge comfortable chair near the front, with a microphone. The stars would talk through the movie here, in comfort, while the attendees watched.

"You're a little early," said Gary, startling Steph. "Sorry."

"You keep sneaking up on me, Gary," said Steph. "I couldn't sleep last night."

"How did your evening with Henry go?"

"It went fine," said Steph. "How did you know about that?"

"A little birdie mentioned it to me."

"A little birdie named Dan?"

"Maaaybe," said Gary. "But I didn't need anyone to tell me about the way you looked at him. Or vice versa."

"Was I that obvious?" asked Steph.

"You're like that wolf, with the heart eyes, from the Tex Avery cartoons," said Gary. "Have you seen Frank this morning?"

"Not yet," said Steph. "Only Bill and Dan were up when I left the mansion. Bill was telling him old war stories about Sam Peckinpah."

"Could you go find him for me?" asked Gary. "He was supposed to be here by now."

"Sure," said Steph. Alarm bells immediately rang out in her mind. Another missing celebrity.

"I'll be back, hopefully with Frank in tow," said Steph,

walking to her golf cart. The line had already grown, picking up a few more fans. Within fifteen minutes the general admission would open, and the place would be swamped. Easier to find Frank now.

She drove to the mansion. Both Bill and Dan had left, and Steph could hear people stirring throughout the house. She went to Frank's room, knocking three times, but there was no answer.

"Frank?" she asked at the door. "Are you there?"

She listened, but heard nothing. What could she do? Just wait here, and hope he got up in time. She imagined Steven lying dead in his bed. Had the same fate happened to Frank?

*Welp, here goes nothing.*

She tried the knob, and it turned. She opened it a crack.

"Frank?" she asked, giving him some warning. Still no answer, and she pushed the door open all the way.

There was no one inside.

"Frank?" she asked again. The door to the bathroom was open, but it was empty.

"Where the hell could he be?" she said. She closed the door behind her after taking a quick peek into the hall. Steph went to his bed and saw his phone plugged in on the nightstand.

Why would he leave his phone behind? She picked it up. Fully charged, too.

A piece of paper lay folded next to the phone, on top of an envelope.

Steph grabbed it and read.

*In the woods? From Mary?*

Steph looked around the room, but nothing else stood out. She studied the note again. Anyone could have left it.

Including Abel.

She knocked on Mary's door. She'd ask directly.

There was no answer, and the handle didn't move when Steph tried it. She knocked three times, but still nothing.

"She left a few minutes ago," said Nancy, standing in her doorway, looking to leave herself. "We have a panel together in an hour or so."

"Did you see her and Frank together last night?" asked Steph.

"No," said Nancy, a look of utter disgust on her face. "Why would they be together?"

"I'm trying to find Frank," said Steph. "He's late for an event."

"Don't look at me," said Nancy. "He's never taken anything seriously in his entire life. Why would he start now?"

Steph smiled politely, and then went back outside to her golf cart. She'd have to find him. She hoped he was okay.

The woods were near the dorms, with unkept underbrush. She switched on the cart and drove over, weaving around the meandering groups of attendees. A huge line waited outside the church, ready for Frank's event.

"Damn it," said Steph. She sped up, the big dormitory building in sight. She turned left at it, and she saw trees in the distance, beginning to cluster past the dorms, and then grouped closer and closer together. A small worn path led the way, and she followed it, looking for any sign of Frank. Maybe he was still out here?

She stayed on the path, and the trees on her right got thicker and thicker. Steph slowed, peering into the woods, when she came to a T-junction, the left path heading back toward the mansion and church, and the path forward leading farther into the wilderness.

She looked desperately for any sign of him. Maybe he was back at the event. Frank might have gone for an early morning walk to clear his head and left his phone behind.

She hoped that's what it was.

Steph was about to give up when she noticed the tracks in the underbrush, dual paths of golf cart tires that had squashed the brush, leaves, and branches underneath them, leading into the trees.

"Where in the hell did you go, Frank?" she asked, and she left the cart, turning it off. Steph followed the tracks as they weaved around trees. She soon lost sight of the road. Had he done this in the dark?

She spotted the golf cart next, the motor dead. Even if the battery was charged, she could see it was stuck on a tree stump. Why hadn't he gone back? Steph continued forward, and within a minute of following beaten down brush, she found a shack.

It looked older than her, cobbled together out of wood and sheet metal, hastily repaired over the years. How old was this building? It seemed to be a remnant of Kalman's time here.

It stood in a clearing, and she had lost any trace of Frank.

"Frank!" she yelled, hoping he could hear her. Maybe he was inside. Had Mary Jo lured him out here and then left him? Had she come out here at all?

No answer.

"Frank!" she yelled again, but still nothing. There wasn't even an echo, the trees absorbing all the sound. She suddenly realized how isolated she was, not even a mile away from thousands of people. Her heart beat harder in her chest.

She walked closer, the thin wooden door swinging slightly on its hinges in the soft breeze. The faint sound of flies buzzing reached her from inside.

*What was that smell?*

Something smelled dark, and earthy, and wrong. Her gut told her to run, but she didn't. She pulled open the door, and first saw the damage to the wall, which she hadn't seen from the path, but that was quickly forgotten.

She had found Frank.

Or what was left of him.

29

Steph's eyes darted around the room. Wherever they went she found blood and gore, the room coated in it. Frank's head lay on the table in the middle of the room, his torso and limbs scattered throughout. Everywhere she looked she saw carnage, and as tears welled in her eyes, the smell overwhelmed her, and she vomited. She ducked back outside, throwing up her breakfast in the grass.

Steph leaned against the side of the shack, sobbing. He had killed him he had killed him—

She tried to catch her breath, but her lungs didn't cooperate, and she coughed. Steph fell to her knees, trying to stay out of the pile of puke nearby.

*No doubt anymore. This was a murder.*

The thought seized her mind and halted her tears. Someone had killed Steven and killed Levi, and now they had murdered Frank too, in a much more brutal fashion.

She wiped her face clean with her shirt and jogged back to her golf cart, back through the well-worn path that Frank had created last night. Thoughts flashed in her mind. Dan hadn't followed Abel back to the lodge. He could have planted the note and lured Frank out here to kill him. He had the strength to overpower Frank.

She needed to tell everyone. She needed to tell Gary. They would get the police there—

Frank's dead body intruded into her thoughts—his arms and legs, strewn around the room, the stench of heavy blood, dried in thick clumps—

She choked back more sobs, and she went to her golf cart, on the trail, and it was like she had stepped into civilization again. Gary was probably still waiting at the church, and she would have to tell him that Frank Buchanon was in pieces out in the woods past the dormitory. She floored the accelerator, getting as much out of the electric motor as she could, the tires spinning out in the dirt. As she got closer to the main area of the compound, she could hear the crowds, as they loitered in the common area, or went to one of the tents set up for concessions.

The legacy screening was running late, but there would be no screening with Frank anymore, his head sat on a table in a shack in the woods, and Steph weaved around and past the assembled fans, frantically honking, trying to get people to move out of the way. They had no idea the news she had.

She got through the worst of the throngs, out to where the buildings were more scattered, and she saw the church in the distance, the high-pointed star standing out.

She skidded to a halt outside, no one waiting in line anymore, and she ran inside. The seats were all full, people all chattering, probably all waiting for Frank to show up so they could watch a movie with their hero.

Her eyes adjusted to the inside of the building, scanning for Gary. He had to be here somewhere.

"There you are," said a voice, but it wasn't Gary's. It was Geno, his face frustrated. "Where the hell is Frank?"

"Where's Gary?" asked Steph.

"I don't know. He went out looking for you," said Geno. "Where is Frank?"

Steph swallowed. She didn't like Geno, but he was in charge. She should tell him what happened.

"He's dead," said Steph.

"What?" asked Geno.

"I was looking for him and I found a note in his room and it led me out to the woods and his body is chopped up in pieces out in a shed in the woods—"

"Calm down," said Geno. "You sure it was him? You sure it wasn't just some animal or something?"

"I saw his face!" said Steph, a little louder than she intended, and a group of attendees' heads all swiveled to look at her.

"Shh," said Geno, pulling her back outside. He waited for the door to close, and then looked around, making sure no one was near them. "You saw Frank's body?"

"Yes," said Steph. "He's out in the woods."

"Show me," said Geno.

"What? We need to call the police, there's a killer—"

"Shh," said Geno, again. "We are not calling the cops out here unless we are sure it's him. Take me to where you found the body, and we can take it from there."

"But Gary—"

"Gary isn't in charge," said Geno. "I am. Now let's go." He gestured to the cart she just drove up in, and Steph jumped into the driver's seat. Despite all the conflicts raging inside her, Geno was right. He was in charge, and they should make sure it was Frank. Now she doubted herself. She had only looked for a second. Maybe she had made it all up.

"Hurry," he said, and Steph didn't need to be told twice. She floored it, quickly driving back the way she came. They were at the road again, and she jumped off the cart, returning through the woods, the underbrush stomped down well from the back-and-forth traffic. Geno followed behind her, and she realized she had questioned herself for nothing. Somebody had tramped through the underbrush, somebody had driven the cart here. She hadn't imagined that.

But maybe it wasn't Frank.

She didn't know if the thought it was some other poor soul made it any better, but it changed things, if only slightly.

"How far is it?" asked Geno.

"We're almost there," she said, and within moments she stepped into the clearing, and she saw the wooden shack, frail wood that contained death.

"He's in there," she said. She walked up to the entrance, but didn't go in, couldn't go in. She couldn't face all that horror again. Geno pushed the door open and went inside, squinting at the lack of light. The door closed behind him.

"Oh God," he said, and pushed back out into the sunlight. He breathed hard, catching his breath. "Fucking hell. They cut him up."

"That's three dead, Geno," said Steph. "Steven wasn't a

suicide. Levi wasn't an accident. Three dead celebrities."

Geno stared at her, and then away, cogs turning in his mind.

"Can we call the police now?" she asked, starting back toward the cart, going to walk through the woods. Geno clutched her arm.

"Wait one minute," he said.

"We need to tell people now," said Steph. "There's a killer here! They're targeting the celebrities!"

"We can't tell anyone," said Geno.

"What?" asked Steph. "People are dying!"

"The premiere is in seven hours," said Geno. "Seven. If people think there's a murderer on the loose, there won't be a premiere. The cops will put us on lockdown, not to mention the people who will leave, and demand a refund."

"You're thinking about money?" asked Steph. "Are you kidding me?"

"You shut your mouth," said Geno. "It's easy to say that when it's not your money on the line. How much do you think this cost? To rent this place, to pay for the insurance, to pay all these actors to come out here? It wasn't cheap, and it sure as hell was way more than Gary could afford."

"It's just money," said Steph. "Frank and Steven and Levi are dead, and there will be more if we don't do something!"

"We will not say a word," said Geno. "Not one mention until after the premiere. After everyone has seen Midnight Star, and then conveniently, we find the body, and we call the police."

"You're crazy," said Steph. "I won't just stand by and say nothing so your stupid premiere can still happen. Let go of me." She shook her arm, but Geno held on.

"You *will* stay quiet," said Geno. "Or all the costs of Splatterfest will fall on poor Gary."

"You can't do that," said Steph.

"Yes, I can," said Geno. "You don't think I didn't have the contracts written the way I wanted them? That gave me all the outs I needed? If Splatterfest fails for any reason, I don't pay the bills, Gary does. Gary has to cover the refunds. Gary has to recoup the costs. Not me."

"You bastard! It'll ruin him!"

"Hey, he signed on the dotted line. I didn't make him. He knew what he was getting himself into."

"Fuck you," said Steph.

"You should really be more polite," said Geno. "If you want your precious video store to stay in business, and Gary not to be buried under a mountain of debt, you'll keep your pretty lips sealed. At least until tonight. After that, we can have the police come, and get poor Frankie taken care of."

"You're a monster," said Steph.

"Frank's not getting any deader," said Geno. "And all the stars will be at the premiere. They'll be safe. It'll all work out."

Geno let go of her then, and Steph wanted to run, run straight to a phone and call the police, and bring everything down, not just for everyone's safety, but just to wipe the slimy smile off of Geno's face.

But there would be no video store if she did that. She believed Geno, and he was enough of an asshole to make sure that Gary got the worst of their contract. There would be no more Splatterfest, and no more video store, and it would ruin Gary. He'd spend the rest of his life paying off the debt. Or going bankrupt.

She could call the police and destroy Gary's life. It was the right thing to do, and it was the choice Gary would have made.

But she wouldn't do it. She couldn't do it.

Steph eyed him.

"See, it won't be so bad," said Geno. "Just do it my way, and everything will be fine."

"I'm calling as soon as the movie is over," said Steph.

"Good," said Geno. "It should make for some great publicity."

# 30

Steph sat to the side of the panel, trying not to think about Frank's dismembered body, chopped up into pieces in a shack in the woods. Someone had killed him, someone had killed Steven and Levi, and Steph couldn't say a word.

"Mary Jo, you got your start in the very first Hallow's Eve movie," said Kyle, sitting on stage next to Mary and Nancy Slaughter. The Scream Queen panel had started, but Steph's thoughts were only on death.

"I did," said Mary. Nancy and Mary sat a few feet apart from each other. Nancy's face was passive. She seemed out of it. Or maybe she was hiding murderous intent. Steph studied her face. She had been the last to see Steven alive. She had hated Frank. All those crocodile tears could hide blood on her hands.

"Some even call you the very first scream queen," said Kyle.

"They need to take some history lessons," said Mary.

"What do you mean?" asked Kyle.

"I mean, there were scream queens in the 50s and 60s," said Mary. "The term didn't come until much later, but there were women who played the murder victims for years before I came along."

"Yes, but nothing had codified the slasher like Hallow's Eve," said Kyle. "It is responsible for the glut of slashers in the late 70s and early 80s. There wouldn't be a Jason if Hallow's Eve hadn't happened."

"That's probably true," said Mary. She looked out into the crowd. "Is Abel here?" The fans laughed. Nancy remembered Mary's bitter words the night before. Had she been preparing to kill Frank? She could turn the charm on and off so quickly. Was there something else she hid?

"I don't think so," said Kyle. "And Nancy, your first role came only two years after Hallow's Eve, before you changed your name."

"Yes," said Nancy. "I was Nancy Slater back then."

"It was in a movie called Killer Psycho," said Kyle.

"It wasn't very good," said Nancy. "But it got my foot in the door."

"And that got you your role in Dismembered, which put you on the map, and was also your first movie billed as Nancy Slaughter."

"That's right," said Nancy.

"Why the name change?" asked Kyle.

"It seemed like the right decision," said Nancy. "I never really cared about my last name anyway, and I didn't have a famous name to grab people's attention. So I changed it. I don't regret it."

Nancy's subtle dig at Mary didn't go unnoticed. Steph saw Mary's eyes narrow at the remark. Mary's parents were actors themselves, famous in the 50s and 60s.

"Mary, you only did one more horror movie, at least for a long time, a much lesser known one, called Road Kill, in 1982. One of my favorites, actually."

"Well, thank you. It's still a good movie. Anyone out there who hasn't seen it should track it down."

"But after that, you branched out, and became a certifiable movie star. You didn't do another horror film until the 2000s, when you starred in a reboot slash sequel of Hallow's Eve. Why the gap?"

"Oh, it's easy to look back at all that time and try and ascribe some motive to it, but I just didn't get any offers that I considered worth my time. If I had to put a reason on it, I wanted to keep my options open, and if I kept playing the same kind of roles, I'd get typecast. Then I'd be playing a damsel in distress through my twenties, my thirties, even in my forties." Mary's eyes went to Nancy as she said this. A strike back at Nancy's earlier dig. Nancy remained stone-faced.

Kyle grinned, but Steph could see the unease in his eyes. Steph knew these two hated each other, and yet they both smiled. She had seen it for the entire festival, seen it from all the celebrities. They all hated each other. They all sniped and picked from their vantages, attacking whenever they saw weakness. Over and over again. Taking advantage of anyone they could. They had killed Steven. They had killed Frank and Levi.

She remembered the note on Frank's nightstand, from Mary calling him out to the woods. To isolate him, to separate him from the herd and cull him. To slaughter him just like the way he killed in his movies, to rub it in his face.

But anyone could have forged that note. Nancy, Joe, Abel, or Geno himself.

*Oh god.*

Steph realized that Geno could have done it, and now could use her to cover up his own crimes. She felt sick suddenly, and she got up, and ran to the nearest bathroom, slamming the door shut behind her and throwing up into the sink, mostly bile, all of her breakfast thrown up earlier.

Geno wouldn't have, would he? He had so much to lose. Why would he kill any of them? But Steph thought back to the look in Geno's eyes outside of the shack, thinking not about Frank's destroyed body, but to the publicity it would get his movie. Everyone hated him.

Steph turned on the water and washed out her mouth, swallowing a couple handfuls. She exited the bathroom to hear Mary and Nancy openly insulting each other now, oblivious to the crowds. Kyle sat there, looking overwhelmed.

*I can't do this.*

Steph left the hall, back into the open air of the compound. Hundreds loitered outside, grabbing a bite to eat between showings or signings or panels. None of them knew Frank's body still cooled, or realized a killer stalked among them. They had found the dead bodies there, decades ago, strewn about the common area, and everyone was sitting there, and they'd be dead again, if she didn't do something.

"You alright, dear?" asked a voice, and Steph looked, and

it was Velma, the old woman from Frank's line. She sat by herself, and Steph had wandered right by her.

"I'm—I'm not feeling great," said Steph.

"Why don't you sit down here, next to me?" she asked, and Steph did, trying to catch her breath. "What's wrong? Feeling sick?"

"It's complicated," said Steph. "I feel—I feel like I'm getting pulled in a bunch of directions. Between my friends and doing the right thing."

"Want to tell me about it?" asked Velma.

"I can't," said Steph. "I don't want to lay it all on you. It wouldn't be fair." Steph thought to Velma's excitement when she met Frank. Frank had held her hand, and they had even hugged, and Velma practically glowed as she walked away from his table. Now he was dead, cut into pieces out in the woods, and it was her responsibility to tell someone. It would break her heart, it would *break her heart*—

"I'm sorry, Velma, I've got to go," said Steph, and she left without a glance back.

She had to tell somebody. She couldn't keep this a secret. Screw Midnight Star and screw Geno. She would find Gary and tell him.

She jumped into her golf cart and sped toward the mansion. He would have to go back and get ready before the premiere. She would tell him and let him decide.

*You know what he'll do. He'll do the right thing, even if it costs him everything.*

Steph kept driving, and she was at the lodge within minutes. It would be empty, and she could regroup. She jumped out and opened the door, pushing through. She hit someone and knocked them down.

It was Henry. He looked a little stunned.

"Oh god," she said.

"What? What's wrong?" asked Henry.

"Frank is dead, Henry," said Steph.

"What?"

"Somebody chopped him up, out in the woods, and they killed Steven, and Levi too, and Geno—"

"Calm down, Steph," said Henry, quietly, softly grabbing her hand. He stood up. "Let's sit down." He pulled her to a side room, the den, and they sat in the two leather chairs within. Steph felt the emotions well up inside her again, but she wouldn't let herself cry, not now.

"What happened?" asked Henry.

Steph told him everything from when she woke up to when she barged through the door, leaving nothing out. Henry tried to stay calm, but his face betrayed him.

"You sure it was Frank?" asked Henry.

"Yes," said Steph.

"Okay," said Henry. Henry did math in his head. "Do you think it was Abel?"

"I don't know," said Steph. "I didn't stop and look for the midnight star. I should have, I should have, but I saw him cut up like that, and I couldn't—"

"It's alright," said Henry. He sighed. "We're between a rock and a hard place."

"I was coming to tell Gary about the murder," said Steph. "I couldn't deal with the guilt anymore."

"Geno will follow through on his threat," said Henry. "I don't have any doubt about that. It explains his behavior to-day, though. I just talked to him, and he was dialed up to a thousand."

"I don't want anyone else to die," said Steph.

"Are we sure it's Abel?" asked Henry.

"Who else would it be? We were together last night. It's not Dan or Gary. Mary, Nancy, or Bill don't have the strength to subdue Frank. William was out of the room when the tape was moved for Levi."

"Could it be Ted?" asked Henry.

"Oh god," said Steph.

"What?"

"Gary couldn't find him yesterday. I hope he's okay."

"So he's not a suspect?" asked Henry.

"No," said Steph. "He wouldn't hurt a fly."

"Then there's no one else," said Henry. "It's Abel, or Abel and Joe working together. Geno said you could call the cops after the premiere, right?"

"Yes," said Steph. "A few hours from now."

"Joe and Abel's last event is going on right now," said Henry. "They'll be back here soon to get ready. I'll be at the premiere, and I can watch them. Closer than anyone. It's my job. While I'm doing that, you look for proof in their room, before they hide it. Premiere happens, we call the cops, we have the evidence, and Gary gets to keep his store."

"All of that seems very precarious," said Steph.

"It's the best I can come up with," said Henry.

"I think it's the best we can do," said Steph. "I just hope they don't have anything disastrous planned for the premiere."

"I'll be there to head off disaster," said Henry. "I also have this." He reached into his pocket and handed her a key, heavy and thick.

"For the rooms?" asked Steph.

"Yes," said Henry. "It should work on them all."

Steph stared at it, rolling it in her hand. John Kalman once held this key. She imagined his touch on it, and a shiver ran through her.

"Are you alright?" asked Henry.

"I can't take much more of this," said Steph.

"Just a few more hours," said Henry. "And it will all be over. Just hold yourself together until then."

"I'll do my best—" and then Henry kissed her, and she kissed him back. It felt right. It felt good.

"We'll get through this," said Henry. "I have to go. Message me if anything comes up. Be careful."

"I'm always careful," said Steph.

# 31

Steph waited while all the celebrities got ready for the premiere. Geno had insisted on the whole nine yards, a red carpet and everything. The VIPs would walk it, along with the celebs. The general public were being ushered to their buses, leaving the compound for the last time. Stephanie envied them. They'd be safe.

She sat in her room, hearing the noises throughout the mansion as people dressed. She wanted to go out, to do *something*, but she had to wait. Her stomach grumbled, and she realized she hadn't eaten anything since breakfast, and she would need food for whatever faced her tonight. Would they find the killer? Henry had left, orchestrating the grounds for the premiere. It was up to her, but she couldn't do it on an empty stomach.

Steph walked to the kitchen, hoping to find no one. She would grab something and eat it in her room. She didn't want to be found, didn't want to have to keep up this charade, to cover for Geno, who might very well have killed three people already.

She ran into Gary instead, eating a sandwich at the table, dressed in a full tuxedo.

"Hey kiddo," he said, smiling.

Steph stopped in her tracks.

"You alright?" asked Gary. "You look like you've seen a ghost."

*Cover, Steph.*

"I—just—I didn't recognize you. I don't think I've ever seen you dress up," she said.

"Oh, come on," said Gary. "There was that one time—wait, no—but that other time—oh, no, I wore a utilikilt to that—"

"Gary, have you ever worn a tuxedo in your whole life, until today?"

"No," said Gary. "I had to rent this. It doesn't fit great."

"You look good," said Steph. "Although I don't know why you thought eating a sandwich right after you got dressed was a good idea. Looks like you're about to have some stains to worry about."

Gary hastily dropped the sandwich onto the plate, bright yellow mustard leaking out the sides.

"Good catch," said Gary. He swiped a finger around the edges of the bread and ate the excess.

"Nothing but the best manners," said Steph. "My mom would scream at you."

"Good thing she's not here," said Gary, smiling again. He

looked better than he had the previous couple days, if only exhausted now. "God, I'm ready to go home."

"The tuxedo is that bad, huh?" asked Steph. She made her own sandwich, turning her back to Gary. She couldn't look at him anymore. She would spill the beans, tell him about the ghastly scene at the shack.

"It's bad enough, but this has probably been the most stressful weekend of my life. And that was before Steven killed himself, Levi's accident, and Frank drank himself into a stupor. Geno told me he's missing the premiere. Can you believe that? Maybe I should have gone on a bender, and I could have stayed in my room the whole day."

Steph only took a deep breath, spreading some mayo on a couple pieces of bread. If she opened her mouth now, it all would come tumbling out, and Gary would call off everything immediately. She had to bite her tongue.

"It's almost over, though," said Gary. "We have the premiere, and the afterparty, and then we can all go home tomorrow. No more celebrities, no more planning, and no more Geno."

"It's almost over," said Steph, quietly.

"Are you not getting ready for the premiere?" asked Gary.

"I will be, shortly," said Steph. "I'm ready for this all to be over, too. I'll probably be as late as I can. Got my dress picked out and everything."

"At least that will be neat," said Gary. "I've never walked a red carpet before. But I'm ready to be back in the video store. I think I've come up with a way for Splatterfest to just be Splatterfest again. No more Geno, and no more celebrities."

"Really?" asked Steph.

"With the money we made this year," said Gary. "I'm going to invest it back into the business. Diversify a little more. Push harder as a place for community, and less direct sales. What do you think about opening a bar on site?"

"I don't know," said Steph. She didn't even know if they'd get through the night. "Maybe." She forced a smile.

"It's just an idea," said Gary. "We'll have a meeting when we get back." Gary picked up his sandwich and finished it, making sure not to spill anything on his tux.

"I'll see you at the premiere," he said. "Thank you for everything you've done. This couldn't have happened without you." He patted her on the back, and Steph forced herself to hold back tears. She held her breath and bit the inside of her cheek. She couldn't tell him.

"I'll be right behind you," said Steph, finally. Gary walked away, and she finished making her sandwich, putting it on a small plate, grabbing a soda from the fridge and hurrying back to her room. She ate and drank quickly.

Everyone left as time ticked by, and the premiere drew closer and closer. She waited well past the time everyone should have left by and then exited her room. She waited, listening at every door as she passed, but no one was there.

*Easy peasy.*

As she walked upstairs, the mansion was quiet. She went into Joe's room and found it almost pristine. The bed was made, the bathroom still spotless, only a few pieces of closed luggage sitting on the bed. She opened them, but it was only clothes, all untouched. She dug through them, but they hid nothing. Confusion hit her briefly, and then she realized, and went over to Abel's room. A lot of the rooms had shared doors between them, but most of them were locked.

Not Joe and Abel's.

They had been using Abel's room together, with Joe's room now a closet. It looked similar to the others, with open luggage strewn everywhere, and piles of clothes randomly stacked. The place was a mess, a single room containing all the stuff of two people. Steph searched.

The bathroom came first, and there wasn't much there, aside from the normal soap and beauty products. She left the bathroom and began digging through the piles of clothes. Steph didn't care about leaving signs that she'd been there, and rifled through the piles, looking for any blood, anywhere.

A sudden sound from downstairs froze her, and she waited, listening for more. The AC kicked on, trying to push out the Texas heat, the whirring air creating more noise. She tried to listen through it, waited for anything else, but that was it. She continued searching.

There was nothing. She dug through piles of clothing from both men, and there was nothing. It seemed impossible. The shack was covered in blood, and the killer would have caught some of the spray. And they couldn't walk back to the mansion naked, they couldn't. Maybe they dumped the clothes, or burned them, and then changed.

Abel and Joe were their main suspects, their only actual suspects. Abel's obsession with the Midnight Star. Frank, Steven, and Levi's spats with Joe. Everyone's knowledge of them living in the closet. Any of those reasons could have driven Abel to kill.

But there was no evidence. Steph looked through the room, pulled open every drawer, and found nothing.

The faint smell of smoke hit her nose, and she smelled

around again. It stank like burnt toast. She dismissed it.

*Focus, Stephanie. There had to be something, somewhere.*

Her eyes darted around the room, looking for anything she missed. Then she saw it, so obvious, right in front of her face. A grandfather clock, old, big, sat to the side. Her eyes had passed right over it. It stood seven feet tall, and she reached to the top, feeling for anything strange. She poked with the edges of her fingers, standing on her tiptoes, and she felt something move, and she pulled on it, and a small pouch came away in her hand.

It was black leather, and she unzipped it, her hands shaking. The contents were simple.

A syringe.

A bottle of unmarked liquid, clear.

The rising tension in her stomach burned hard, but the doubt also eased in her mind. She and Henry had been right. And Joe and Abel had killed both Steven, Frank, and Levi. It would have required a lot of strength to kill Frank that way, and Abel was a big guy.

They had killed all of them before the premiere of their own movie. She couldn't imagine either had acted alone.

Steph zipped up the bag and left it there, on top of the clock. They would come back and find it, and both of them would be done for.

She had to warn Henry, warn everyone. She ran to her room to grab her things. She didn't know when she'd be back. She got out her phone to message him, but the message wouldn't send. The wi-fi was down.

*Perfect.*

But a piece of folded paper sat underneath her phone, that she noticed now. Her name was written in a scrawled script.

Steph grabbed it, flipped it open.

*We need to talk. Find me at the after party.*

*-Linda*

What? What did Linda have to tell her? Had Linda seen something from Abel and Joe? Steph needed to get there anyway, and she left her room hastily.

She'd have to hurry there and convince everyone of the truth. The movie would be over by now, with everyone moving onto the after party. She had to hurry.

She hurried out of her room and toward the front door. The smell was even stronger now, but more pungent, with the smell of smoke. Something was burning in the house. The whole place would burn down.

Steph listened, and she could hear crackling now, and pops. It came from the den.

*The fireplace.*

She ran to the den. Smoke poured from underneath the door, and the smell rankled her nostrils. Had they set a fire?

Steph opened the door and more smoke poured out into the hall. She looked to the fireplace and saw the source of the flames.

It was Bill, his frail body crammed into the stone fireplace. He burned, his skin blackened. He still held a hand-rolled joint.

Steph dry heaved and turned away, trying to find breath. She wanted to run, to warn everyone of another dead, but she couldn't leave him like this. She ran to the bathroom, and grabbed all the towels she could carry, returning to the den. The smoke was strong, and she tried to breathe through her mouth, covering it with a washcloth.

She had to get the body out of there. One of his feet still poked out from the hearth, and she clutched it, pulling on him with all her strength, leaning back. Bill didn't weigh much, and she tugged him out. He still burned, and now he threatened to light the den on fire. She covered him in towels, first his legs, patting out the flames, and then his torso and head. She could barely recognize him, but he no longer burned.

*How? When?*

Henry had said he would watch Abel. She pulled out her phone to message him, but the internet was still down. Something was going on, but Steph couldn't keep it straight in her mind.

She sat on her knees next to him, his body covered. Tears wanted to come, but she held them back. She didn't have time for sorrow, not now. Another was dead, and she was the only one who could stop them.

She left Bill's body. She hurried outside, and finding no golf carts, she ran.

# 32

Steph squeezed her hands as she ran, feeling ash between her fingers. Ash from Bill's corpse that had half burnt away. Killed by Joe and Abel. He had died while she sat in her room, waiting for everyone to leave. The thought made her wince. She concentrated on her breath.

She wasn't in good shape, and the main part of the compound was at least a mile away. Without the golf cart, it would be hard, but she pushed herself. If she threw up, so be it.

How had they gotten here? Had Joe and Abel lost their minds? There was no way they'd get away with it, not after four deaths. Was Abel working alone? It was a possibility. Maybe all that time playing killers had driven him to it. Maybe he was tired of the snide comments. Or maybe he had just lost his mind.

She couldn't worry about motive now. The bodies weren't imagined, and neither was that syringe. She ran, her flashlight bobbing in the darkness. Her thoughts flashed to Frank's dismembered corpse, to Bill, burning in the fire-place. She pushed them away and ran.

A small light appeared in the distance. Another flash-light? She ran harder. She had made it halfway, maybe, she couldn't tell in the dark. The dim lights that lit the outside of the reception hall were still out of sight. Steph ran for the light, hoping it wasn't Abel, or Joe. Hoping it was someone friendly. Why were they out here without a golf cart, in no-man's-land?

As she drew closer to the light, she could make out the rough shape, and it wasn't Abel, the silhouette much small-er. Steph approached it and realized it was Dan.

"Oh thank god," she said, as she stopped for a second to catch her breath. She drew deep breaths, bent over, with her hands on her knees.

"Are you alright?" asked Dan. "I was wondering where you were. You missed the movie! Okay, it wasn't that great, but it was kinda neat, walking a red carpet and every-thing—"

"Dan—"

"—You know, seeing the stars all dressed up, and having your picture taken—"

"Dan—"

"—and did you see Gary in his tuxedo? I don't think I've ever seen him not wearing his suspenders. That was a trip—"

"Dan!" said Steph, her voice hard. "Stop. Abel and Joe

killed more people."

"More?" asked Dan. "How? They've been busy at the premiere."

"I found Frank's body out in the woods behind the dormitory. They chopped him up with a chainsaw, like in The Vile Buried."

"What? Are you kidding?" he asked.

"Geno wouldn't let me talk. He said he'd pull his money out and bankrupt Gary if I told anyone. He wanted his premiere. I told Henry. He was going to watch Abel. Protect everyone. I found a syringe and chemicals in Abel and Joe's room. They used it to kill Steven."

"Jesus Christ. There's your proof. And people definitely don't chainsaw themselves to death."

"No. But they didn't stop there. I just found Bill stuffed into the fireplace. He's dead."

"What? Fucking hell," said Dan, his hands on his face. Steph remembered her reaction to finding Frank. "I was coming to find him. He didn't show for the premiere, and Geno sent me to get him. The phones aren't working, and the wi-fi is down. I couldn't get any of the golf carts to start."

"The phones aren't working?" asked Steph.

"Dead lines," said Dan. "Not even a dial tone."

"Something's not right," said Steph. "Abel and Joe couldn't take out phone lines."

"We should get back," said Dan. "We can tell Gary, and figure out what to do then. Abel and Joe were at the after party with everyone."

"At least there's a crowd there," said Steph. "They won't hurt anyone if there are witnesses."

They turned and ran toward the reception hall, but earlier doubts had returned in Steph's mind. Something wasn't adding up. How could Abel and Joe take out phone lines while they're at the premiere? Why *would* they kill Bill? It didn't make any sense, no matter how angry they were about perceived slights. Their combined careers were taking off, with more and more success for both of them. Why would they kill here, and now? Sure, celebrities had killed before, but almost always out of sudden anger, never with this much planning. Had playing Kalman driven Abel mad? Did they both worship the Midnight Star?

Still, she ran next to Dan, both of them panting. The reception hall was visible in the distance.

"We're close," said Steph.

"Good, because I'm going to throw up," said Dan. "I don't think I've run since high school gym. And I didn't really do it then."

As they approached they slowed down, both of them catching their breath.

"Something's wrong," said Dan.

Even with their flashlights and the dim outdoor lights of the hall, Steph immediately saw something had happened. There was no music, no faint distant thud of the DJ playing dance music. And no one loitered outside. Every single night so far you could find a couple groups hanging outside, smoking, or just shooting the shit. The music got loud inside, and it was nice to enjoy the quiet stillness the compound provided. But there wasn't anyone outside.

But then Steph saw the bodies.

A dozen people lay scattered on the ground outside the reception hall.

"What the fuck?" asked Dan.

"VIPs," said Steph. She recognized one, a dude named Darrell she had talked to once or twice over the weekend. She didn't know any of the others, but they all wore the VIP lanyard they had spent their hard earned money for.

"Oh no," said Dan. "This—"

"Let's look inside," said Steph. She pushed through the double doors, into the reception hall. The bodies outside were only a start. Dozens of bodies laid inside, at tables, on the dance floor, near catering. The DJ had died draped over her workstation.

"Oh my god," said Dan. "They've killed them all. How?"

Steph walked around the room, filled with eerie quiet. Her steps echoed as she stepped past the dozens of dead. They didn't seem to have any marks on them. She bent down next to one man, foam on his lips.

*Oh no. Oh no no no.*

"Poison," said Steph.

"All of them?" asked Dan.

"They could have poisoned the champagne, the punch, everything. It was the after party, the last dinner of the weekend."

"Everyone would be drinking," said Dan, finishing her thought.

Steph looked over each body, one by one. Then she saw it, Velma's signature beehive. Steph went to her body. She was cold, like the rest of them, and Steph felt her eyes fill with tears. She squeezed them shut, squeezed them away.

"Do you see Gary?" asked Dan, fear in his voice.

"No," said Steph. "Only VIPs. Gary's not here. Neither is Henry, or the rest of the celebrities." The burrow of anxiety grew inside of Steph.

*Rest of the celebrities. There were only four now. Nancy, Mary Jo, Abel, and Joe.*

"Geno's not here either," said Dan, looking at the faces of the dead.

Steph thought back to her first day at the compound, touring the area. Remembered the vision of hundreds dead. It would have looked like this.

"Abel and Joe didn't do this," said Steph. "This is the work of John Kalman."

"What?" asked Dan. "John Kalman is dead."

"Yes," said Steph. "But this is what he did. He lured a bunch of people to his compound and then poisoned them. He hated celebrities. He hated fame. Abel's been infected by the philosophy. He's making a show of it. Killing all the people here with poison. Killing all the stars using stuff from the movies. Leaving the midnight star. He's trying to prove a point."

"But there's no way he can get away with it, not anymore," said Dan. "He can't hide from this."

"Maybe he doesn't want to hide," said Steph. "Maybe he thinks he can awaken the star god."

"If that's true, he's definitely lost his mind. What about Joe?"

"I don't know," said Steph. "If he didn't know before, he knows now."

Dan looked around at all the bodies. He shook his head. "I don't know. But if he wants to kill the celebrities, why aren't their bodies here?"

"He doesn't want them to die like this," said Steph. "Steven died in his sleep. Frank was killed by a chainsaw. Bill was burnt to death. He's making fun of them, even as they die. A final insult, for all of them."

"I get Steven, and Levi, and Frank, but why burn Bill?"

"You burn the bodies," said Steph. "Remember? After the alien revealed itself, you had to burn the bodies."

"Oh god," said Dan. He bent down, his hands on his knees again. "I talked to him last night, Steph. He was looking forward to his next tour. He was going to play music with his son. He was so happy—"

"Take a deep breath," said Steph. "We can't let it overwhelm us. We have to get out of here. We have to save Gary, Henry, everyone. Did you see Linda at the premiere?"

"No," said Dan. "Another one who was missing. Henry kept asking if anyone had seen her."

"She left me a note, saying to find her at the after party. That she needed to talk to me."

"Maybe she saw something," said Dan.

"But why me?" asked Steph. "Why not Henry or Gary?"

"I don't know," said Dan. "But I don't think her disappearance is a coincidence."

"We'll find her," said Steph.

"Where do we start, though?" asked Dan.

They heard a terrible scream then, hoarse and full of terror, coming from a nearby building.

"We start there," said Steph.

# 33

They ran for the voice, coming from a nondescript utility building on the edge of the central area.

It looked like a portable that Steph had used in high school. The outside walls were painted beige, speckled with dirt, thrown onto it by wind and never cleaned.

Steph didn't know what to expect when she opened the door, with Dan right behind her. But whatever it was, it wasn't what she found.

Steel bars greeted her as she stepped into the one room building, a narrow foyer after the door, with metal bars cutting off the rest of the room. A prison style door stood in the middle, closed. Her eyes went wide as she saw beyond the bars.

*Oh no.*

"Grab the door!" yelled Steph, quickly, and Dan caught it with his foot.

"Ow," he said, as he pulled the door open again. Steph thought it had seemed heavy. The facade matched the outside of the building, but the actual door was steel or iron. "Why do we need to keep the door op—oh, oh fuck."

Dan saw what lay behind the bars now too, and he recognized it, just like Steph did. They had seen the movie together. Death Puzzle 2. Directed by Joe Banshee, starring Abel Goffin as the Puzzle Killer. It had indulged further in the ridiculous mechanical traps and games that had been present in the first movie, without a lot of unimportant things like plot or story to get in the way.

Joe and Abel were caught in a recreation of one of the signature death puzzles in the movie, on the other side of the bars.

Abel lay bound to an iron table, his wrists and ankles both bolted to it by thick metal bands. Another thick band wrapped around his neck. He was gagged, dense layers of duct tape over his mouth. He struggled, trying to get free, but the metal didn't budge. He was topless, a crude red X painted on his stomach.

Joe stood next to him, on the other side of the table from Steph and Dan and the iron bars. Joe had been the one screaming. He was still dressed in the tuxedo he wore to the premiere, slightly dirty and disheveled. The only difference is what he carried in his hands. A scalpel in one hand, a gun in the other.

Behind him, within his reach, was a panel, with a large digital timer, counting down. It read 8:57, ticking away, second by second. Less than nine minutes before it was up. The walls were bare, except for the wall on Steph's left, which read in big bold block lettering, stenciled in red spray paint

X MARKS THE SPOT

The room was identical to the room in Death Puzzle 2.

"Oh, thank Christ you're here," said Joe. "Come in here and help us, kids."

Steph froze. This didn't make sense. Abel and Joe, captive? But she had found the evidence in their room. Abel's threat. What was happening?

"Kids! Please!" yelled Joe.

Steph shook the steel prison door. It wouldn't budge.

"Door's not opening," said Steph. "How did you get in here?"

"I don't know," said Joe. "We all drank a toast at the after party, and then I don't remember anything until I woke up here. I'm chained to the floor, to my ankle."

"There's a killer loose," said Steph. *I thought it was you.*

"What the fuck," said Joe. "I—I don't—"

Abel thrashed on the table.

"Can you drop the scalpel and the gun?" asked Dan.

"My hands are glued to them," said Joe. "It's just like the fucking movie."

"Can you cut open Abel's gag?" asked Steph. "It might make it easier for him to breathe."

"Yeah, I can try," said Joe. "Stay still Abe."

Joe bent over, stretching out from the shackle that attached his ankle to the floor. He leaned over Abel and slowly slid the scalpel through the duct tape, cutting away layer after layer. He slowed as he got closer to Abel's mouth, and then Steph could hear a great gasp as Abel breathed easily again. Her eyes never left the timer on the wall though. It was under seven minutes now. She knew what it meant, and she knew they were running out of time. Steph and Dan could leave. Joe and Abel couldn't.

"Are you okay?" asked Abel.

"I'm fine for now," said Joe. "Got a killer fucking headache, though."

"You see what he's done, right?" asked Abel.

"Yeah," said Joe. "He expects me to cut you open to save myself."

"And probably us too," said Steph. "But we caught the door in time." Dan still stood in front of the door. In the movie, the witness came in, and it swung shut behind them, locking them in with the two participants. The timer on the wall was attached to a firebomb that would ignite the room and burn them all.

The only way to stop it was with a code that was inside Abel's stomach. And Joe had the tools he needed right in his hands. A gun to kill Abel, to ease his suffering, and a scalpel to slice him open.

"I'm not doing any of that shit. I'm not playing this game," said Joe.

"He'll kill us both, Joe," said Abel. "Just do it."

"Are you kidding me?" asked Joe. "I can't shoot you. I couldn't do it if I wanted to. I can't even kill spiders. I'm supposed to shoot you, and cut you open?"

"We have less than five minutes," said Abel. "And then we'll both be dead."

"I don't care," said Joe. "I'm not living the rest of my life knowing I lived only because you died. I'd rather die with you."

They argued back and forth, Abel yelling as much as he

could through the sliced duct tape, while Joe denied him, over and over again. Steph could only look at the timer as it counted down.

"Stop, both of you!" she yelled. "We have four minutes. Stop and think. What happened in the movie?"

They both stopped. Joe looked at her.

"The character killed her bound lover and cut him open. The code was inside him, and she found it, and stopped the bomb at the last second."

"For what reason would this work like the movie? How did he get the code into Abel? Why would he want you to live at all? Whatever his plan is, it's killing you both, and to make sure you suffer."

"Then what do we do?" asked Joe.

"Good question," said Steph. "I'd start with the timer. It is attached to anything? Is it real?"

Joe turned and studied it. It ticked below four minutes while he looked. The timer was attached to a simple 12 button panel, with number, enter, and cancel keys.

"It's hard to tell," said Joe.

"Tap on it," said Steph. "Is the panel hollow? Or is it filled with explosives?" asked Steph.

Joe tapped. Steph could hear the empty thunk from by the door.

"It's hollow," said Joe. "What does that mean?"

"What *does* that mean?" asked Dan, he whispered, to Steph. "Since when are you an expert?"

"It means there's nothing attached to that timer," said Steph.

"That's good, right?" asked Joe.

"I don't think so," said Steph. "I think it's bad. The Puzzle

Killer in the movies always had a lesson for his victims."

"So?" asked Joe.

"It was always something. The victims would have done something bad, and the Puzzle Killer would teach them how to repent. How to fix their lives. It would always be ironic. The person who lied to friends would have to cut out their own tongue to survive. The compulsive gambler would have to push their luck to live. But what is he trying to teach you?"

"I have no fucking clue," said Joe, sweat dripping over his face. The timer had ticked down below two minutes now. "I fucking thought Steven had overdosed until about ten minutes ago."

"Kalman hated celebrity," said Steph. "And I don't think there's a way out of this. I think he just wants to teach you that there's no end for you but death."

"Well, fucking lovely," said Joe. "Thanks for the help, kids. If the timer isn't attached to anything, then what's going to kill us? I'm content to wait here for the cavalry to arrive."

"The phone lines are down, and so is the internet," said Dan. "We're cut off."

"But still," said Joe. "If you don't think the timer is going to do anything—"

"I don't know," said Steph. "I'm just spit balling—"

"Helpful," said Joe. "Well, I'm tired of this shit, and if we're going out, we're doing it on my terms. I'd leave the room, kids."

"What are you doing?" asked Steph, but Dan grabbed her, pulling her outside. Dan pulled her down the steps, two at a time. The door slammed shut behind them.

A gunshot rang out from inside. And then another. Then silence.

"He didn't—" said Dan.

"I don't know," said Steph. But the timer would have run down by now, and there was no sounds of fire, or explosion. They gave it another thirty seconds, but still nothing.

"Are we going back in?" asked Dan.

"We have to," said Steph, and she climbed the short staircase to the door, and swung it open, carefully. It opened, pushing in, and Steph prepared herself for the worst.

Joe stood there, next to Abel.

"So you came back," said Joe.

"What did you do?" asked Steph.

"I shot the timer," said Joe. "What did you think I did? I said I wasn't going to play any games."

Steph looked to her left, the panel a wreck, with two bullet holes penetrating it. The timer had frozen at just under thirty seconds.

"And?"

"And nothing happened," said Joe. "But I realized the timer wasn't attached to anything, as far as I could tell. You were right." He swung open the panel the timer was attached to, and that's when she realized Joe's hands were no longer attached to the scalpel or gun.

"It had glue solvent inside," said Joe. "It dissolved the superglue." He bent down and then came back up. "And a key to our restraints."

"Thank Christ you didn't listen to me," said Abel.

"My poor listening skills finally paid off," said Joe.

"Now let's you get out of there, and we can track that fucker down—"

Joe thrust the key into the lock by Abel's neck, and then he convulsed, frozen in place, a hard grunt coming from him, a low hum filling the room. Abel shook in his restraints.

Steph and Dan froze, shocked. After a few moments, Joe fell over, dead. Abel continued to convulse on the table.

"Jesus Christ. Jesus fucking Christ," said Dan.

"The key," said Steph. "It completed the circuit. And Joe left it in." Abel was dead, but his body still danced as god knows how much voltage ripped through it. Within moments, he was smoking.

"What do we do?" asked Dan.

"We leave," said Steph. "They're already gone."

"But—I mean—"

"What do you mean to do, Dan?" asked Steph. "He's killed them. We have to go find everyone else."

It was her turn to pull him back outside, the door slamming shut behind them. The soft hum of a motor still filled the air.

"It was supposed to be them!" said Steph. "Everything pointed to Abel. Everything."

"Well, that clearly isn't the case," said Dan, trying to catch his breath. "Who's left? Who could it be?"

"I don't know," said Steph. "Everyone else had an alibi."

Dan stared at the ground, thinking. He looked to her. "William. Who else could it be? Who else could take out the internet and phone lines?"

"But he wasn't in the room when Levi's mark was moved," said Steph. "He wasn't—"

"Who else could it be?" asked Dan. "He's an orphan of the Midnight Star. He knows the place better than anyone, and he can get in and out of anywhere without trouble. He could have planted evidence in Abel and Joe's room."

"I guess," said Steph. "Something is going on."

"We'll figure it out. That's two more dead," said Dan.

"We have to find him," said Steph. "And stop him from getting the rest."

# 34

"What do we do?"

Steph didn't know. Death had followed her wherever she went. She had found poor Bill's body, and then the dozens of dead VIPs. And now, the death trap for Abel and Joe. She looked to Dan. His face was full of confusion, of sadness, of exhaustion. The weekend had tired them out, and then they were dropped into an emergency scenario neither of them had prepared for.

*Except for William. He had been ready. He'd been preparing this for months.*

"I don't know," said Steph. "What are our options?"

"We could run and get help," said Dan. "If William hasn't sabotaged the bridge. But by the time we get back—"

Dan didn't need to finish the sentence. William would

have killed anyone left by then, if he hadn't already. Getting caught wasn't a concern for him. Steph didn't know what sadistic urge had driven him to kill so many, but she doubted if he was worried about the authorities. He wanted to finish his mission, and damn the consequences.

"We can't run," said Steph. "We have to try and stop him. Gary is still out there. So is Henry and Linda. And we haven't found Nancy or Mary yet. They might be alive."

Steph thought to Gary, and his plans for the future, and a pang of guilt struck her. She should have said something, she had the chance, but she let him stroll right into the lion's den—

*Stop it, Stephanie. You had no choice. This was Geno's fault.*

"There's Geno, too," said Dan.

"Yeah, let's not forget him," said Steph. "But still, where do we go?"

"Well, if we think William is the killer, we start there," said Dan. "We go to the caretaker's house, and to his work shed."

"What, unarmed, after he's killed so many people?" asked Steph. "He'll slaughter us."

"I didn't say we just lay down and let him kill us," said Dan. "We arm ourselves first, and then we look for him. The compound is big and spread out, but it's not infinite. And anything loud will carry for miles now—"

"Now that most of us are dead," said Steph.

"Well—yeah," said Dan. "Where are there weapons?"

"There are knives back at the mansion," said Steph. "In the kitchen. There's a fireplace poker. I'm sure there's something else, but either of those will do for now."

"Do you think he has a gun?" asked Dan.

"I don't know," said Steph. "He hasn't shot anyone yet. He doesn't want to just kill them. He wants to prove a point."

"And what point is that?"

"I don't know," said Steph. "Maybe it's just that we shouldn't have come here."

"Well, he's proved it to me," said Dan. "I promise to never come back."

"Let's get moving," said Steph. "I hope you're wearing your running shoes."

"Now that you mention it," said Dan. "I've already got blisters, but they're the least of my worries."

They jogged as fast as they could at a steady pace. Steph breathed hard, her heart pounding in her chest, but she pushed through. They didn't have time to walk.

Both of them were covered in sweat by the time they reached the mansion. Steph peeked inside and listened, but there was no sound, and they crept into the kitchen. Dan hurriedly drank a glass of water while Steph pulled the chef's knife from the block. It was long and sharp, and would do the job if it had to. She tested a quick slice, the grip firm in her hand.

"I've never been in a fight," said Dan.

"Neither have I," said Steph. She squeezed the knife. She didn't know if she could stab someone. Real violence and death scared the shit out of her. Horror movies were one thing, real life was another. But then she thought to all the dead. The second Kalman massacre, and it made the thought a little bit easier.

They left the kitchen, checking every corner, but there was no sign of William, or anyone here. Steph hurried to the den. She braced herself for seeing poor Bill again, but the fireplace poker was inside, and would make a good weapon.

She pushed open the door and Bill's corpse was still there, half burnt. The smell had filled the room, and Dan backed away, and she heard him retch in the hallway. She held her breath and grabbed the poker before retreating and closing the door behind her.

Dan was doubled over, his hands on his knees. Steph put a tentative hand on his back.

"Are you okay?" asked Steph.

"Bill," said Dan. "I saw him there, and the smell—"

"It's okay," said Steph. "Let's go." She handed Dan the poker, and they left the mansion behind them.

"William's shed is a half mile to the west," said Dan. "Near the mine."

"The mine to nowhere," said Steph, quietly.

Their flashlights lit the way as they jogged. Steph's feet burned in her tennis shoes, and she could feel liquid slosh between her toes. Blisters had formed and then burst, and the pain had all merged into a burning sensation covering both feet. She pushed it away. She would have to do more running tonight, and her feet would have to make do with the suffering.

The buildings out here were sparse and separated. There was a mish-mash of them, mobile homes, wooden structures, and cinder-block construction, all laid down randomly, probably as members had joined Kalman originally, each laying claim to a plot of land they'd only live on for a few months. Steph tried to avoid the larger pieces of rock, both of them running on a rough path formed by William and his ATV.

"Did you see inside the shed?" asked Steph.

"No," said Dan. "When we got the chairs the other day, they were already sitting outside. But it was big. God knows what he could have had in there. It could be full of anything."

"I didn't go in either, when I helped him," said Steph. "At least we know where he's been building everything. He's had a long time to plan."

"What set him off?" asked Dan. "He didn't seem to like Kalman."

"I don't know," said Steph. "All this isolation, in this place. It could have done things to him. He didn't seem violent. I would have sworn it was Abel."

"We turn here," said Dan, approaching a T-junction in the path, and they turned right down it. Trees grew a little more often as they went down the trail. There was still no sound except for their footsteps, the ground crunching beneath them, their harried breaths coming in quick gasps.

"We're almost there," said Dan, and slowed down. "We should be more careful." Steph stopped too, catching her breath as they walked. They got off the path, walking through the rocky soil and around trees. Steph listened for anything else, but there was nothing.

"Are you sure we're heading the right direction?" she asked, in a harsh whisper.

"Yes. Shh," said Dan. "Look, there it is." He turned off his flashlight and motioned her to do the same. She clicked it off, and the barn was there, through the trees. Its outdoor light illuminated the surrounding space as bright as day. Steph remembered it from helping William the day before.

"What's the plan?" whispered Steph.

"I don't know," said Dan. "I was going to ask you."

They waited a minute, but there was no movement, and no noise.

"I guess we go inside," said Steph. "And see what we find. What else do we have to go on? There has to be something in there."

They crept closer, and Steph kept her head on a swivel, looking all around, looking for any other lights, any other movement. William's ATV wasn't here, which means the coast was clear, for now.

"He's not here," said Steph. "Let's go inside."

They hurried to the door, plain and wooden in the side of the barn. Steph put her ear to it. She heard something from inside, a creaking noise. What could it be?

Steph tried the door, expecting to find it locked, but it swung open, and she quickly saw the source of the noise.

"What the fuck?" asked Dan, as he followed her in.

The outer edges of the building were covered in desks and workspace, with power tools of all kinds covering them. Different wood and metalworking projects covered every available space. But that's not what Dan had seen.

A large wooden platform dominated the center of the space. They had found Mary Jo, Nancy, and Linda. They stood on top of—

*A gallows, Stephanie. The right word is gallows.*

They each stood on a chair on the gallows, the platform seven or eight feet off the ground. Each had a noose tied tight around their neck, the other end of the rope tied to a wooden bar in an upside down L shape, even higher up. The creaking noise she had heard was the wooden chairs they each stood on, the only thing keeping them from hanging.

Each chair only had three legs, another sadistic game as all of them balanced precariously on tiptoes, to not fall and die.

"Oh my god," said Steph. They stared at them, their mouths gagged, their hands tied behind their backs. At seeing them, they all tried to yell, but it only came out as muffled noises.

"Keep them stable, and I'll try and find something to stand on to cut them down," said Steph, her eyes already searching the room for anything tall. She could cut through the nooses and finally save someone. No more death.

Dan ran up the stairs to the platform and tried his best to help steady any of the three that seemed to struggle. All of them continued to try to talk through their gags. Steph searched around the room and only saw pieces of things, nothing to stand on, how, how did William do it in the first place.

The sound of the door opening broke her from her focus, and she grabbed the knife hard, ready to defend herself, and she looked to the door, but it wasn't William.

It was Henry.

"Oh my God!" he exclaimed. Then he looked to her. "Stephanie! Oh, thank God you're alright." He ran to her and embraced her. She hugged him tight, the embrace feeling good.

"Go help Dan," said Steph.

"What's happening?" he asked.

"It's William," said Steph. "He's doing all of this. We can figure out the rest later, go help Dan and I'll be up in a second to cut them down." Henry nodded and went up the stairs. Steph turned and looked for anything to stand on. She saw something, finally, a wooden crate she could turn on its side. It would be sturdy enough to work. She grabbed it and turned back to the gallows just in time to see Dan thud to the ground. He grunted, dazed, and rolled over, grabbing his shoulder.

*What?*

She looked up to the platform. Steph hadn't glanced up since Henry had arrived, but all three of the women were screaming into their gags. Linda's eyes stared into Steph's, a frantic terror in them. Henry stood behind her.

Steph remembered Linda's note too late. Linda had needed to talk to her. To tell her something important.

Henry kicked out the chair from under Linda and the noose snapped tight as Linda choked. She thrashed in the air.

"Sorry for the subterfuge, Steph," said Henry, staring at her. "But it couldn't be helped."

# 35

Steph's heart thudded hard in her chest. Pain shot through her body.

Linda was dying, and she had to do something.

Steph charged toward the stairs, her knife out.

"Nuh uh uh," said Henry, moving behind Nancy, ready to kick her chair out. "One foot on those stairs and Nancy dies too." Nancy's eyes locked on Steph, pleading for her to stay put, even as Linda convulsed, her brain using her last bit of oxygen. If Steph didn't do something now, Linda would die in moments.

Her inaction had already cost too many lives, and she charged up the stairs, her knife out. Henry sighed and kicked out Nancy's chair, and she dropped, the noose cutting off her oxygen. She grunted once and then made wet choking sounds. She kicked hard in the air, trying desperately to find breath.

Steph ran up the stairs and found Henry at the top of them, waiting for her. She sliced once, aiming for his throat, but he dodged her, watching for the blade to pass before grabbing her wrist of the hand that held the knife, and locking down on it with his grip. He pulled hard, down and back, and Steph had to let go of the blade, the torque too much, and then her body flipped over, and she felt Henry move her in mid-air, with strength she didn't realize he had.

As she fell from the platform, she remembered his soft touch on the overlook, and then she hit the ground with a thud, all the air leaving her lungs. Her back flared up in agony and stars flashed in her vision. She gasped, trying to breathe, her body in pain.

"I told you," said Henry. He reached down and picked up the blade. "Do you think I'm unprepared? I've been planning this for *years*, Steph. You charging at me with a knife won't stop me. I've been taking Krav Maga for a decade."

Linda stopped moving now, and Steph could do nothing but watch as she died. Nancy thrashed in the air, desperately trying to do anything, but she was just as helpless as Steph was.

Dan was on his feet again and moved toward the stairs.

"Don't do it, Dan," said Henry, moving behind Mary Jo, the last one still balancing on a three-legged chair. "Her death will be on your hands."

Dan stopped at the bottom stair, Mary's eyes cocked at him, as she did her best to keep the chair level.

"That's a good boy," said Henry. "You're learning."

Nancy struggled for a few seconds longer, and then

stopped, and then died. Tears welled in Steph's eyes, her chest aching. More death, and she could do nothing.

"Why?" she asked, the only word she could muster, looking up at Henry. He stared down at her.

"Why? Are you kidding me?" asked Henry. "Have you been paying attention, Steph? I thought you understood that, at least. These people are scum. They are a pathogen. They are evil. You've been exposed to it for what, a couple days? How did it feel? To see the stars you idolized and worshiped show their true colors? The infighting, the pettiness, the shallowness, the banality. The abuse, the lies. So, so much, from all of them."

"And that's worth killing them for?" asked Steph.

"Oh, Stephanie," said Henry. "Yes, yes. Of course. I've been in it for years. For years, and so many times I struggled. After a star lied to my face, or insulted me, or treated me like a slave, a lesser, like dirt. Screamed at me, used me. And I wondered why continue? Why do this to myself? I'm smart, and capable. I could do anything I wanted. But you know what got me through it all, all that abuse, all that pain?"

Steph didn't answer, her lips pursed.

"These moments," said Henry. "Knowing that it would all be worth it. That would I get to punish them for all their transgressions, all of their sins. That they would taste a small return of all the vile and evil they dish out. And you know what? It was worth it. I'd do it all again." He gestured to Nancy. "They finally get what they deserve."

"Revenge?" asked Steph. "All of this for simple revenge?"

Henry stared at her in confusion, and squinted his eyes, trying to read her. "You're serious, aren't you?"

"Wha—"

"You *are* serious," said Henry, smiling and shaking his head. "I thought you were smarter than that, Steph. But I guess I can't blame you. Sometimes you're looking in the fridge, and you can't find the eggs, even when they're right in front of your face. This isn't about revenge, even if I did take pleasure in exacting it."

"Then fucking what is it?" asked Dan, yelling.

"Shh shh shh," said Henry. "Not so loud, Dan. I might get a little squirrelly up here and Mary Jo might accidentally take a tumble. And you don't want that." Mary's eyes darted between Steph and Dan, looking to them for help, but what could they do? Trying to save her would condemn her to death.

"Well?" asked Steph. "I know you want to tell us."

"John Kalman was a great man," said Henry. "He was trying to create a new society. Create a new Earth. But the government wouldn't allow it. Those in power want to remain in power, and they couldn't handle that being threatened. They knew he was close and they put a stop to it before he could finish his dream. But I am here, to succeed where he failed, to not just reach his goals, but to push past them, to go further than he ever did."

"You've lost your mind," said Steph.

"No," said Henry. "I'm the only sane one here. Me and William. William understood, understood the whole time. When I approached him, he didn't believe me at first. But the blood tests proved it out, and after that, we figured out a plan. And we executed."

Steph stared at him in confusion. *Blood tests?*

And then she remembered William's story. Only a few

kids had gotten out.

"You were here too," said Steph. "William is your brother."

"You're almost there, Steph," said Henry, smiling.

"And Kalman was your father," said Steph.

"Ding ding ding," said Henry. "And William is my *half* brother, technically. But we share a strength in belief of father. He was a brilliant man, and I studied his teachings, and I taught William. And together, we set this all up."

"You sure like talking a lot," said Dan. "Why, fucko?"

Henry glared at him.

"Because they would turn us into a publicity stunt. Because they would turn us into a joke. And that couldn't happen, I couldn't allow it, and then inspiration struck, and gave us the chance to re-ignite the dreams of the Midnight Star. For the Star God to re-awaken, there must be a holy sacrifice. Father wrote that righteous punishment would bring down our Holy Lord from the heavens above, and then transform the world, the worshipers new kings upon the Earth."

Henry held his hands high, looking into the air.

"The Midnight Star will rule the Earth, and it will start right here, with the sacrifice of these unbelievers, of these charlatans, of these monsters. And you might not thank me now, but you will thank me later, when our new Earth is upon us."

"You lied to me," said Steph.

"Of course," said Henry. "You were getting wise to our plan. You believed Nancy. You spotted when I moved Levi's mark. So I had to distract you while William worked. It caused us a little extra work, but we both knew that no plan survives contact with the enemy."

*I can't believe I fucking kissed him.*

"You monster—"

"Did you know Mary Jo's character has died in only one movie she's been in?" asked Henry. He walked closer to her again. "Even in her extensive filmography, only one movie, and it was an early one, a smaller part, where she got hanged. Nancy here, on the other hand, as I'm sure you're both aware, died dozens of times on screen, usually by the hand of some mindless monster. So I gave Nancy a taste of Mary's life. It seems like it's what she wanted. Mary, on the other hand—"

Henry kicked out the chair, and Mary fell, the noose snapping tight, and she made a terrible noise as her throat cinched shut. She struggled in mid-air.

"Mary seemed happy with her choices, so she gets to choke on them."

Suddenly arms wrapped around Steph from the back, and she realized William was there and he could feel his hot breath on the back of her neck. She fought, trying to pull herself loose, but William was strong, his grip like iron. She tried to kick him, to drive her heels into him, but he kept her away from him, and he dragged her.

"Bring her up here, William," said Henry. "She was useful while she lasted."

And then Dan was on William's back, beating on him with his fists. She felt the weight of him as he did his best to hurt William, to try to break his iron grip. He clocked William on the head, over and over, and William's grip loosened, if only a little, and Steph gained enough leverage to drive her elbow into his stomach, once, twice, three times, each time harder until William let go completely. Dan grabbed a nearby wooden box and brought it down on William's skull, and he fell, finally, and Steph ran. A hand caught her ankle, and she stumbled. William had reached out and snagged her. She kicked once, twice, driving her foot into his face, and she heard a SNAP as his nose broke, and blood poured out from it.

William's face was full of anger, but he let go, and Dan grabbed Steph and ran. Steph looked back once, to see Henry still standing next to Mary, as Mary stopped moving, her last breath leaving her body.

"There's no use running," Henry yelled after them. "This is our place now. You cannot escape the Midnight Star. The Star God is coming!"

# 36

Steph and Dan ran out the door of the barn. Her feet flared with pain, and Dan ran alongside her, clutching his side.

"Head for the trees," said Steph.

"I'll try," said Dan. "I think I broke a rib when I fell. It hurts every time I move."

"Well, I've got some bad news for you," said Steph. "We've got a lot of moving in our future." They hit the first copse of trees and moved around it, the rocks crunching beneath their feet. They heard the ATV start up behind them. William would be after them, on top of them.

"There's nowhere to run," said Dan. "William will catch up in seconds."

"That's not true," said Steph. "The mine. He can't take it into the mine. And the trees will slow him down. He'll stick to the path."

"How do we get there?" asked Dan. "I have no idea where we are anymore."

"This way," said Steph. "I think." She pointed away from the path where the trees grew thicker, where scrub grass and bushes had overgrown the ground. "If we cut through here, we'll get there."

"What the fuck are we doing?"

"We're trying not to die," said Steph. "It was both of them. Henry. He lied to me."

"He lied to all of us," said Dan. "He orchestrated this whole thing. He still has Gary."

"Well," said Steph. "If you want to know what we're doing—we're trying to save Gary, and get the fuck out of here."

Dan grunted in pain.

"You gonna make it?" asked Steph.

"I'll have to," said Dan. "There is no fucking way I'm going to die in this godforsaken place. I didn't even get to eat dinner."

Steph smiled despite herself. They ran, crashing through scrub bushes and dashing around trees. The ATV cruised by out on the road, and a spotlight would occasionally break through the tree cover, looking for them.

"He's searching for us," said Dan.

"Good," said Steph. "Because when we're close enough to the mine, I want him to see us."

"What?" asked Dan.

"We're not getting back to Gary while William is still standing and has that ATV. We have to take him out and get his wheels. We need him to follow us into the mine."

"And then what?" asked Dan.

"I'm not quite sure," said Steph. "Let me know if you think of something."

The trees were thinning out, and the ground was clearer, and then Steph saw the ATV path again, carved out of the earth.

"There," said Steph. "See that light, over there? That's the mine. Once we break tree cover, stay on the path. And if you're holding back anything, now's the time to let loose. We'll have to sprint our asses off. Because William will see us as soon as we're out in the open, with our lights. And he'll be speeding toward us on the ATV. But once we hit the fence, he'll have to stop. We can scale it and head down into the mine. You ready?"

"No," said Dan. "I think my heart is going to explode."

"Run like your life depends on it," said Steph. "Because it does."

They both sprinted, their flashlights bobbing as they pumped their legs. Steph couldn't breathe, but she ran anyway, her heart pounding as hard as it ever had. She heard the ATV behind her. It got louder as William turned toward them, their lights giving them away. The mine drew incrementally closer. They only had to reach the fence.

But even that seemed a mile away, and the ATV was much faster than them.

*Please, a flat tire, an engine failure, anything.*

The engine grew louder, and she glanced back to see the headlights, farther away than she thought. But it grew closer quickly, and it got louder as William hit the gas, pushing it as fast as he could.

"Almost there," said Dan, and he was right. She didn't believe it, but they had made ground on the fence quickly.

Steph had never run so hard in her entire life, and she had nothing left in the tank, but still she didn't stop. She thought of all the dead. The two of them wouldn't be added to the tally. They would make it out alive.

The ATV accelerated, and she felt it at her heels. Its headlights got brighter and brighter behind her, silhouetting her. He would run her over in the road, and that'd be the end of her, Jesus Christ, she was just helping at a movie festival, what the fuck, and then Dan's flashlight rested on the chainlink fence that segmented the mine and he jumped onto it with an awful grunt of pain, but climbed, and pulled himself up and over, and thank Christ there wasn't any barbwire, and she felt the ATV behind her, and then she jumped, and she pulled herself over, god she never could do pull-ups, but she pulled and she was over, and she flipped over the other side and fell onto the dirt, scrambling onto her feet.

She doubled over, trying to breathe, with Dan doing the same next to her. The ATV skidded to a halt next to the fence. William sat on it, gave them a quick glance, and then sped toward the entrance another half mile down the path.

"We're not out of the woods yet," said Dan, and they both started jogging toward the opening of the mine, only a minute away. Darkness filled the yawning portal, and their flashlights cut narrow swathes through it.

They entered, with Steph leading the way.

"We can go down to the storage area," said Steph. "We can use the boxes as cover."

"It's as good a plan as any," said Dan. "We need weapons."

They jogged down the incline, the sound of their breath and feet filling the space. She remembered the trip down with Abel and Joe. It felt like a million years ago.

"What's that smell?" asked Dan.

"I don't know," said Steph, sniffing. "But it's awful."

They soon came to the boxes, crates stacked to the ceiling. Steph went to one and pulled it down. She scanned the room with her flashlight and found what she was looking for, a crowbar leaning against a pallet in the corner. She grabbed it and pried open the box.

"What's in there?" asked Dan.

"MREs," said Steph.

"They really think the apocalypse is coming, don't they?" asked Dan.

The stench had only gotten worse, though. She sniffed around.

"God, it reeks," said Dan.

"It smells like—"

*Something's died in here* is what she was going to say, but she stopped herself, looking behind the rows of crates.

"I found the smell," said Steph.

"What is it?" asked Dan.

"It's Ted."

"Fucking hell," said Dan. "What's the plan?"

"This is as good a place as any to set the trap. Do you want to be the bait, or should I?"

"Who can swing a crowbar harder?" asked Dan.

"Probably you, even with some broken ribs," said Steph. "That makes me the bait. Don't let him kill me."

"I'll do my best," said Dan.

"Hide behind that stack over there," said Steph. "I'll hide, but give myself away. When he comes for me, swing the pointy end straight into his head."

"Yes, ma'am," said Dan, and disappeared into the darkness, turning off his flashlight. The noise of the ATV echoed down the cave. William had arrived at the entrance to the mine. Steph stood behind a narrow stack of boxes, but left an elbow obtrusively sticking out. The engine of the ATV turned off.

"Hey Steph," said Dan, in a whisper.

"Shut up," said Steph.

"I love you," said Dan.

"I love you too," said Steph. She took a deep breath and tried to calm the anxious beating of her heart. She could feel her hands shake, and she squeezed them hard to try to stop them.

They waited in total darkness. William's footsteps echoed in the dark, and she realized now their footprints were probably easy to follow. It didn't matter. They had made a mess in this area. He would see her first. She was sure of it. And if he didn't, she'd make sure he did.

She heard his breathing as he approached, and soon his powerful flashlight illuminated a fair chunk of the cave.

"You shouldn't have come down here," he said, his voice echoing. "You shouldn't have come here at all. But Henry is right. You need to pay."

He was close. His deep drawl reverberated through the closed cave. His light was in the room now, and it passed over her hiding spot.

"Girl," he said. "Come out. Don't make me drag you."

*Good.*

Steph stepped out from behind the boxes, into full view of his flashlight, blinding her, and she put a hand over her eyes so she could see him. He carried a shovel with a sharpened end for cutting through hard Texas topsoil.

"You shouldn't have come down here," he said again. "Where's the boy?"

Dan stepped out and swung the crowbar hard, with all his body weight behind it. He aimed for William's head, but William sensed him and moved at the last second, and it caught him high on his shoulder, near where it met his neck. It made a sickening THUNK noise as it sunk into William's flesh. Steph thought it would have still been enough to stop him, but William didn't fall. He turned and swung with his shovel, not seeing Dan, only knowing he was there, and the metal hit Dan's leg with a hard CRACK and Dan screamed, falling, letting go of the crowbar.

"Boy," said William, pulling the crowbar out of his shoulder and throwing it aside with a CLANG. Blood poured from the wound. William turned and looked down at Dan. Dan's leg was broken, his shinbone poking through the skin. Dan's hands shook as he clutched his leg.

"You're gonna get worse than that," said William, and raised his shovel. Steph charged and jumped onto his back, putting one arm around his neck and sinking the other hand into the gash on his shoulder. William showed that he was human, yelling out in pain. He turned in circles, dropping the shovel, trying to throw her off. She squeezed harder, digging into the deep wound with her fingernails. He finally reached around with his other arm and got a hold of her and pulled her off, tossing her with an incredible strength.

"Bitch," he said. "You can't stop this. We're almost done." She scrabbled backwards in the rough dirt, looking for the crowbar, but it lay across the room. William advanced on her quickly, and grabbed her throat, pulling her to her feet, and then off the ground. He squeezed hard, and Steph couldn't breathe anymore. She remembered Linda, Nancy, Mary, all suffocating in front of her. She beat the arm of William, but it did nothing. Her vision started going black.

SHUNK.

Dan didn't miss this time, shoving the point of the shovel into the back of William's skull. His grip loosened, and Steph gasped in a deep breath of air. William's eyes twitched, twitched, and then he fell over, the shovel still stuck in his head. Dan stood behind him on one leg.

"That was for Bill, you fuck," he said, and then fell over, cradling his leg.

# 37

"Holy shit, this hurts," said Dan.

Steph stepped around the body of William and crouched next to Dan.

"It looks—"

"It looks fucking awful," said Dan. "I do my best to keep my bones inside my body."

"We have to get you up," said Steph, trying to put an arm under his shoulder.

"No, no," said Dan, pushing her away. "We don't have time for this. I couldn't help you, anyway. The worst I could do was bleed on him. Leave me. Go find Gary."

"Are you sure?" asked Steph.

"I'm sure," said Dan. "I can barely move. Go get his ATV and stop Henry. I'll be waiting for you."

Steph nodded and then hugged him. Dan returned the hug, and then she was running, taking William's big flashlight and the crowbar. It wasn't a lot, but it was something. She ran back up the cave, her body aching. The toll of injuries were adding up. Her feet, her back, her throat all screamed in pain, but she pushed it all away.

*Almost done, Stephanie.*

The ATV was parked at the entrance to the mine, and she jumped in the driver's seat. She had never driven one before. The keys were already in the ignition, and she turned it on. It was an automatic, and she threw it into drive, and twisted the throttle carefully. The vehicle shot forward, and she held on, testing the steering. It wouldn't do to crash and break her neck on the way to save the day.

Steph steered toward the exit to the mine area and then accelerated on the path.

*But where am I heading? Where would he take them?*

Neither Gary or Geno had any ironic deaths in store. They weren't at the mansion, or the main hall. Henry had said that they were summoning the Star God. He used the word sacrifice, and ritual.

It hit her suddenly, obvious now.

The church. He would be at the church.

She sped up and the wheels spun for a second before the ATV surged ahead. The powerful headlights of the ATV illuminated the path before her, and within a few minutes, she'd be there. She hoped she wasn't too late.

The dry air rushed past her face, and she did her best to push away all the thoughts of death, but they kept resurfacing in her mind. Of all the dead.

*You could have stopped this.*

She shook the thought away. This wasn't her fault. She hadn't killed anyone. It was Henry, who had lied to her face, who had misled her, who had manipulated all of them. How far back did it go? Geno said that this was his idea, for the premiere to happen here, but was it really? Had Henry gotten into his ear and suggested that they take Splatterfest here? To use that as an excuse for slaughter?

She didn't know, but she couldn't put it past him. He had played her, told her exactly what she had wanted to hear. Had misled her into chasing false leads, to give him and William time to kill everyone.

To what end? Did he actually believe that he could awaken his Star God?

The silhouette of the church's star shaped steeple came into view, dark against the night sky. But the building's lights were on, bright light streaming through the high windows, and she knew she was right. Henry was inside, with Gary, with Geno.

She slowed as she pulled up, but there would be no hiding the noise of the engine. Henry would hear her coming. He had controlled every encounter they'd had, but she had no other options.

She grabbed the crowbar, and then looked through the storage area in the back of the vehicle, hoping there would be something she could use. It was mostly trash and junk, a spare coil of rope, a bag of mulch, a set of five-minute flares, a small can of gas, a toolbox.

Steph searched the outside of the church and saw the propane tank. She would prepare a surprise of her own, but she'd have to hurry.

Within a minute she entered, crowbar in hand. She

didn't know what to expect. The space looked much like it had on their first day, before the festival. She counted in her head. She had 300 seconds.

*278, 277, 276*

Henry stood in the middle of the room, lighting a candle, outlined on the floor in the same star shape as the steeple, as the huge carving on the wall. The white candles dripped wax onto the ground, and red lines of paint connected the candles, finishing the shape. Gary sat on his knees inside the star, his arms and legs bound behind him. He was gagged.

Steph spotted Geno off to one side. He was bound and gagged similarly, his nose bleeding. His eyes widened when he saw her.

"Did you have any trouble with them?" asked Henry, not turning around.

"William broke Dan's leg pretty bad, but Dan'll make it," said Steph. "Don't think William will pull through, though. Not after we jammed the shovel into his head."

Henry turned, his eyes showing surprise, looking alien on his face.

"Steph," he said. "I wasn't expecting you. William is always so capable."

"Sorry to surprise you," she said.

"I doubt that, actually," he said. "But there are contingency plans in place. It's a tragedy that William won't get to see His arrival. He was so instrumental in all of this happening. But he was just a small piece. Just like me."

Steph took a step toward him and Henry put a hand out.

"Wouldn't do that," said Henry, pulling the same knife Steph had dropped earlier from his belt. He held it to Gary's throat.

She stopped.

*199, 198, 197*

"Good girl," he said. The edge of the blade rested against Gary's skin.

"Do you really think you're going to summon a god?" asked Steph.

"Yes," said Henry. "The prophecy said so. It spoke of a Star God, of one who feasted on righteous death of the sinners from the evil city."

"All written by Kalman," said Steph.

"Yes," said Henry. "My father was shown the truth, and the government intruded on him before he could realize it."

Steph looked into Henry's eyes. He believed what he said.

"Why would you kill Gary?" asked Steph. "What did he ever do?"

"He founded this," said Henry. "He gave birth to it."

Steph shook her head.

*121, 120, 119*

"He's one of the best men I know," said Steph. "He doesn't deserve this. Even if I believed that all the others did, I know Gary. He's a force for good in the world."

Henry's eyes wavered for a second.

"And why is Geno still alive?" asked Steph. She gestured toward him, and Geno shook his head, hoping to be forgotten. "Is he not sinful enough to warrant destruction?"

"A contingency plan," said Henry. "Just in case."

"Ah, I see," said Steph. "So just in case your apocalyptic scenario doesn't work out, you have some sleazy producer?"

Henry didn't answer. He just stared at her, his eyes full of hate.

"I will awaken the Star God with the blood of a sacrifice,"

said Henry.

"Why did you kill all those people?" asked Steph, ignoring him, staring right back.

*78, 77, 76*

"I told you! They were vacuous, banal, empty monsters! They acted as if everyone was below them. They perpetuate a culture of filth and—"

"So?"

Henry glared at her interruption.

"It's not worth killing for," said Steph. "They made movies, Henry. Most of them were just crappy horror flicks to watch with your friends. What, they were *mean* to you, so they deserved to die?"

"They—"

"What about all those VIPs? Those poor people that saved for *years* for this, just to meet some celebrities and watch some movies, and you killed them without thought."

"They supported it!" he yelled, his face red. Steph couldn't recognize him anymore. Henry the shapeshifter. The doppelganger, the changeling.

"So they deserved to die?" asked Steph. "Why do you get to decide?"

*25, 24, 23*

"Because I am the inheritor! I am the descendant! I carry the blood—"

"John Kalman was a nobody crackpot, Henry," said Steph. "He tricked a bunch of innocents, including your mother, to come out here after he washed out of Hollywood. And then he killed them."

"No, those are lies, he—"

"He was a nobody, Henry," said Steph. "Who wrote a lot

of crap, trying to get people to believe. And you were dumb enough to believe right along with them."

"No!" he yelled, holding the blade closer to Gary's throat. "You shut up, or Gary dies now." *Need to get the knife away from Gary.*

"You're a coward, Henry," said Steph. "Threatening an old man to keep a woman away from you? You're still trying to manipulate me, like you've been doing to me all weekend. Do you have a single honest relationship?"

Henry glared at her and pulled the knife away from Gary's throat. He pointed the blade at her. "You don't know me—"

*3, 2, 1*

"Gary, hit the deck!" she yelled, and dove to the ground. Gary's eyes went wide and did the same.

"What are you doing?" asked Henry.

And then there was silence, and Steph thought the trigger hadn't worked, that the flare hadn't set off the gasoline, but then the ground shook, and the wall disappeared as a massive explosion and fireball ripped through the building. An immense wave of heat rolled over her, and the sound of concrete and debris spraying across the room filled her ears. She braced herself, but only some dirt and dust hit her.

She peeked up, surveying the damage.

The gas can had lit after the flare had burned down, igniting it, and then the propane tank, which exploded. It had destroyed the entire wall of the church, and she could see the night sky. The lights were out now, with only the flaming wreckage providing a dim glow.

"Gary," she called out. "Are you okay?"

She only heard a mumble back. She forgot the gag.

Steph pushed herself off the floor and turned on her flashlight. She walked over to Gary, who laid in the middle of the star shape, his hands and feet still tied. She hastily untied him and pulled off his gag.

"Are you okay?" asked Steph.

"I don't think we're getting our deposit back," said Gary.

"I'll take that as a yes," said Steph.

"Yeah, I'm fine," said Gary. "Where's the psycho?"

Steph whirled her light around the room, looking for Henry. She couldn't spot him at first. Had he run in the aftermath of the explosion?

But then she saw him. The shrapnel had hit him with full force. A length of rebar pinned him to the back wall, punched through his chest and into it. He laid slumped against it, the huge symbol of the star directly above him.

"He didn't make it," said Steph.

"Thank god," said Gary.

There was another muffled noise, and Steph turned toward it. It came from beneath a pile of rubble, and she went over, pulling the rocks away. Geno lay there, below it. She untied him and pulled off his gag.

"Holy shit, I'm alive," said Geno.

"Did anyone else make it?" asked Gary.

"Dan," said Steph. "He's back at the mine with a broken leg."

"But no one else?" asked Gary.

"No," said Steph. "We've only found dead. All the celebrities. All the VIPs."

"Oh god," said Gary. He sat on the floor, his head down. "Those poor people."

Steph sat next to him and hugged him.

# 38

"So, what do you think?"

"I think it looks great," said Steph. "I'm just worried."

"You're worried?" asked Gary. "It feels like I haven't slept in a month."

They both stood in the newly renovated and redesigned Video Store. They had gutted half of it. The shelving, the displays, the various relics of decades in operation had all been taken away, sold, put in storage, or tossed in the dumpster. The other half had been cleared of all the thousands of VHS tapes, DVDs, Blu-Rays, Laserdiscs, and every other form of media known to man. Steph and Dan had gone through *all* of them, doing an extensive inventory.

"It was overdue," said Steph. "It needed to change."

"You're right," said Gary. "You two have dragged me

kicking and screaming into the 21st century."

They did an extensive inventory because The Video Store finally was moving online, moving most of their stock into warehouse space, and selling both through their website and eBay. They stocked the remaining shelf space with only the best stuff. The most limited edition films, the special collection DVDs, and all the most eye-catching movie memorabilia were all put out front to catch people's eyes.

The other, empty half had been replaced with a bar, cafe, and general hangout spot with a simple walk-up counter with a row of taps for local craft brews, and an extensive fridge for other tastes. Multiple coffee machines sat behind it, ready to meet whatever needs a customer would have. Local artists had come and decorated the walls with multiple murals, all influenced by trashy films, and clunky CRTs were strapped to every wall, all playing the same movie. Or, they would be, when they opened it up to the public.

"Everyone I know is excited about it," said Steph. "They all want to come and see."

"I just hope they'll spend money," said Gary.

"I think you'll be making more money in beer than you ever did selling videotapes, Gary," said Steph. "And with everything online, people can buy our stuff from all over the world."

"It's scary," he said.

"Is it any scarier than being sacrificed in a ritual to awaken some cult god?" asked Steph.

"Hmm," said Gary. "I'll say no, because I know that's the right answer. But it sure is scary enough."

Splatterfest was fresh on her mind, and she was sure it was on Gary's. It had been a year since the final Splatterfest, a year since Henry and William had murdered over seventy people over a weekend. It had taken days for all the bodies to be removed. William had destroyed the only bridge in or out. The police arrived later the next day, after emergency crews repaired the bridge, to find Gary, Steph, and Dan laid up in the mansion, trying to keep Dan's leg stable. The feds came afterward. They believed everything the three told them, and then informed them about Dave Barclay, who'd been found dead in his home in LA, apparently killed by Henry before he left. One more added to the tally.

There would be no Splatterfest this year, or ever again.

"Man, this place looks amazing," said Dan, coming out from the back.

"Are you trying to say that it didn't look great before?" asked Gary.

"Of course not, Gary," said Dan. "It had a certain gross charm about it, for sure, but this is much more welcoming. You won't just get the lo-fi weirdos in here."

"What's wrong with lo-fi weirdos?" asked Gary.

"Again, nothing," said Dan. "But once in a while, your business might need to make money."

"Fair," said Gary. "You really think this will work?"

"Yes," said Steph. "I do. And it will keep this place alive. More importantly, it will keep the community alive."

"Even without Splatterfest?" asked Gary.

"Well, now that you mention it—"

"I don't like that tone," said Gary.

"It's been a year," said Steph. "And I know, despite every-thing that happened, you still miss it, right?"

Gary looked down at his hands, and then up at her. "Of course," he said, finally. "I mean, I don't know. I just miss everyone gathering in the back room, or the parking lot, and watching some terrible VHS with bad tracking and worse sound and having a good time. I don't need celebrities or premieres. Not that any of them would come close after last year."

"That wasn't your fault," said Dan. "The only one who survived that should have taken any of the blame was Geno, and he got off scot-free."

"He did right by us," said Gary.

"You mean he paid us the money we were rightfully due?" asked Steph.

"Yes," said Gary. "But he didn't have to. He could have kept it."

"Even he wouldn't stoop that low," said Dan. "Especially after Steph saved his life."

"Anyway," said Steph. "I've been thinking about a successor to Splatterfest. Something different, but still captures the charm of the old store and parties."

"A sequel?" asked Gary.

"Splatterfest 2, electric boogaloo?" asked Dan. "This time, with less murder."

"A new name," said Steph. "Obviously. And spread out through the city. We partner with a bunch of other places and hold events all over town. And have a big parking lot bash to end the event."

"When?" asked Gary.

"Next year," said Steph. "Gives us time to plan it, and get everything ready."

"Sounds good to me," said Dan.

"What do we call it?" asked Gary.

"I was thinking Zombie Con."

"Why that?" asked Dan.

"Because we won't stay dead."

# Sign up for your free, exclusive short story!

Sign up for Robbie's newsletter! Monthly sneak peeks at upcoming projects, cover teases, and instant access to a free short story!

www.robbiedorman.com/newsletter

# Acknowledgements

Thank you to my wife Kim, for her patience and support, and my team of beta readers: Andrew, Matt, Megan, Yousef. And thank you for reading.

# About the Author

Robbie Dorman believes in horror. Splatterfest is his sixth novel. When not writing, he's podcasting, playing video games, or petting cats. He lives in Texas with his wife, Kim.

You can follow Robbie on Twitter @robbiedorman